Series by Julie Johnstone

Scottish Medieval Romance Books:

Highlander Vows: Entangled Hearts Series
When a Laird Loves a Lady, Book 1
Wicked Highland Wishes, Book 2
Christmas in the Scot's Arms, Book 3
When a Highlander Loses His Heart, Book 4
How a Scot Surrenders to a Lady, Book 5
When a Warrior Woos a Lass, Book 6
When a Scot Gives His Heart, Book 7
When a Highlander Weds a Hellion, Book 8
How to Heal a Highland Heart, Book 9
Highlander Vows: Entangled Hearts Boxset, Books 1-4

Renegade Scots Series
Outlaw King, Book 1
Highland Defender, Book 2
Highland Avenger, Book 3

Regency Romance Books:

A Whisper of Scandal Series
Bargaining with a Rake, Book 1
Conspiring with a Rogue, Book 2
Dancing with a Devil, Book 3
After Forever, Book 4
The Dangerous Duke of Dinnisfree, Book 5

A Once Upon A Rogue Series

My Fair Duchess, Book 1
My Seductive Innocent, Book 2
My Enchanting Hoyden, Book 3
My Daring Duchess, Book 4

Lords of Deception Series

What a Rogue Wants, Book 1

Danby Regency Christmas Novellas

The Redemption of a Dissolute Earl, Book 1
Season For Surrender, Book 2
It's in the Duke's Kiss, Book 3

Regency Anthologies

A Summons from the Duke of Danby (Regency Christmas Summons, Book 2)
Thwarting the Duke (When the Duke Comes to Town, Book 2)

Regency Romance Box Sets

A Whisper of Scandal Trilogy (Books 1-3)
Dukes, Duchesses & Dashing Noblemen (A Once Upon a Rogue Regency Novels, Books 1-3)

Paranormal Books:

The Siren Saga

Echoes in the Silence, Book 1

How to Heal a Highland Heart

Highlander Vows: Entangled Hearts, Book 9

by
Julie Johnstone

The best way to stay in touch is to subscribe to my newsletter. Go to www.juliejohnstoneauthor.com and subscribe in the box at the top of the page that says Newsletter. If you don't hear from me once a month, please check your spam filter and set up your email to allow my messages through to you so you don't miss the opportunity to win great prizes or hear about appearances.

Dedication

For anyone who has misplaced their inner strength. Don't give up on yourself and keep fighting! You are a warrior!

As always, I have to thank a few people. First my assistant Dee, who keeps me sane and whom I drive insane. A million thanks would not be enough. And I need to thank my editor, Danielle Poiesz. I give her impossible deadlines for the both of us, and she sprinkles her magic editor dust and makes it happen! And for my husband and kids who have heard me say a billion times not to open my office door unless the house is on fire, thanks for being patient with me!

Author's Note

I have taken great pains to make sure the words I used in writing this story were as historically accurate as possible. However, given that I am writing to a modern audience, there are some instances when I chose to use a word that was not in existence in the fourteenth century, as they simply did not have a word at that time to correctly convey the meaning of the sentence.

If you're interested in when my books go on sale, or want to be one of the first to know about my new releases, please follow me on BookBub! You'll get quick book notifications every time there's a new pre-order, book on sale, or new release. You can follow me on BookBub here: www.bookbub.com/authors/julie-johnstone

All the best,
Julie

One

1361
Isle of Skye, Scotland

*W*hen a man discovered his destiny, he could either control it or let it destroy him, and Brodee Blackswell had no intention of being defeated this day or any other.

"What say ye? Will ye accept my reward?" King David asked again. But it was not a question. The men present in the great hall of Dunvegan Castle, the stronghold of the MacLeod clan, knew as well as Brodee did that the King of Scots often disguised a command as a request. The clever king loved to test the extent of his subjects' loyalty, and he was testing Brodee's now.

Uneasy looks were exchanged surreptitiously among the MacLeod brothers, their wives, and the council that served the MacLeod laird. But they were not sly enough, and their expressions revealed the underlying uncertainty of Brodee's response. The doubt did not surprise him. They questioned the extent of the burden he would accept, not his allegiance to the king.

He had proven his devotion over the last year as King David's right hand. He'd recaptured more than twenty castles for the king, driving out men who thought to defy David—or worse, unseat him from the throne. The sieges had earned Brodee the sobriquet of "the Savage Slayer." He suspected the king himself had first whispered the nickname. Brodee had no doubt it was to make those who thought to defy the king—or to support his greatest enemy, his nephew the Steward, who coveted the throne—to reconsider. He didn't mind being called the Savage Slayer, though. He knew it wasn't true, but his enemies did not, making the nickname quite beneficial. It had ended a few battles before they had begun, sparing numerous lives. For that, he could withstand the fear he saw in the eyes of others.

"Blackswell?" The king shifted forward, his hands coming to rest upon the table. His blue gaze delved, attempting to uncover Brodee's answer. A frown appeared on the man's regal face, and the drumming of his fingers broke the silence in the room. His brown eyebrows arched high, David's irritation apparent.

Dangerous situations called for deliberate questions. The king was offering him Silas Kincaide's castle as a reward for killing the man, who had been one of his nephew's biggest supporters. Of course, Brodee would first have to seize the castle from the Kincaides, who still occupied it. That would not be a problem. Silas's younger, weaker brother was now laird and would be easily defeated. The problem, as Brodee saw it, was that the king had also offered Silas's widow as a gift to be Brodee's new bride.

He took a measured breath, and then he spoke. "When would the wedding take place?"

A spark of triumph lit King David's eyes. "Immediately."

The king might as well have said, *I sentence ye to Hell.* Brodee didn't want a damn wife.

Careful, careful. He had to tiptoe. He walked upon a

shore of shells that was the king's pride. "I beg pardon, Sire, what was her name?" Brodee had already forgotten it. Perhaps unconsciously? No, purposely.

Royal lips pressed together in annoyance. "Lady Patience Kincaide, originally of the Bullard clan...the traitors," David spat. "Though I'm told she's a rare beauty."

That was supposed to be an enticement. It wasn't. It was anything but. Still, Brodee gave the expected answer. "I'm pleased to hear it."

A collective sigh came from the occupants of the room, and the spark of triumph moved from the king's eyes to his lips and twisted them into a smirk. Brodee shifted onto his heels, sending the weight of his annoyance away from the king. David thought he'd won, and he had. But only because Brodee would triumph, too. He wanted his own lands, ones he had earned, not property his elder brother had given him. His brother would inherit the lairdship of Clan Blackswell when their father died. He didn't begrudge Broch that. He'd been born a cry before Brodee, thus it was his by the luck of birth order. This desire to gain a holding Brodee had worked for and the loyalty of men pledged to him, was precisely why he'd accepted the king's offer to become his right hand in the first place. He'd figured— correctly, it seemed—that if he served the king well, David would reward him.

What he'd not considered was that the reward of land would include a bride.

Unease danced a jig in his gut.

"Blackswell, do ye accept my gifts or nae?" Irritation laced the king's words.

A hard gaze fell on Brodee, almost like a physical blow. He directed his attention to the man sitting to the king's right, Iain MacLeod. The laird was the king's oldest and closest friend. The MacLeod stared at him, as if searching for his secrets. Brodee had many, but he'd die before revealing them.

A slow smile, one of interest, spread across the Mac-Leod's face, but thankfully, he did not speak. Broch had told Brodee that the MacLeod was an uncommonly observant man, and Brodee did not need the laird noting things that were private. Especially things that might anger the king and cause Brodee to be stripped of the land and castle in question.

"I gladly accept yer gifts," Brodee said, though awarding him a castle teeming with warriors who supported the Steward and who would despise Brodee for killing their laird was hardly a *gift*. It was more like another mission to drive out the men who did not support the king. Except when this one was completed, Brodee would become laird of the castle and create another branch of the Blackswell clan—the Blackswells of Skye.

The king flashed a conqueror's smile, sharp and gleaming, before raising a hand to wave over one of his personal guards. "Send a missive to Laird Bullard. Tell him the Slayer will wed his daughter and will fetch her from the castle."

"Beg pardon, Sire," the guard began when he approached, "but I thought ye were rewarding the Slayer with the castle?"

"I am, ye foolish pup," the king snapped.

To the young guard's credit he did not show any reaction to the public scolding, though his ears did turn red.

"See if ye can follow along," David said, his expression holding a note of mockery. "Bullard dunnae ken that Blackswell will nae simply ride to Crag Donnon Castle and fetch his daughter." He paused, picked up his goblet, took a swig of wine, and plunked the cup down on the dais, all the while keeping his eyes upon the now-fidgeting guard. "Can ye imagine why it may be that I dunnae wish Bullard to ken that Blackswell will take Crag Donnon in my name and make it his by my good graces?"

Brodee sighed inwardly. Whenever the king's voice rose several octaves as it just had it meant he was at the beginning of a speech. Brodee hoped this one was short. He was eager to get to his men.

The guard looked suddenly as if he might be ill. The poor clot-heid was likely terrified to answer, yet he knew he must. David was a good king, but he could be a harsh king, made so by the brutal times during which he reigned.

"I imagine," the guard began, his voice cracking, "that ye wish to prevent the Kincaide warriors from hearing word of the Slayer's siege. That way," the guard continued jerkily, "the Kincaides will nae be able to mount a defense before the Slayer and his men arrive at the castle."

King David slapped both his palms against the dark wood of the table and grinned. "By God, I think ye do have some wits, after all."

"Aye, Sire, thank ye, Sire." The guard's face was now red as a beet.

David pointed at the young man. "Dunnae ye ever forget, the fewer people who ken my plot, the better. Can ye remember that, Farquort?"

The guard blinked in surprise, likely at the king knowing and using his given name. The young man appeared to grow in height. "I pledge nae to ever forget it," Farquort said, his tone now strong with the sense of importance the king had managed to give him by simply knowing who he was.

That was the thing about David. He was wickedly smart and surprising, and underlying his maneuverings for his kingdom was his real regard for his subjects, though he would manipulate them, without a moment of pause, for what he considered the greater good of Scotland.

"Farquort, ye will tell Bullard that the bargain is accepted, and I'll expect him to denounce my nephew publicly and make his support of me kenned immediately, by word and deed."

The guard nodded. "Any particular deed, Sire?"

"Aye. He already kens what is required."

Brodee cleared his throat, hoping to draw the king's attention, as he did not know the terms himself. The king's gaze fell on Brodee. "Ye desire to ken the terms I gave Bullard?"

"Aye. I dunnae wish to be uninformed," Brodee said.

Or wed, but that wish is hopeless now.

"Off with ye, Farquort," the king commanded, holding to his comment that the fewer people privy to his plans, the better.

Once the guard had left the room, the king continued. "After ye get yer new home in order, ye'll join forces with Bullard to take back the Gordon stronghold."

A suspicion rose in Brodee's mind, one he hoped was wrong. "Surely, ye dunnae trust Bullard to help stop another enemy simply because he weds his daughter to me?"

A dark look crossed the king's face. Whether because of the thought of treachery or because Brodee was questioning his decision, Brodee couldn't say. David swiped a hand over his jaw, his nostrils flaring. "I will trust him as much as I trust any man who was formerly aligned against me unless he proves I should nae trust him at all. He is the one who warned us that Kincaide and his men would try to overcome me on my trip to Edinburgh."

The desire to point out that Bullard may well have sacrificed Kincaide to gain something greater, like King David's favor, made Brodee's teeth ache, but he clenched them together to hold in the words. David would not like his decisions being questioned—twice—in front of so many others.

"I'm pleased ye've accepted my gifts of land and wife." The king did look pleased. With himself.

Brodee could do no more than nod. His thoughts were locked on his impending marriage. Was Lady Kincaide a viper like her father? It didn't matter. Brodee would wed her because he had to in order to get what he desired. He had no doubt if he refused the lass, being laird of the castle would not be his for the taking. The king was a prideful man who did not like to be rejected, and he would surely consider Brodee not wanting half of what the king offered him a rejection.

"Ye will be my eyes, as always, Blackswell," David added.

Brodee nodded. There was no choice but to do so. He'd hoped once he had land that he could have peace, but it seemed peace would have to wait.

The king picked up his goblet then, took a swig of wine, and stared for a long moment over the rim at Brodee. "Bullard specifically requested ye for his daughter."

"Requested?" Brodee asked, frowning. "This was Bullard's proposal?" Warning bells sounded in his mind.

"I was already decided upon giving ye the land, but then Bullard approached me and said he wished to pledge his fealty to me and offered his daughter for ye, my most valuable warrior, as proof of his intentions."

The warning bells became near deafening. "Sire—"

The king shook his head. "I already told ye," he said, his

voice grave, "I trust him as much as any man who was once my enemy and now claims to be my ally. And ye are even less trusting than I am, so all will be well."

Brodee nodded, a feeling of impending treachery making him tense.

"I accepted his pledge of fealty, of course," David continued, "but told him I'd need deeds to prove it beyond the offer of his daughter, which I took for ye."

The king took another swig of wine, and the pause, Brodee knew, was intended for him to show his gratitude yet again. "Thank ye, Sire."

David inclined his head. "'Tis the least I could do for ye after all ye have given to me. Now then," the king boomed, apparently pleased that Brodee was appropriately grateful. "Once his daughter and his pledge were accepted, I told him what else I required." He chuckled. "I dunnae believe he expected me to require him to go on a siege with ye."

"Hopefully, he'll nae try to kill me during it. Or mayhap he simply intends to use his daughter to spy on me," Brodee said, unable to contain his doubts any longer. Damned the punishment if the king became angry that he'd voiced his concerns. He'd rather be alive and in the king's disfavor than dead because he'd not wanted to incur the king's ire.

"I thought of that, as well," David said, one corner of his mouth twisting upward. "Ye and I think verra much alike, Blackswell. 'Tis why we have been so successful since ye became my right hand. I've nae a single doubt that ye'll take a care with yer new wife. Bed her but dunnae give her yer trust."

He didn't plan to. "And if Bullard proves treacherous?" In Brodee's mind, the question was *when* Bullard proved treacherous.

"Then we will crush him." The severe words rang with

finality.

It was a good thing Brodee had no need for a happy marriage. "Will that be all for now, Sire?"

"Aye."

Brodee inclined his head and made for the door, eager to seek out his men. He wanted to ensure they were ready to take the castle. Four steps out of the great hall, and the door squeaked open behind him.

"Hold."

Damnation. Brodee swiveled to face the deep voice. The MacLeod stood in front of the now-closed door, a wry look upon his face. "Ye dunnae wish for a wife, do ye?"

Broch's words regarding Iain MacLeod came to mind: *Fair. Honorable. Fierce. Loyal. Utterly devoted to his wife. Reasonably devoted to their king.* Meaning, the MacLeod knew the king was a man who made errors like all mere mortals. This was in addition to being dangerously observant...

Brodee frowned. "What makes ye say that?"

"Experience. I recognize the signs. But dunnae fash yerself, the king dunnae see what I see."

"Do ye have a point?" Brodee asked, refusing to acknowledge the MacLeod's comment about what he saw in Brodee.

"Aye. If ye dunnae consummate the marriage, it can be dissolved."

"Was that yer plan when the king ordered ye to wed yer Sassenach wife?" Brodee tried to keep the amusement out of his voice, but he failed.

The MacLeod's eyes glazed with exasperation. "First of all, he did nae order me. He asked."

Brodee just stared. The MacLeod knew as well as Brodee how the king maneuvered to get what he wanted.

"And secondly," the MacLeod said, scowling, "I took

one look at my wife, and lust overcame me."

"Ye sound weak to me," Brodee said, purposely prodding the man.

The MacLeod smirked. "Ye're witty. And witty men
tend to hide things."

Brodee snorted. "Ye're too personal with yer questions.
Can ye keep a secret?"

The MacLeod nodded and leaned closer.

"I can too," Brodee whispered, allowing his amusement
to come through in his tone this time.

The MacLeod chuckled. "It seems we're both flawed."

"Seems so," Brodee agreed. He liked the MacLeod.

The laird grinned. "My point is, dunnae let lust or emotion overcome ye, and ye'll be fine."

"I never have," Brodee said, even as he was struck by
the untruth of his own words. Once, he *had* allowed lust
and emotion to swallow him up like the sea, and he'd
almost drowned because of it.

But that was his secret to keep.

Two

"My lady, are these the gowns ye desire?"

Patience Kincaide looked up from the trunk she'd been delving through. Jane, her new lady's maid for the last sennight—appointed to Patience by her late husband's sister—stood partially in the doorway. With one foot in the bedchamber and one foot out, Jane looked ready to flee should the need arise. Patience's stomach sank. Apparently, Jane had finally heard the rumors that Patience was a witch, and from the looks of her, she believed the unfounded nonsense, just like everyone else.

Jane looked positively petrified, as if Patience might cast a deadly spell upon her. Patience had half a mind to pretend to do just that to spite the woman, but that would not help anything. Instead, she swallowed past a lump of aching loneliness. She was a fool. She should have known, though Jane was new to working in the castle herself, it would not take long for her to be brought into the fold of the others, a group Patience had never belonged to. Yet Patience had not known or she had simply ignored her reality. She had hoped, since Jane had not long ago wed into the Kincaide clan, and had not formed any close friendships with the other Kincaide women, that she and Jane would bond, and then the rumors would not matter to the woman.

Patience slid her teeth back and forth, trying to ignore

the emptiness filling her chest. Somehow, it was even more hurtful that Jane, who had come to the castle from the isolated job of tending the sheep with her reclusive husband, was now aligned against Patience. They had been fellow outsiders here at Crag Donnon Castle, even if Patience had been the only one to see it and recognize it.

Wariness darkened the young woman's eyes as she waited for Patience to respond. In Jane's right hand she clutched a red silk gown, tattered not from age but from the violence with which her first husband, Ivan, had ripped it from Patience's body. Jane gripped a black gown in her other hand. It, however, was pristine. A different viciousness had dwelled in her second husband, Silas. He had used words and games to cruelly control her, but mercifully, he'd finally gotten the death he deserved, but the damage he'd inflicted was seared upon her soul and marked upon her skin.

What if she had fled her father and Silas instead of submitting to the wedding? No, that had not been an option. Still… Where would she be now? Would she be so pathetic? Would she be alive? Would she be so alone? She inhaled a sharp breath. She hated when her mind played the "if only" game, yet she could not help herself as memories flooded her. Her father's face, twisting with rage, infuriated beyond words, because she had dared to say again that she did not want to wed Silas. The slap, right before he'd shoved Patience at her second evil husband-to-be. That hit had been very loud and very clear. *Do or die.*

That was always his threat: *Do or die.* Some days she wished to God she would just choose to die. But she couldn't. Her father had threatened to punish her younger brother, Duff, if she did not do as he bade, and she didn't doubt that he meant it. In her mind, she could see the nasty scar that made a jagged path down her brother's right cheek, which he'd received from their father for siding with her when she'd first refused to wed a second time.

Duff had vowed to her in secrecy after her second wedding, before Silas had taken her from her home, that if it came to a third wedding he would stop Father. Was he out there now trying to do that somehow? She wanted to hope, yet hope had been no friend of hers.

"My lady?"

Patience blinked. Did Duff even know a third forced marriage for her was on the horizon?

Dunnae hope. Dunnae do it. A pressure built to near unbearable in her chest. Blasted, foolish hope—it kept her alive while breaking her heart.

God, oh dear, merciful, possibly deaf God. Please let Duff appear before the newest man comes to wed me.

This husband might be her last. The Savage Slayer— that was what her father, the laird of the Bullard clan, had said her new betrothed was called. Father had not written of when she'd be collected, nor had he made any mention in his missive of when he would see her. It seemed she was to be wed to a stranger, surrounded by nothing but strangers, feeling very much like she always had, utterly alone. Suddenly, she felt the need to sit, or crumble, into a ball on the floor and cry.

"Lady Kincaide?" Jane asked. "The gowns?"

Pushing her pity and hope away, Patience asked, "Where did ye find them?" She shoved a pile of discarded ones out of the way so she could stand without slipping.

"Oddest thing," Jane said. "They were stuffed under the bed in Laird Kincaide's chamber."

Ah, yes. Patience had forgotten to retrieve them from Silas's room after the last time he had played one of his games. That one had been called "Strip the Whore Bride." And he had. Of her pride. He'd made her don each gown and he would slowly take it off while telling her all her faults. She knew every flaw her body and character possessed, according to her late husband, from her dull wit and duller dark hair, to her odd second toes that were longer than her first.

Reflexively, she curled her toes in her slippers. "Burn them."

Jane gasped, and looked as if Patience had just recited a dangerous spell. "But my lady—"

Something in Patience snapped, and she stalked toward Jane, accidentally bumping a table balancing a full wine goblet. Patience detested wine. Jane had brought it to her daily, but Patience never drank it. Jane's gesture of kindness in bringing Patience the wine was the first anyone in this castle had ever shown her, so she did not refuse the woman's kindness. Instead, she simply let it sit, assuming Jane might eventually take note and no longer bring it. The goblet clattered to the floor, the red liquid flowing onto the dark wood.

"I'll go fetch something to clean the mess," Jane said, giving Patience a fearful look that she'd seen all too often in the eyes of other Kincaides. It was entirely too bad that she was not truly a witch. Or perhaps it was good, because in this moment, had she possessed powers, Jane would be croaking at her.

"Dunnae bother," Patience said, skittering around the wine to retrieve the gowns from Jane. Her life was a much bigger mess than that wine.

Jane stumbled backward, crossing herself. "My lady, please—"

"Oh, do hush," Patience said, taking the gowns.

Patience had no control over any part of her life, but she *could* control what happened to these horrid gowns. She would burn them.

Her eyes met Jane's. Curiosity and a hefty dose of fear gleamed in the woman's gaze. And was that a sliver of pity? Had Jane also heard the names they called Patience? Likely. But it didn't matter. It didn't hurt her any longer.

She stiffened her spine. "Please put away the remaining things."

When Jane did not move, Patience tensed, expecting that the woman had decided she did not have to do Patience's bidding any longer. No one else did; Silas had seen to that.

Jane looked down at the pile of linens and silks. "Aye, my lady."

A release of breath left Patience feeling empty and slightly grateful. Then memories surged like a tide once more: *Ye're nae any better than the dirt on the floor. Even the servants ken it.*

She squeezed her eyes shut for one moment, willing Silas's voice to silence. *Go back to yer grave.*

Jane's eyes bugged wide. "Pardon?"

"I did nae say anything," Patience lied, shifting the gowns and turning away to hide the flush of hot mortification that she'd spoken her inner thought aloud.

Jane would think she was touched in the head now, and she would likely gossip. Then everyone would not only call her "Plain Patience" and "Perverted Patience," they'd call her "Peculiar Patience." She forced one foot in front of the other to walk out of her bedchamber toward the stairs. As she trod down the steps, passing servants who looked down their noses at her, the last name kept rolling through her mind. *Peculiar Patience.* Being thought of as mad might not be so horrid. It had to be better than people thinking she was dealing with the Devil.

She exited into the inner courtyard, pleased to find it empty. The sky, glimmering with the burgeoning moon, revealed why no one was afoot. Silas's people would all be in the great hall for supper. She was not welcome there; she was not one of them. Silas had quite enjoyed ensuring she was ostracized, hated, and slightly feared. He had been so masterful at convincing everyone that she practiced black magic and that he had personally dedicated his life to making her a better person. Public humiliations were a regular part of his "aiding her." She'd tried to contradict it, but no one had believed her.

Shifting the gowns to a single hand, she grabbed one of the torches flickering by the door and made her way to the fire pit in the center of the courtyard. She dropped the gowns into the pit and set them alight. Heat licked her face as the flames consumed the gowns, and then the fire began to grow hotter and higher, burning away her past.

Sweat trickled down her back, dampened under her arms and breasts, and even the back of her neck where her hair lay heavy. She tugged on the laces of her gown, feeling suffocated. How could she feel unable to breathe when she stood outside? A quick glance around the courtyard confirmed she was alone, and she yanked on the laces until the front of her gown gaped open and the cool air hit her chest. It still wasn't enough.

Not the burning of the gowns.

Not the little niggle of hope to which she clung.

Perhaps she truly was going mad...

A desperate inhalation left her worse than she'd been a breath before. She kicked off her slippers, grasped her hair, and twined it into a knot. Then she tugged up her skirts and tied them at her thighs, letting the cool air caress her legs.

She needed freedom. At least for a moment. If she was going to survive, if she was going to remain sane, she needed to feel free for one blessed moment in her life.

She took another glance around the firelit courtyard. Still alone. Her heart thundered so hard she thought it might burst.

Ye're worthless.

"I'm free," she argued aloud. And she willed it to be so for one heartbeat. *Two.* She closed her eyes, threw her arms wide, and twirled around, the air washing her anew, cooling her more, saving her. She used to dance when her mother was alive so, so very long ago. In the privacy of her mother's chamber, that was. To do so elsewhere would have been folly.

"I'm free," she said again, louder this time. Her twirling grew faster. Her heart beat even harder. Blood rushed through her veins, awakening her body, revitalizing her spirit, singing in her ears, and drowning out Silas's whispers.

"Is that yer bride?"

The voice, like a clap of thunder, stopped her twirling and her heart. Patience opened her eyes and sucked in a sharp breath. Two men stood almost within arm's reach of her. Behind the men, more warriors than could quickly be counted were positioned in perfectly formed lines and among the ferocious looking men was a plump man dressed in priest's robes. Torches flickered to life among the warriors, and one was passed up the lines and handed to a man at the front of the group.

It glowed just brightly enough that the man's face became clear. And what a face it was—ruggedly, wildly handsome with an inherent strength. Yet it was severe. Narrowed eyes impaled her. Shadows cast by the torchlight shifted across his angular face, highlighting sharp cheek-bones. His strong jawline held tense. Quite visibly. His profile, dark against the moonlight, looked perfectly proportioned. He was the most handsome man she'd ever seen. It was unsettling, really, and it made her feel plainer than she already felt.

Still, she found herself unable to look away. His hair appeared to be russet, and it grazed his broad, corded shoulders in waves. He was tall, his legs long and powerful. The large hand that was not holding the torch rested on the hilt of an enormous sword. "Are ye Lady Kincaide?" White teeth flashed in the darkness. Not a smile. No. More like lips curling back from teeth, rather like a wolf. It mesmerized her for a moment. "I'm Blackswell, and these are my men." He motioned to the man closest to him. "This is William MacLean." The Savage Slayer's voice had a warm quality she would never have expected. "Are ye Lady Kincaide?" he asked again, more curt this time.

"Nay." She didn't want to be linked with Silas anymore.

He closed the distance between them so fast she gasped. "Where is yer mistress, lass?"

He didn't sound like a killer, like the Savage Slayer. A warrior, yes, but not a man without emotion. Then again, what did she know. *Ye're stupid.*

Shut up.

"What?" The man brought the torch between them, and for one brief moment, she thought she saw his eyes widen, but a blink later, they were narrowed again.

Dear God. Why had she suddenly developed the habit of speaking her inner thoughts aloud? People truly *would* think she was touched. And if this man thought her mad, life could be worse than it had been. Or...

An idea suddenly struck her. Life could be *better*. Tolerable even, forced as she was bound to be into another unwanted marriage. If her new husband thought her mad, maybe he'd leave her in peace. Or perhaps he'd be wary of her once Silas's people told him she spoke with the Devil. Or he could put her in the dungeon, but that would hardly matter. She was already caged. It was invisible, but it was there.

She waved her hands on either side of her head, as if swatting at something. "Voices in my ears. They'll nae quit talking."

"I see," the man said. "I'm terribly sorry."

He sounded impatient possibly, definitely not sorry.

"Good thing this one is nae yer betrothed. She's bonny, but mad," another man added.

"Cease talking, William." The three words, spoken barely above a whisper, held an intensity that she could feel. It washed over her.

"Is yer mistress in the great hall?" The Slayer asked her.

She took a step back so she could properly meet the man's eyes. She still had to arch her neck to do so. "I'm my own mistress now."

"Where is Lady Kincaide in the castle?" Definite impatience punctuated his words.

God, but she'd had her belly full of men who were bossy and impatient, among a million other horrid qualities. "Lady Kincaide is in the courtyard." Her audacity—*where the devil had it come from*—astonished her.

He glanced around the courtyard, then his eyes rested on her again before he blew out a breath. "Are. Ye. Lady. Kincaide?"

He thought her either a simpleton or mad. Either way, it was perfect. She'd not felt real joy in years, but she rocked back on her heels in happiness and grinned. Why the devil not? Weren't mad people supposed to go around smiling a great deal?

"I was. But. Silas. Is. Dead."

There. Let him see how it felt to be talked to like a fool.

He said nothing, but it was the *way* he said nothing. He exhaled another long, slow breath, as if his tolerance was nearly dissipated. He withdrew his sword from the sheath at his hip, put the tip to the ground, and leaned on it as if debating whether to use it on her or not.

She bit her lip. Perhaps she'd gone too far with the last bit. "Now, I'm simply Patience."

"What the devil sort of name is *Patience?*" he asked.

Plain Patience. Perverted Patience, she heard in her head again. Silas was awfully loud for a man in his grave.

"A long-suffering one," she said, sighing.

"Lady Kincaide—"

"Patience," she repeated. "Unless ye wish to think of me as Silas's still."

"Ye are mine now." He sounded as unhappy about it as she was. Somehow, that gave her hope. "Did yer father tell ye we are to wed?"

"Aye," she said, hearing the bitterness in her voice but finding she could not suppress it. "As caring as ever, he sent me a letter. I received it just this morning informing me he was wedding me to a stranger yet again. I take it ye are the Slayer?"

His brows dipped together. "Ye are nae close to yer father." It was a statement, not a question.

She frowned. "Ye sound pleased."

"I am," he said.

She waited a beat, sure he would elaborate, but he simply stared at her.

"So," she said, realizing he'd not confirmed his identity.

"Are ye the Slayer?"

"Ye will call me Brodee." It was a command. Just like a man, but not exactly like Silas or Ivan, or even her father. Brodee's order was not harsh. The quiet words had contained an almost gentle cadence.

"I'm told ye're called the Slayer," she pressed.

Whatever was possessing her? She knew better than to speak in such a manner to her betrothed. Raising her hands to her chest, palms splayed to ask forgiveness, she took a step back. She had no wish to be struck. His fists looked huge, even bigger than Ivan's, and his hit had hurt something fierce. One day into her marriage to Ivan was all it had taken to learn to hold her tongue, which made her all the more surprised she was acting so recklessly now, as if she did not know better.

"I am." He reached out and grasped her by the wrist, pulling her to him. Not hard or hurtful but with definite purpose. His strong, calloused fingers easily encircled her wrist. His touch was hot, as if he contained a fire within him. He smelled of smoke, woods, and grass. And perhaps a smidge of wine. She hoped he was not one to over imbibe and become angry. Both Silas and Ivan had done that—one with words, the other with his fists.

"I will nae ever hit ye," he said, his voice still low.

She believed him. She didn't know why. It was truly madness. Regardless, she nodded and murmured, "God has finally blessed me with the perfect husband." Her mouth parted at her own surprise of the flippant words she'd spoken. It was like her lips had taken on a mind of their own and had decided they no longer needed to check with her before talking.

"Are ye mad?" Brodee whispered.

Was he referring to her daring to speak so glibly to him

or did he truly wonder about her sanity? Fear rose in her then, but it was herself she feared in this moment. "I might be," she whispered back, completely unsure.

He squeezed her wrist once and released her. "Where are yer men?"

She frowned. "My men?"

"Yer guards? Laird Kincaide's men."

"Oh, ye mean Lamond's men? Silas's brother? Lamond is laird now."

Brodee nodded. "Aye, I'm referring to Lamond." Distaste weighed his words. "But he is nae laird here anymore."

She snorted. "Then I do believe Lamond did nae get the missive from the king," she said jokingly. Lamond was very much alive and was acting very much the laird now that Silas was gone and had no heirs.

"I'm the missive," Brodee said, not a trace of humor in his tone.

Confused and nervous, she cleared her throat. "I dunnae ken…"

Brodee raised his hand, and the men behind him withdrew their swords as one, causing a singing of iron to fill the air.

"What are ye doing?" she asked, her breath hitching.

"Taking what's mine," he said with cool authority.

"Ye need all these men to collect me?"

He laughed then, but it immediately died—or rather, it sounded like he'd stopped it with the force of his will. His hearty mirth surprised her. Somehow, she'd not thought a man with the moniker *the Savage Slayer* ever laughed. Suddenly, his hand snaked around her waist, and her body went rigid with a flood of bad memories.

A derisive noise came from deep within him. "William, take her," he said, his tone controlled and still low. It almost seemed as though he did not want to alert anyone to his presence. It hit her then that the horn announcing visitors had not blown as it normally did, and a suspicion rose.

"I'm nae going to be relegated to the position of watching yer mad wife," William whispered, interrupting her thought.

Her spine stiffened at the man's insulting words. Though she was certain it would behoove her to be thought touched in the head, she found she did not much care for it. Still, desperate people could not cling to pride, and she was desperate. Yet she was also pleased to discover she still had a shred of pride left in her. Honestly, she'd thought Silas had destroyed it all.

Brodee shoved her at the man. "Will, other than myself, ye are the best fighter I ken. I trust ye above all others to keep her safe."

"Flatterer," William said, flashing a large, toothy smile. Then his hands came to her waist, and she could not stop the hiss and the moan from escaping her.

"God's teeth, Will," Brodee snapped, his voice louder than it had been since he'd first spoken. "Be gentle with the lass, or I'll cut off yer hands."

"He was gentle," she rushed out, fearing for the man. Now she understood exactly why Brodee Blackswell was called the Savage Slayer. If he would cut off his comrades hands for irritating him, what else was the man capable of? "'Tis nae him. 'Tis me."

"I suppose 'tis good, in a way, that Silas had her fealty," William whispered, speaking as if she were not there.

Brodee's response was a grunt. She could correct the man William, but then again, it might be good for the Slayer to think Silas had her heart and that she clung to the memory of him. It would go far in helping her appear mad.

Especially if she could not get her problem of blurting her thoughts aloud under control.

"Where do ye wish me to take the lass?" William asked.

Brodee turned to her. "Where's the safest place in Crag Donnon, Patience?"

"The chapel," she said. "Nae anyone has darkened the door, except for me, since I was wed there."

"Nae even the priest?" Astonishment tinged Brodee's voice.

Patience could not help but laugh. "Especially nae the priest."

She despised Father Bisby. He had helped Silas spread the gossip that she dabbled in black magic, and how it was only by Silas's good graces, and the priest's regular cleansing of her soul, were they able to aid her in driving the Devil from her body enough that she was permitted to live.

"Take her to the chapel," he said to William. "Ye ken what to do. I'll send for ye when I'm done with the Kincaide men."

"Try nae to shed too much blood," William said.

The amusement in his voice made her suck in a sharp breath of complete understanding. "Ye're nae here to take me," she stated.

"Oh aye, I am, but nae just ye," Brodee said. "I'm here to take the castle."

He started to turn away, but she grasped at his arm, driven surely by madness. Under her fingertips, his muscles tensed, and the sheer power leashed there filled her with awe and fear. "Please, ye must nae kill them."

He pried her fingertips from his arm, his rebuttal of her plea stinging her. Things would be no different with this man from how they had been with her first two husbands. She would be less than nothing to him, especially since it did not seem she would ever provide heirs.

Brodee gave her a grave look. "I dunnae ever fell any man unless he tries to fell me. That, ye can count upon."

Around them, the men had begun moving—or creeping more specifically—toward the door to the castle. The way they flowed silently, like a shadow, swept gooseflesh over her skin and left it tingling.

Brodee passed the torch silently to William, and then the night swallowed up the Savage Slayer, who might not be quite as savage as rumor would have her believe. She smiled at that, then frowned that it even mattered to her.

She knew better than to care.

Three

Several hours later, Brodee sat on the dais in the great hall of his new home. He surveyed the room. Tables and chairs had been overturned during the fight to claim the castle, and now the line of Kincaide men prepared to bend the knee to him and pledge their loyalty to both him and King David was trailing out of the room. He knew not to put much stock in words of loyalty, though. Only when those words were backed up by action, repeatedly, would he give more trust to the men; he would exile those who proved their oaths meant nothing.

A commotion at the door caught his attention. When he saw the guard he'd sent to look for Father Murdock enter the great hall, Brodee thought the man must have found the priest whom Brodee had instructed to hide in the kitchens during the attack on the castle. He had brought the MacLeod clan priest with him at the offer of the MacLeod. If time had permitted, Brodee would have traveled home to Hightower Castle to collect Father Donnely for the wedding, but they did not have much time and the MacLeod had offered his priest. And since Brodee had not wished to rely on his enemies priest to faithfully wed him to Patience, he'd taken MacLeod's offer.

Yet instead of Father Murdock's voice, he heard a woman's voice suddenly at the entrance to the great hall. His heart beat increased with the expectation that Patience Kincaide was about to appear. He had summoned her and William from the chapel, but a different woman—*lovely but no comparison to Patience,* he thought, surprising himself— picked her way through the great hall. She held her head high and had a haughty tilt to her chin. As she approached him, his guards stepped forward and pointed their swords at her.

He waved a hand for them to stand down. "The day I need guarding from a lass is the day ye all should look for a new laird." God's teeth, but it felt odd to think of himself as a laird now.

Laughter rolled through his men and even some of the Kincaide men, who were lined up before him.

He first turned his attention to the guard he'd sent to fetch Father Murdock. "Where is the priest?"

The guard pressed his lips together. "In the kitchens. He refuses to leave. He claims ye instructed him to stay there until William came to fetch him." Brodee let out an annoyed sigh. He had said that, but he'd not expected Father Murdock, a man who loved his drink more than God, to follow Brodee's instructions so faithfully. A suspicion rose. "Is there wine in the kitchens?"

"Aye," the guard said grimly.

Brodee gave a nod. He'd send William to deal with Father Murdock soon enough. Decision made, he focused on the woman before him. "How may I help ye?" he asked.

She cut in front of the man who was next in line to bend the knee and strolled right up to Brodee, stopping within touching distance. She offered a slow, welcoming smile. "I'm here to aid ye."

Another wave of laughter, one of assumption, went through his men, but this time, Brodee waved them to immediate silence. Even if Patience was addled, he had no intention of taking another woman to his bed. Vows made before God were sacred, whether he wanted to make them or not. When he gave them, he'd honor them.

"How are ye here to aid me?" he asked.

"Ye'll need a wife to run this castle properly," the woman said, leaning forward and giving him a clear view of her ample breasts.

Even if he wasn't to wed Patience, he had no time or tolerance for a woman who was trying to wind him around her finger. He'd been coiled tightly around a woman's finger once before, put there by his own desires, and the pain that had resulted from the loop would never be forgotten. "I'm afraid, Lady—"

"Kincaide," she said, smiling slowly, rather like a cat. An evil one waiting to claw him.

"Sister to Silas and Lamond?" he asked, surprised their sister would be offering herself to him like that.

She nodded. "I am Lady *Kinsey* Kincaide, aye. Ye killed my brother Silas."

It was a flat statement with no emotion. He answered in kind. "I did, but only because he tried to kill me first."

She inclined her head at that. "I heard ye sent Lamond to his death, too."

He stiffened at that. "I sent yer brother to the king for justice after he refused to bend the knee once I took the castle in the king's name. This was commanded by the king himself."

"Seems the rumors of ye being fair are true."

"I'm pleased ye think so," he said.

She nodded, as if she'd expected him to say just that, as if she'd assessed him and thought she knew him. God, if the woman truly knew him, she'd not be standing here. "Ye'll make a fine ruler of my home," she said.

"Crag Donnon Castle belongs to us Blackswells now," one of Brodee's younger guards piped up.

"Crag Donnon Castle," Brodee said, "belongs to the Blackswells *and* the Kincaides from this day forward."

"Ye mean the men," Kinsey muttered.

Now he saw why she had come. She feared for her place with her brothers gone. The thought of Patience, his possibly mad betrothed who had yet to appear, made him frown. Where the devil were she and William?

"All Kincaides are welcome to join my clan, as long as they are loyal. That includes the women, who are an important part of every clan."

He wanted to unite the Blackswells and the Kincaides if he could, not divide them. Division bred hatred, disobedience, and bloodshed. He wanted no part of any of those things. He wanted peace, and he hoped to God to find it here. It had proven damned elusive thus far in his life. The disquiet that had hounded him as a child and at the home he'd grown up in had followed him on every mission he'd embarked on for the king over the past year.

Kinsey's mouth turned up into a satisfied smile. "What better way to show ye mean that than by wedding me, a true Kincaide."

"I'm to wed Lady Patience by the king's orders," he said, careful not to allow his displeasure with the impending wedding to be revealed by his voice. He may not want to wed Patience, but he was, and he would have her respected.

The look of surprise on Kinsey's face told Brodee she had not known. An image of Lady Patience as he'd first seen her, turning in circles in the courtyard with her hair unbound, feet bare, arms thrown wide while wearing nothing more than an almost-sheer léine, came to his mind.

The perfect silhouette of her high, firm breasts was
apparently seared in his memory. He didn't like that. But he
was pleased with her unintended revelation that her father
held no favor with her. In fact, the man sounded as if he'd
been uncaring. It did not soothe Brodee to think she'd been
hurt by her father, but it did alleviate some of his worry that
she was to spy on him. Some. Not all. He was not a fool.

He clenched his teeth. Why was he thinking upon Patience? Never did his thoughts turn to a lass he had bedded
or would bed unless she was lying in front of him. Neither
before nor after the joining. Just in the moment during it
because that's all he had to give—a few moments of sin.
The women he joined with had known it before the first
kiss was ever exchanged. A mingling of bodies did not mean
an intertwining of lives, and that rule would not change for
Patience. That rule was his shield.

"Ye should ken that some whisper she is *ban-druidh*,"
Kinsey told him.

He studied Kinsey's face. He could not tell if she was
regretful to deliver the gossip or not. "What do ye believe?"

She cocked her head, as if carefully considering the
question and selecting the perfect answer. "I dunnae. I have
nae gotten to ken her much in the time she's been here, but
my brother believed it, and he was her husband." Those
words alone would be damning if Brodee had trusted
Kincaide, but the man had possessed no honor. He'd not say
that to the man's sister, though.

"I'll take what ye've told me into account."

She studied him for a moment, and he got a strange
feeling the woman was assessing him and judging him for
something. She licked her lips, then slowly said, "Ye may
also wish to speak to Father Bisby. He's our priest, and he
cleansed her soul regularly."

He inclined his head to show he'd heard her as he considered her comments. His gut told him Lady Patience was no more a witch than he a savage beast, but he could not ignore the allegation. To do so would make him look weak. He stood, pushing his chair back, and swept his gaze over the gathered men. He would send for the priest, but first he'd hear what those gathered here had to say. "Does anyone have proof to offer that Patience Kincaide is *bandruidh?*"

Patience came to a halt upon the threshold of the great hall and sucked in a sharp breath. Black magic, indeed! Why could the Kincaides not focus on the fact that a man named the Savage Slayer was to be their laird? After all, Brodee Blackswell stood like a giant oak—no, not a tree, more like a deadly wolf—in front of the dais glowering like…like the Devil himself! She grinned, rather pleased with her comparison, but the happiness was as fleeting as time itself.

"She made me ill!" Alfred, a younger Kincaide warrior, shouted.

She glared at his back from the shadows of the hood she had pulled over her face. She'd tried to be nice to Alfred, but Silas had convinced the man that he'd gotten sick because she'd put a spell on him.

"Ye've proof?" her soon-to-be, possibly ruthless husband asked.

Except he sounded, well, quite reasonable. As she nodded her approval at his sensibleness, the hood on the cape she'd donned when she'd dashed away from William—he had meant to drag her into the great hall dressed only in her léine!—slipped backward, exposing her face.

"Here she is!" a man beside her bellowed, and before she knew what was happening, she was being jostled, then shoved forward. Solid hands pushed her so hard that she staggered, got her foot caught in the hem of her cape, and fell to her knees.

"Hold!" Brodee roared, making her flinch and her ears ring. The hands that had been touching her immediately dropped away. Patience stared at the rushes covering the floor and blinked back the tears that threatened to fall. She knew she needed to stand and face everyone, but not before she got herself under control.

"The next man to lay a hand upon my betrothed," he continued, "will soon be a man who is missing a hand."

Brodee Blackswell certainly did have an obsession with cutting off hands. The gruesome thought made her giggle nervously. She slapped a hand over her mouth to muffle it, but she didn't think it had done much good. Heat rushed to her face and down to her neck, blood rushing in her ears at her embarrassment.

'Tis nae as horrible as ye think, Patience.

The tips of two deerskin shoes suddenly appeared in her line of sight. She blinked to ensure she was not seeing things. Indeed, she was not. The wearer of the shoes rocked back on his heels as if waiting for her to look up. Not feeling ready, she decided to trail her gaze upward slowly to gather her courage. The ankles seemed like an average man's ankles. That was good. Surely, if Brodee was standing in front of her, the ankles before her would be larger. A man with skinny ankles couldn't very well be called the Savage Slayer. Of course, these were average ankles, not skinny ones.

She gave her head a little shake to jostle her rambling thoughts to silence and continued her inspection of the man before her. Devil take it! The man's calves were *not* average. They bulged with a swell of sinewy muscle that most definitely could be her prospective husband's. The farther up she got, the more certain she was that Brodee Blackswell stood before her. He had long, extremely well-made legs that he probably used quite adeptly when he fought so as to earn his reputation. And those thighs! She swallowed as her belly tightened.

Marauding Viking thighs are what these are.

"I assure ye, I dunnae pillage, but I am descended from Viking stock," came a deep voice from above her.

Her already-growing flush was suddenly a raging fire burning up her chest. She tore her gaze from those fine legs and looked up, up, up, past narrow hips and over an impressive expanse of bronzed, banded muscles that made up Brodee's stomach, and then farther upward, skimming his corded neck and finally settling on his face.

Too handsome to be called the Slayer.

He cocked a russet eyebrow in a perfect arch. "Do ye think so?"

She'd done it again! Let her inner thoughts out.

I need to stuff a piece of cloth in my mouth.

The man's lips tugged strangely, as if they were trying to form a smile but did not quite know how. "I dunnae believe cloth will be necessary."

She pressed her own lips together to ensure no more words escaped her. This was horrid. But then again, if she was going to convince Brodee she was mad, her inability to control her inner thoughts and odd, ill-timed nervous giggling might very well do the trick. The Slayer—No, Brodee—heaven above, she was unsure how to think of this man—held his hand out to her, and she grasped it. Strong, warm, calloused fingers closed around hers, and then he pulled her up as if she were a feather.

She fully expected him to release her, but instead, he brought their interlocked hands between them and faced her. "Were ye injured in yer fall?"

The concern glittering in his eyes and strumming through his voice sucked the air from her lungs. Was this a wishful imagining? She squeezed her eyes shut, sure she must be seeing what she wanted to, and when she opened them again, he was looking at her with a mixture of pity and wariness. This man could not be what people said he was. That didn't mean he couldn't be other things, things that made one cower in his presence, but a coldblooded murderer? No.

"Were ye injured in yer fall?" he asked again, slower this time, as if he spoke to a person who was cracked.

She had to bite the inside of her cheek not to smile at how well her pretense seemed to be going. "Nay."

"Good. Where is William?"

Patience winced. She'd told the man she'd seen Silas's ghost in the solar as he dragged her past it on the journey to the great hall, and when he'd stepped inside, she'd locked him in. "I only wanted a cape to cover myself," she said.

"Where is he?" Brodee demanded, his tone turning hard.

"I'm here," William said, his voice coming from behind Patience. She whirled around to find the man standing in the doorway of the great hall. His gaze narrowed on her. "Ghost, indeed."

She notched her chin up. "I could nae verra well allow ye to drag me in here in naught but my léine. 'Tis indecent."

"Will, explain," Brodee said, the command lashing the air.

"The lass said she saw a ghost, and—"

"See there!" someone called out. "She practices black magic if she sees ghosts!"

"Nay!" Patience cried out. She moved to flee, but Brodee shot his hand out and grabbed her. The bottoms of her feet had just healed from Father Bisby's latest "soul cleansing." The man enjoyed delivering physical pain, that much was for certain. And he seemed to have an endless imagination in regard to ways to drive the Devil from her. Funny, they all involved watching her writhe in excruciating pain. "Let me go," she hissed and tried to twist away.

Brodee's fingers curled around her arm, the grip a steel vise she knew she'd not escape, which made her only try harder. As she maneuvered her arm in an attempt to break free, he said, "Ye, Alfred, fetch this Father Bisby. Now I will decide why my betrothed is thought to be *ban-druidh*."

Alfred gave her a mocking smile as he rushed to do Brodee's bidding. William, on the other hand, frowned. "Brodee. I dunnae ken, the lass—"

Brodee simply shook his head at William, and much to her dismay, the man fell silent.

"Go fetch Father Murdock, William. He's in the kitchens with the wine." William smirked at that. Apparently this Father Murdock had a known proclivity for wine. "Apprise him of what has occurred, and tell him that after I have dealt with this, he will perform his duties, and I expect him to do so without slurring a single word."

William gave a brief nod as his eyes alighted on her for a brief moment, but she could not read the man's emotions. He nodded to Brodee and left the room.

Excited chatter hummed through the great hall. Thanks to Silas, none here would stand up for her. None here liked her.

Oh God. What duties does the new priest perform? Is he like

Father Bisby? I think I'd rather die than face more fire and water.

Brodee jerked his head toward her, and his blue gaze captured hers. His eyes seemed to probe to her very soul as he stood there staring at her. "Be calm," he ordered.

Calm?

He nodded at the thought she'd apparently voiced again.

"We should burn her!" one of the men shouted, capturing her attention. Her blood roared in her ears as she skimmed the crowd.

"Or drown her!" another man yelled.

Her heart exploded, and she looked back at Brodee. She jerked on her arm as he seemed to be assessing her.

"Be still," he said, the words soft, spoken only for her.

"Please," she said, unable to keep the rising hysteria from her voice. "I'm nae *ban-druidh*, I vow it."

"Laird, we can tie her to a chair so ye dunnae have to hold her," someone suggested.

She struggled mightily then, but it was no use. Brodee's fingers had become like iron, and his jaw had tensed. At his right eye, a tic began, and his pulse hammered visibly at his neck. Was he excited by her fear as Silas and Ivan had always been? She didn't know. She didn't know *him*. All she knew of men who were supposed to protect her were Silas, Ivan, and her father, and not a one of them had guarded her.

"She will stand with me," Brodee said. "As I'm the one to do what must be done."

Dear God above. How will he kill me? Fire? Water?

Brodee scowled at her. "If I were going to kill ye, it would nae be fire or water. That is a coward's way."

"Yer words do bring me such relief," she said, her voice purposely flat.

"Laird Blackswell," Kinsey said, walking toward them. "I'll stand with ye in judgment of her."

Was Kinsey trying to aid her or crucify her? Patience looked to her former sister-in-law, and the woman gave her an encouraging smile. Kinsey had never been friendly, but Patience had wondered if Silas had ordered his sister to be cold to her. Kinsey had, to be fair, appointed Jane to aid Patience after Silas's death.

"Why? Do ye have something to say in her defense?" her betrothed demanded, his tone like a wintery wind. He had a look on his face that Patience could not quite decipher. Was it anger? Expectation?

"I—" She glanced toward Patience. "I am the last true Kincaide here. I thought it would be good if we both sat in judgment, a Kincaide and a Blackswell, our clans united."

Still, Patience had no notion if Kinsey was trying to aid her or not.

"Are nae all Kincaides true Kincaides?" Brodee asked, his eyebrows arched.

Irritation fluttered across Kinsey's face, but it disappeared as fast as it had appeared. "Well, aye, but—"

"Then ye dunnae need to represent yer clan. Ye can stand with everyone else and listen."

Kinsey's lips pressed into a thin line. "As ye wish, Laird Blackswell."

Patience stole a glance at Brodee, surprised to find him looking at her instead of Kinsey. No one ever paid Patience notice, but Kinsey had the respect of everyone in the Kincaide clan. His observant eyes softened as if he had somehow read her thoughts. He squeezed her wrist once, and said, "Dunnae move, Patience," and then he released her. She wanted to flee. God help her, she did. But she knew it was hopeless.

Her betrothed took out his sword, drawing it up, and
then banged the blade down upon the table beside him. The
hit resounded like a clap of thunder, and the chatter
instantly ceased. "Ye will all be quiet, or ye will leave."

Men nodded immediately, and Brodee's hand came to
the small of her back, where he pressed slightly. "We will
stand before the dais to hear what this Father Bisby has to
say."

"Why?" she asked, trying to dig in her heels so as not to
be moved from the door, which seemed her only path to
freedom, whether hopeless or not.

"Because at the dais," he said, giving her a gentle push
that forced her to move, "men are nae at my back."

"Ye dunnae like men at yer back?" she asked as his hand
caught hers, and he fairly tugged her to the dais.

When he did not answer her, she assumed he would
not, but at the dais, when it was only the two of them with
the nearest man several feet away, Brodee pitched his voice
low. "I dunnae like my enemies at my back."

She sucked in a breath of hope. "I vow I'm nae *ban-
druidh*," she whispered, praying he would believe her.

"Just a touch cracked, aye?" He did not smile, but his
eyes did crinkle with what appeared to be amusement.

She bit her lip, uncertain it was wise in this moment to
continue the charade, but fear of the unknown, fear that this
man would be cruel to her, had her nodding. "Just a touch
mad, I believe. 'Tis nae a crime."

His lips did that odd pulling thing again, as if he might
smile. "Nay, Patience. 'Tis nae a crime."

The door to the great hall opened with a bang, and
Father Bisby entered, his robes billowing at his ankles. "I'm
here to punish the *ban-druidh*!"

Four

The stodgy, red-faced, bulbous-nosed man who swept into the room made the tic that had started at Brodee's right eye worsen. But when Patience tensed beside him and inhaled sharply, Brodee wanted to punch the priest. He may be wearing robes of the cloth, but one look at the anticipatory glee in the man's dull brown eyes confirmed what Brodee had suspected: Father Bisby was no true man of God. Men who held God in their hearts did not enjoy the pain and suffering of others.

Brodee stole a swift glance at Patience. The paleness of her face and the slight trembling of her body bespoke her fear. He didn't for a moment believe she was a witch. If she were, she would have simply put a curse on Brodee rather than wed him, as it was quite obvious she had no desire to do so. Neither did he believe she was touched in the head, as she wished him to think. No doubt it was a ploy she'd come up with in the hope that he might not wed her. If only things were that simple.

But nothing was. He had taken this castle, but he could not take loyalty. It had to be won, and he'd rather have the Kincaide men's loyalty than more deaths. And to get that, he had to show he was willing to listen and judge whether Patience was a witch. He just wished he'd had a moment of privacy to reassure her, and he *really* wished he didn't care that she needed reassuring. Caring brought complications, but he was no more capable of stopping the tide of protectiveness that had risen when she'd been shoved to the ground than he was capable of halting the need to draw breath.

He assessed the priest. Rings on every finger. *Greed.* Eyes affixed to Patience's breasts. *Lust.* Brodee clenched his teeth against the urge to throttle the man. Brown eyes glancing swiftly between Brodee and back to Patience. "Let me take the *ban-druidh* lass from yer sight, Laird Blackswell. I'll take her to my chambers, and—"

"Nay." *Ye covetous swine.*

Brodee didn't need to be a seer to read the burning desire on the man's face. Did he satisfy that unfulfilled hunger for Patience by punishing her? Is that why she trembled? Would she even tell him if Brodee asked? Not likely. The lass feared him. Trust would take time. "My betrothed stays with me, and if she needs punishing, my priest will be the one to do it."

Father Bisby frowned. "I was told ye called me here to—"

"I called ye here to tell me what proof ye have that Lady Patience is *ban-druidh*. I assume ye have some since I'm told by Lady Kinsey that ye have been cleansing Lady Patience's soul."

"I have," the priest said, his tone boastful.

"Then what did the lady do to cause ye to think her soul needed cleansing?"

The priest looked disdainfully at Patience. "She talks to herself."

"That dunnae mean she's *ban-druidh*," Brodee said, thinking of his own past and times his father would make him feel worthless. Brodee would talk to himself because he could never admit his feelings to anyone else.

"She made Alfred ill," the priest said, pointing at her.

"What is yer proof?" Brodee asked. He'd been thought a murderer in his lifetime because one person had whispered it, and the whisper had spread like fire. When the priest did not answer, Brodee went on. "I suspect ye dunnae have any, Father."

"Are ye accusing me of...of...lying?" the priest demanded.

Brodee raised his hand and flicked it forward, a silent command for his men to grasp the priest, which two of Brodee's guards did immediately, one taking each of the man's arms.

"Unhand me!" the priest shouted.

"Bring him forth," Brodee commanded. Patience's leg suddenly brushed his, and he looked to her, realizing his betrothed was practically trying to hide herself behind him. He had to clench his jaw on a curse at the fear this priest elicited in her.

When one Kincaide guard stepped forth as if to stop Brodee's men, Brodee said, loud enough to be heard over the den of noise that had set in, "I'd nae if I were ye."

The man's eyes met Brodee's and narrowed, but he stepped back out of the Blackswell guards' path. When the priest stood before Brodee and Patience, who was hovering at Brodee's back now, Brodee motioned for his guards to release the man.

Father Bisby huffed and jerked his arms away. "How dare ye have yer men treat a man of God thusly!"

The man was challenging him. That was fine. He'd been challenged many times before, and he'd yet to lose. "I ask again, what is yer proof that Lady Patience is a *bandruidh*?"

A flicker of apprehension crossed the priest's face. "She…she…she's nae had a bairn after two husbands!"

Patience sniffled behind him, and he wondered for a moment if was she crying. Damn the man before him. "That is nae proof. Mayhap her husbands did nae perform properly."

"Are ye faulting my laird?" the priest demanded.

Brodee leaned forward and down until his face was a hairsbreadth from Father Bisby's. "*I* am yer laird now."

The priest's mouth slipped open, and then he said, "I, well, aye, of course." Finally fear had set in. Brodee could smell it and see it. "Silas told me she was *ban-druidh*. I simply did as he bade."

"So ye cleansed her soul regularly because Kincaide claimed his wife was *ban-druidh?*"

"Aye. What else could I have done?" The priest spread his hands as if he were helpless, which Brodee sincerely doubted.

"Ye could have refused," Brodee said plainly.

"Laird, surely ye ken that to refuse would have angered my laird, and I would have put myself in grave peril."

"Aye, I ken it perfectly."

The priest practically sagged before Brodee, and Kinsey said, "See here, how fair and understanding our new laird is!"

Rousing cheers went up in the great hall from the Kincaides. Brodee's men stood silent, knowing him as they did.

Once the cheering died down and everyone was looking at him expectantly, he turned to Patience. She stepped back, surprised, but he caught her by one slender wrist. "Ye must trust me."

Her wary gaze met his, but as he pulled her to his side, she did not fight him. He brought her close and then swept his hand toward her. "Tell me, Father Bisby, how did ye cleanse Lady Patience's soul?" The man's beady eyes darted between Patience and Brodee. "Did ye pray for her?" Brodee asked.

"I, well, ye see, I deemed it necessary to use harsher measures," the priest sputtered.

Harsher measures. Brodee could only imagine what that meant. He could not stop his fist from curling at his side, and he took grim pleasure in Father Bisby's gaze going to Brodee's clenched fist.

"And why did ye 'deem it necessary'?" he asked. "Did she fight ye?"

"Nay, but—"

"Protest?" Brodee interrupted.

"Well, aye, but—"

"Without any real proof, did ye nae deem it *necessary* to be as restrained as ye could with the soul cleansing, perhaps consider yer laird was leading ye astray?" Brodee's blood was boiling now. He could see the answer in the man's eyes. He'd enjoyed punishing Patience, and he knew damn well she was no witch. "How did ye cleanse her soul?" he asked, repeating his earlier question.

"I, well, I—"

"He made me walk on smoldering wood," Patience said, her voice very small. Brodee hissed in a breath.

When the priest opened his mouth to speak, Brodee said, "Dunnae ye even dare."

The priest clamped his jaw shut, and Patience continued. "He held me underwater. Quite regularly. He seared me with the mark of the cross."

Shock yielded to fury when Patience pulled up the right sleeve of her gown and showed him the brand on the tender skin of her right arm. The puckered red skin stood in stark contrast to the rest of her unblemished olive skin. She looked up at Brodee then, her gaze imploring and making his chest ache with the raw vulnerability he saw there.

"I dunnae wish to continue," she whispered.

He went to place a hand on her shoulder, and she flinched away. He had to wonder, if the priest had done all this under the directive of her husband, what had that man done to her directly?

"Ye dunnae need to," he assured her. He had heard more than enough to deal with the priest, and the Kincaides had seen that he'd listened and would judge accordingly. "Father Bisby, for yer crimes against the mistress of this castle, I punish ye to death."

Buzzing immediately started in the hall once more, and the priest began to wail his protest.

"Nae, death," Patience protested above the din.

Immediately, silence fell once more. "Ye argue for leniency for this man who has hurt ye?"

"Nay," she said, her face setting like stone. "Death is too quick."

Brodee's eyes widened at her words. For a fragile-looking lass there was mettle hiding under that facade. "What do ye wish?"

"I wish him to endure every punishment he ever gave me, and then I wish him to be cast from this castle forever."

"So be it," Brodee pronounced, which set the great hall to buzzing once more. "Guards!" he called, and they came forth to grasp the priest by each of his arms. "Take him to the courtyard. Start a fire, bring water, and bring my branding iron."

Patience gasped. "Ye have yer own branding iron?"

"Aye." He didn't bother to explain that he'd had it fashioned some time ago in the hopes of one day owning his own land and his own sheep. That was too personal, and it made him look sentimental and weak. Two faults that he needed to overcome, something he'd heard growing up more times than he could count.

"Have mercy!" Father Bisby begged, rushing toward Patience.

Brodee moved to shield her, but she pushed his hand away, her chin going up in a sudden show of bravery. "Mercy?" The word was a hiss of disgust. "What *mercy* did ye have for me? I begged ye," she said, voice low.

The priest's lips curled back in a vicious smile. "And I enjoyed it, Pa—"

Brodee sent his fist flying into the priest's nose. Bone cracked, and blood spurted. The priest sagged in the guards' arms, and Brodee stepped forward to yank up the man's lolling head. "I verra much enjoyed that," he said through gritted teeth. "And I'd verra much enjoy killing ye, so if ye wish to live, I suggest ye refrain from speaking another word, or I will send my sword through yer gut with much glee, despite Lady Patience's wishes. I'm the Savage Slayer, remember? Ye will do well nae to forget it." With that warning, he released his hold on the priest's head and stepped back to Patience's side.

When his gaze caught hers for a moment, fear and awe dwelled in her eyes. "Should I fear ye, Savage Slayer?" she asked so only he could hear.

He could have told her no. He had never raised a hand to a soul who had not been attempting to do him bodily harm, or in this case harm to his soon to be wife. He wanted her trust, but he didn't want complications, nor did he want her to have expectations of him that he could never meet. The best way forward seemed to allow her ruse to continue—for now. "I would nae ever hurt a lass who's touched in the head."

Her eyes widened at that, but she nodded. He held his hand out to her. "Come. We will watch the punishment of the priest, and then we will wed."

"I dunnae wish to watch it," she said, shaking her head.

"Ye must." He grasped her hand when she did not put hers in his. "Ye will look weak otherwise, and ye kinnae be weak."

"Why nae? I'm mad, remember?"

He had to stifle his desire to laugh. She spoke too logically to convince anyone she was truly cracked, but he wouldn't tell her that. "I recall. But I'm laird, and I will nae have a weak wife."

"Ye kinnae command me to be strong," she protested.

He pulled her along toward the door to the great hall, careful to tug her just hard enough that she had no choice but to follow, yet not so much as to trip her or hurt her wrist with his hold. "I just did, Patience," he said as they exited the great hall and headed down the passage toward the courtyard. Behind them, he heard the people filing out of the great hall after them. Without pausing or looking back, he said, "Ye will either make yerself strong or I will do it for ye."

If she appeared weak, the men and women would never respect her. He could command them to treat her with respect, but that was not the same thing as being respected. When she did not answer, he stopped at the door and turned to look at her. Her mouth had dropped open, and she'd gone pale again.

God's teeth. He'd only meant he'd work with her not to fear things, but he could see he'd stirred up a ghost for her. Likely that of one—or both—of her two dead husbands.

"I will do it," she said in a choked whisper. "I dunnae

need yer aid."

He frowned. Why did he feel a flash of disappointment instead of an immediate rush of relief? This woman affected him strangely, and the less time they spent together, the better. In fact, no time together at all would likely be best. Well, except when they joined. He was a man, after all, and he had needs. His gaze fixed on her full mouth, and damned if the mere suggestive curve of her lips did not make him hard as stone.

"Go out," he commanded, stepping aside and waving her forward. The unbridled lust a simple glance at her mouth stirred in him unsettled him.

"Woof," she said, glaring at him and not moving.

This time, it was his mouth that slipped open. "Dunnae disobey me, Patience."

"Ye told me to be braw," she said, crossing her arms. But when he narrowed his eyes, a shadow of alarm touched her face. There was most definitely an inner fire in his betrothed, as well as a hefty dose of fear. He would prefer her inner fire, he realized with a start. Even if it caused him trouble, which he suspected it very well could, once she had more faith in herself. There had been a time in his life when he had no belief in himself, and he'd not wish that miserable existence on anyone.

"I do wish ye to be braw *with others*, but ye must be obedient to me," he clarified.

She quirked her dark eyebrows. "So with ye, I'm to obey mindlessly?"

"Aye." Now she was understanding. He gave her an encouraging little push out the door and into the night. Torches cast a glow around the courtyard; the guards he'd sent ahead had already started a fire in the center as he'd ordered.

He caught her by the elbow as he came to her side and guided her toward his men, seeing William and Father Murdock, who must have encountered his guards when William and the priest were on their way to the great hall. "Father Murdock," he said, releasing Patience, "this is Lady Patience. Ye will wed us tonight after I deliver justice to the priest I'll need ye to temporarily replace until I can get a new one here."

"Ah, the cracked bride-to-be!" Father Murdock exclaimed in a slur of words that made Brodee grind his teeth. Apparently the priest had already over indulged by the time William found him. Father Murdock gave a bow that almost landed him on his face.

Brodee glared at William, who shrugged helplessly. "He was in this state when I located him, and I thought it prudent to apprise him of the situation."

"Father Murdock," Brodee began, "ye will be respectful to Lady Patience *always*, or else—"

"He's likely to threaten to cut off yer hands," Patience cut in, as if she were relaying what was being served for supper.

"Patience," Brodee warned as his clanspeople started to file out of the castle and walk toward them.

"Woof," Patience said again, but this time she took a step away from him, as if she could not quite yet believe he'd not hurt her, even as the brave woman inside her was dying to surface.

"Ah, poor lass," Father Murdock said and patted Patience on the arm. "I see now the affliction ye suffer. Ye believe yerself to be a dog."

Patience's eyes widened as the clanspeople approached, and she looked suspiciously as if she were struggling not to laugh. Finally, she pressed her lips into a hard, thin line and nodded. And then his mischievous betrothed had the audacity to bring her hands up like a dog and pant. He had to turn away from her so she would not see his own smile, which had shocked him when his lips had pulled up.

William, who faced him, stepped quickly forward and drew close to whisper, "I heard murmurs in the hall that the Kincaides believe yer reputation inflated. That ye can be killed and replaced by one of their own."

Brodee nodded his appreciation of the warning and narrowed his eyes on the approaching men. He wanted peace in his life, but to get it, it seemed he'd have to pretend to be the Savage Slayer a bit longer.

Patience had determined the character of her first husband in the space of a breath, and her second in two. And she'd sinfully wished to God above that both would die by breath three. A moment after meeting Ivan, he'd slapped her in front of the priest who was to wed them, for God, her father, and all her clanspeople gathered to bear witness of how he was going to treat her. No one had raised their voice in protest, not even her brother. That had stung worse than Ivan's hit.

Of course, Duff had explained that Father had given Duff the warning look, the one that only Father could give. *Disobey and die.* Their father had two looks he reserved for them, and neither were filled with love: *Do or die* and *Do and die.* Neither ended well. It was a rather final ending, which was what really mattered. So Patience had forgiven her brother, for how could she not? Hadn't she been moved like a chess piece by the threat of death enough times over the years? Who was she to judge Duff?

She swallowed, her mouth dry, as she stared at Brodee's very broad back. Thankfully, he'd relegated her to the outer circle with William once again as her keeper, while her future husband oversaw the punishment of Father Bisby. The priest had been shoved underwater, branded property of Brodee with the word *Blackswell*, made to walk on burning logs, and now he was being stripped of his robes, which Brodee had pronounced he was not fit to wear.

It wasn't that she had changed her mind, or that she thought Father Bisby undeserving of all the punishment he was receiving. The man deserved it all, perhaps more, but she found that she had no heart or wish to stand here and witness it. In fact, his continued squealing like a pig who'd just lost his bollocks was making her stomach roil and her head feel light. Too light, as if she would swoon. But worse, frightfully worse, was that her betrothed had not blinked, flinched, or shown even the slightest hint that delivering the punishment to Father Bisby bothered him in the least.

When she glimpsed Brodee's face, it had been stony, as if nothing could crack his ruthless demeanor and touch his heart.

Who is he? The Savage Slayer or another man altogether?

Her nails bit into her skin as her worry mounted. Earlier, she'd sworn she'd seen compassion and protectiveness in him, but perhaps it was Brodee's natural tendency to simply protect what he believed was his. That was quite different from being a kind and good man.

Silas had been a man like that, one who had showed one face to the world and another to her. She'd been introduced to him by her father, and Silas had been all smiles, bows, and a press of his lips, albeit cold, to her hand. But when the solar door had closed and her father had stepped out of the room under the pretense of tending to an urgent matter, Silas had ordered her on her knees. When she'd hesitated, he'd kicked her feet out from under her so that she'd fallen. Once he was towering over her, he'd told her never to forget that she would always be below him, only to rise above others when he permitted it. Every protection she had would only come to her if she pleased him, and if she didn't, his men could do with her what they wished. And then he'd described in gory detail what they might wish.

She shuddered recalling it.

"Take him outside the protection of Blackswell land," Brodee announced, drawing Patience's attention, "and leave him."

"What am I to do?" Father Bisby wailed. "I will be attacked."

The torch Brodee was holding lit his face as he looked at the priest. Patience sucked in a breath. Her betrothed was savagely handsome, but was he savage? She sifted through the shadows of his face but saw no mercy.

"What was Patience to do when ye tortured her and she had to endure it?" Brodee's face was as hard as his voice.

"I'll die," the priest said, dropping to his knees. "Mercy. I beg ye for mercy."

"I dunnae have mercy for someone who has lied to me," Brodee said, his tone like steel.

As much as Patience despised Father Bisby, she'd never be able to close her eyes in peace again if she sat there and said nothing. She had said she wanted him to suffer, but standing here, she realized that she could not be party to what equated to allowing him to go to his death. If he should find it later, without her knowledge, well, that was God's justice. Yet she had to be careful what she said and how she said it. If she was going to convince Brodee she was touched, she could not let her pretense falter. "Silas says to give the priest a dagger," she announced, moving from her place in the outer circle.

Silence fell, and Brodee motioned her forward. She took a step, and he waved his hand for her to come closer. She didn't want to. Her body really didn't want to aid her, either. Her legs trembled and her feet felt encased in thick, unmovable muck. But she forced herself to walk, knowing if she didn't, he'd likely simply come to her. She did not want to look weak anymore. Never would she have chosen to appear cracked, but at least it had been *her choice*, and that made her feel better than she had in a very long time. She almost felt proud of herself.

Father Bisby scrambled to his feet, and when he moved to step toward her, she flinched. Brodee shot his arm out and shoved the man back. "If ye value yer life, ye will nae even blink at Patience."

"Of course, of course," Father Bisby hurriedly agreed.

In one long stride toward Patience, Brodee closed the distance between them. Heat and power radiated from the man. As her gaze slowly inched up his corded chest to his face, a dozen thoughts filled her head, one louder than all others.

Do yer enemies tremble when they see ye coming?

"Aye," he said, making her cringe with the realization that her thoughts were escaping her again. She clenched her jaw, deciding she'd keep it this way until he asked her a direct question.

"Ye say yer dead husband told ye to equip Father Bisby with a dagger?" Brodee asked, incredulous.

Heaven above, that had been a stupid lie, but she could not turn back now. "Aye."

Through the shifting torchlight, she could just make out

the way he crooked his mouth, as if he knew she was lying.

"And do ye often commune with the dead?" he asked.

Hmm. It seemed best to keep the lie simple, so it would be easier to remember. "Just Silas."

"And ye expect me to believe—"

"She loved him greatly," Kinsey blurted, breaking away from her own place in the circle and rushing to link arms with Patience. She was so dumbfounded by the show of support that she could do no more than stare in wonder and suspicion at the woman who'd acted as if Patience did not exist since the day she'd arrived.

Brodee's brows dipped together with obvious displeasure. "I must say, I'm surprised to hear this."

"Well, she did," Kinsey responded. "I mean, she does! Patience told me just yesterday that she could never imagine loving anyone but my brother."

She was so startled by Kinsey's lie that Patience opened and closed her mouth several times before she could make words come out. "I...I..."

"Poor Patience." Kinsey patted her hand. "She gets quite tongue-tied when nervous."

Patience took a deep breath to rebuff what Kinsey was saying, but Brodee's words popped into her head: *I dunnae have mercy for someone who has lied to me.* Patience nibbled on her lip, trying to decide what to do. If she revealed Kinsey's lie, what would happen to the woman? She had no loyalty to Kinsey, but neither did she want her to lose her hands— or worse. Patience did not know Brodee well enough to judge what he would truly do. So she simply shrugged, as if Kinsey spoke the truth, and made herself a liar, as well. Even more than lying, she hated for anyone to think there had been anything remotely worth loving in Silas, because there had never been.

"Is this true, Patience?" Brodee demanded.

Blast. Why did he have to make her give specific agreement? It somehow seemed to make things even more reprehensible. "Aye," she said, unable to get her voice above a threadbare whisper.

He stared at her for a long, silent moment, and then he asked, "What is Kincaide wearing when he speaks to ye?"

"What's he wearing?" she repeated. When Brodee nodded, she frowned. Why in God's name did he want to know that? Mayhap *he* was the one touched in the head. "His plaid."

"Oh, aye? Nae anything else?"

Was he supposed to be wearing something else? Mayhap Brodee knew a fae or a seer, who'd told him of ghosts. "Some braies.

"Why, of course!" he pronounced. "Everyone kens ghosts wear braies, dunnae they, Father Murdock?"

The priest, who still stood at the outer circle, coughed a bit and then said, "Aye. We all ken it."

"Deerskin shoes, too," Brodee said. "Ghosts always wear deerskin shoes, so their feet stay warm."

She had a suspicion she was somehow being tested, and whether she agreed or disagreed, she doubted she'd pass. She stepped back, recalling Ivan's hits when he was irritated with her. "Aye," she said, "and deerskin shoes."

Brodee nodded. "Ye speak the truth, then. Ye've proven it. I'm glad to ken ye're so honest, Patience."

She could not make herself agree with the statement, and she was awfully glad she held no torch because he'd surely see the blush of shame that was singeing her face. "Will ye give Father Bisby the dagger now?"

"Aye," Brodee said. "William, take the priest off my land and give him one dagger to make his way with, courtesy of my kind, *honest* betrothed." Before anything could be said or done, Brodee spoke again. "I'm laird here now, and what I say is law. I am fair, but I demand complete fealty and that every man and woman do their part to ensure the success of the clan. Ye can earn a higher place or a better position in the clan if ye show ye are worthy of it, and that is the *only* way ye can earn it. If ye kinnae give me complete fealty and ye are too lazy to work, ye should leave now. I'll give ye food rations and weapons to make yer way to where it is ye wish to go. But if ye stay and ye cross me, or ye think to overturn me as laird, or ye dunnae do yer work, or ye are nae honest, I will nae have tolerance for that. And I will nae be merciful."

With that, Brodee looked to her, and try as she might, she could not stop herself from squirming. His eyes narrowed almost infinitesimally. Unease trickled through her. Did he know she was lying?

Five

$\mathcal{I}$t had been too many years to count since Brodee had thought to wed and bind himself to a woman, heart and soul. He stole a glance at Patience, who stood trembling beside him. In moments, they would be wed and bound. Not heart and soul, but bound just the same.

Oh, the irony. There had been a time he'd wanted nothing more than to wed and it had been denied him, and now he wanted no part of a marriage, did not want his life being complicated by her. Yet here he was, unable to obtain his dream of a castle and lands to call his own without gaining a bride. Damn the king.

Brodee shifted impatiently, glaring at Father Murdock's back. What the devil was taking the priest so long to prepare to say a few words? Brodee didn't like standing still. Doing so allowed memories to stir, just as they were doing now. He'd given his heart once, and Arabel had given hers in return. His mind tried to conjure a picture of her face. He could still see her, yet he could no longer capture the essence, and it infuriated him. She'd died because she'd loved him, and he could no longer even remember the exact shape of her eyes, the richness of their color. His chest twisted in pain for her loss, for his failure to protect her. He'd not seen the enemy. He'd not even known who had killed Arabel until years later.

That's what giving one's heart did. It made one blind and vulnerable, and invited in pain. He wanted no part in it ever again. He would be a loyal husband and a good protector to Patience, but beyond that, he could offer nothing.

Father Murdock turned to them, holding the strip of Blackswell plaid Brodee had given him and the strip of cloth Patience had ripped from her cape so the priest could bind their hands during the ceremony. Beside Brodee, Patience inhaled a sharp breath. Was her apprehension because of his reputation or because she truly had loved Kincaide? Based on the way she flinched and that haunted look in her eye, he would have wagered that Kincaide had been cruel to Patience. The man had allowed her to be punished by the priest, after all, when she was clearly not a witch. She wasn't touched in the head, either, but she was wholeheartedly, rather comically, pretending to be. She'd clearly not spoken with Kincaide's ghost. It had been blatantly apparent on her face, and even more apparent in the way he'd easily led her to say what Kincaide's ghost had been wearing.

Deerskin shoes to keep the ghost's feet warm! Och!

The question was, why? If she'd loved Kincaide and did not want to be wed to or touched by Brodee, her wariness would make sense. Perhaps that was it. His gut told him otherwise, but he refused to delve any deeper to ascertain the reason. He did not need the reason. They would join eventually to consummate the marriage, but he could wait until she was more at ease with him. The ice-cold water of the loch would help alleviate any lust she might stir in him.

"Face each other please and hold out a hand," Father Murdock instructed, interrupting Brodee's thoughts.

Brodeee turned toward Patience and frowned. She was facing forward still, looking very much like a hunted deer.

He was glad in this moment that he'd decided to wed in the chapel in privacy, with only William to bear witness, instead of standing in front of the kirk for all the gathered clan to watch. He'd learned to live with people thinking him brutal, but he didn't particularly care for people seeing how scared his betrothed was to wed him.

"Patience," he said and waited a beat.

When she didn't appear to have heard him, he reached out and gripped her shoulders. Her reaction was immediate. Her body tensed and her head whipped toward him, but her lowered lashes prevented him from reading her emotions.

That same gut instinct that told him Patience's actions were driven by much more than mourning the loss of a great love stirred within Brodee.

Dunnae delve. State facts, he reminded himself.

She could keep her secrets just as he would keep his. He did not drop his hands from her shoulders. "Ye need nae fear me, Patience. Nae ever."

"Words," she said, looking down at her slippers. "Just words."

He hooked a finger under her chin and gently raised her face to his. Her beauty struck him speechless for a moment. Everything about her was dark, from her black, glossy hair and lowered lashes, to her olive skin, to her eyes with their obsidian color that was only broken by flecks of gold. She reminded him of shadows where treasure lay, shadows that beckoned for a man to partake, to come closer, to chance the danger ahead. "I will nae ever fail to keep my word to ye."

She looked up then, disbelief etched upon her face, making her look like a goddess who'd been turned to stone. A long ,slow breath broke the spell. "I dunnae ken ye," she said. "I dunnae ken if I can believe ye."

"Ye will ken me eventually, and ye will believe."

She glanced away.

"As if it matters," he heard. "As if my father gave me a choice in wedding ye. As if he has ever given me a choice or even cared."

Her words made him hurt for her, but they stung him as well, even though they shouldn't. Even though it was best she did not want to wed him. She'd want less from him that way. Yet they nicked his pride, which had been perforated a million times before by harsh comments from his father. "And ye think I've a choice?" he asked, wincing at how harsh his voiced sounded.

She turned her head slowly toward him again, those dark, unfathomable eyes locking with his. Lines appeared between her brows. "But ye're the Savage Slayer."

A bitter laugh he'd not expected escaped him, and her gaze widened. "Aye." He nodded, not uttering his unspoken truths. He'd been a man with no home to own, no lands to rule, and to get it, he had to sacrifice. Did he have a choice? He frowned. He wasn't certain he had. If he wanted anything truly his own, to feel any worth, he could not go back to the home in which he was raised, which meant he did what he must to lay claim to his own home.

"And still," he finally said, "I stand here. Hold out yer hand." It was a command, yet when her chin notched up, he recognized he was the one puncturing her now. Little nicks at her worth that might eventually kill her soul. "Please," he added. William began to cough behind him, no doubt in disbelief at Brodee's words. He felt shock himself, but he'd have made the same choice again.

Hesitantly, she held out her slender arm, and he reached out and clasped her tiny hand, setting his rough, battle-scarred hands upon her silky skin. The desire the touch unleashed was almost unbearable. God's teeth, he'd need to take a swim in the loch directly after this.

He looked to Father Murdock, who was gaping at him, and nodded. "Begin."

◄◦❦◦►

Patience trembled so bad she was certain Brodee must feel it, but he did not look at her, and when the priest bowed his head and Brodee did as well, she did the same.

"Lord," Father Murdock began, "help Lady Patience and Blackswell to remember when they first met."

Patience looked up in surprise and found Brodee had done the same. He was frowning as he stared at the priest, whose head was still bowed, his hands folded in front of him. Patience inhaled a long breath and frowned. The smell of wine swirled off the priest.

"Help them to recall the strong love that grew between them," he said.

"Father Murdock, we met yesterday," Brodee said, a shadow of annoyance on his face and underlying his tone. "Ye can skip the prayer and move straight to the ceremony."

"Lass?" the priest asked, as if he expected her to protest.

Heat warmed her cheeks. She nodded. "Aye, ye can go straight to the ceremony."

Father Murdock shrugged. "If ye both say so."

"We do," Brodee said, his lips pressing together.

Father Murdock brought the Blackswell plaid to Brodee's and Patience's hands and started winding the cloth around their wrists to tie it in a knot. "Brodee Blackswell, Laird of Clan Blackswell, say yer vows."

Patience frowned. She'd only just ever stood in front of

the priest and said her name and that she wished to wed the man beside her. Were those the vows he meant? They'd been lies. They'd meant less than nothing to her.

Brodee took a deep breath and began to speak. "Ye kinnae possess me, for I belong to myself." She sucked in a sharp breath at the words, and a gentle, shocking smile pulled at his lips. "I thought ye might like that," he said, looking at her as if they were the only two in the chapel, which of course they were not. Still, the way his gaze simmered as it held hers caused warmth to flow through her, and suddenly, she stopped trembling.

"Blackswell, ye kinnae stop during yer vows," Father Murdock complained, and then her betrothed, the man known as Savage Slayer, did the most shocking thing—he winked at her. She felt her own lips pull into an outrageous grin.

His forefinger of the hand atop of hers trailed back and forth as soft as a feather over the skin of her wrist. It was the gentlest touch she'd ever felt from a man, and she was at once both intrigued and frightened, because it made her belly tighten with emotions she had never experienced while it made her heart quicken with the one feeling she knew all too well—fear. Did he truly intend to be tender with her, or was he simply playing a game as Silas had loved so much to do?

She did not dare to hope it was the former, yet her pulse began to beat erratically as his smoldering gaze delved into her.

His smile touched his eyes, and he continued. "But while we both wish it, I give ye that which is mine to give. Ye kinnae command me, for I am a free person, but I shall serve ye in those ways ye require." Something about the look that suddenly appeared in his gaze made her even warmer. "And the honeycomb will taste sweeter coming from my hand. I pledge to ye that yers will be the name I cry aloud in the night and the eyes into which I smile in the morning. I pledge to ye the first bite from my meat and the first drink from my cup. I pledge to ye my living and dying, equally in yer care, and to tell no strangers our grievances. This is my wedding vow to ye. This is a marriage of equals."

He didn't mean it. He couldn't mean it. But her heart squeezed into a tight ball just the same. "Those are the most beautiful words I've ever heard," she said.

"Ye are the most beautiful woman I've ever seen," he replied, and then his eyes went wide, and she knew in that instant that he'd not intended to say the thought aloud, which led her to believe he'd actually meant it.

Her eyes widened in shock. "Ye think me beautiful?"

He gave her a searching look. "Dunnae sound so stunned. I'm certain I'm nae yer first husband to tell ye so."

The reminder of her past husbands felt akin to his throwing a bucket of freezing loch water on her. She could not stop the shiver that swept through her. He was not the first to tell her she was lovely, no. Ivan had always told her it was her fault he beat her because she was so bonny that he was forced to be jealous, so he had to make her understand never to be disloyal.

"Ye kinnae talk during the ceremony," Father Murdock said and glared at them both.

She nodded quickly, glad to have an excuse not to answer Brodee's question. She looked to the priest. "Do I repeat the vows?"

"Only if ye wish to be wed this day, lass." Father Murdock gave a her a look that said he had his doubts.

For a breath, she considered what would come to pass if she simply refused to say the vows and wed Brodee. Her father's voice rang in her head. *Do or die, Patience.* She wondered then what her father was gaining from this marriage. She did not know. He had not revealed it in his letter nor had he bothered to come to tell her that he'd basically once again used her. There had to be a gain for him, of that much she was certain.

"I'm ready," she said, fixing her gaze on Brodee's broad chest. She feared if she looked at his face, he'd read the terror in her eyes, and she did not wish him to see just how scared she was. Father Murdock began to read her vows and she repeated them, her belly clenching tight with worry for what would come after. Would Brodee parade her through the great hall and drag her to the marriage bed for all to witness the consummation? That's what both Silas and Ivan had done. The thought of having to go through a public bedding a third time made her sway.

A gentle, steadying hand came to her elbow, and she raised her eyes to find him watching her. "Are ye all right?"

His intense scrutiny made her nervous, and she blurted, "I had hoped to nae ever say wedding vows again."

Brodee's brows dipped into a frown. "Because ye loved Kincaide?" His tone sounded almost jealous, and it struck her speechless. "Ye need nae bother answering. Yer silence says it all." All she could do was stare, stuck in a trap of her own creation because she'd gone along with Kinsey's story. "Ye will forget him."

It was a command. A cold and very firm one. And it infuriated her, which was ridiculous because that was precisely what she wanted to do: forget Silas. And Ivan. And her father. And all men, honestly. But she was heartily sick of being commanded and obeying like a scared dog. "I will try, but it may be difficult since Silas does visit me daily to talk to me."

For one moment, her new husband—wait, were they wed now?—looked as if he would cheerily throttle her. She bit her lip and started to step away from him, but he snaked a hand firmly around her neck. "What are ye doing?" she asked, her body tensing and preparing for the worst.

"Kissing ye, of course, lass. That is how ye end the wedding ceremony and begin the life of a *happily* wedded couple."

As his face drew closer she tried to pull back, but moving him was like trying to move a boulder—pointless. "I've nae ever heard of such a custom," she said, her heart pounding in her ears.

A devilish gleam came to his eyes. "Well, now ye have."

"But—" She did not get the chance to finish her objection. His lips brushed over hers, and whatever she was going to say, promptly fled her head.

The kiss started slow and thoughtful, the softness of it surprising. She'd been prepared for pain, punishment, anger, but this…this caress of his lips to hers sent the pit of her stomach into an odd, wild swirl, and she found herself curious and suddenly leaning toward him rather than straining to get away. A slide of his tongue over the crease of her lips made her gasp. It was darkly alluring, that velvet warmth. His lips massaged hers, coaxed and parted them, and her heart jolted when his tongue tangled with hers. Deep at her core, a throb began, and a moan escaped her.

A clearing of a throat brought her reeling back to her senses. As Brodee broke the kiss and gave her a look of primal possession, she pressed her hand against her thundering heart. What had just happened? That kiss was… Well, it was the most magical thing she'd ever experienced. She hadn't known anything like that was even possible. A spark of hope flared in her, and then Brodee said, "Ye may go. Have yer chambermaid wash ye and dress ye in a gown for the obligatory wedding celebration."

Humiliation burned her cheeks. He'd dismissed her like a dog with yet another command. And one that would lead to the public bedding. All hope died where it had first sparked. She supposed she had her answer now, at least. She was wed once again, and it seemed that it was to yet another intolerable man.

Six

"For a man who has long claimed he dunnae have a desire to be wed, ye certainly kissed yer new wife with what appeared, to my discerning eye, as an abundance of enthusiasm," William said just before he took a swig of the wine he'd helped himself to in what was now Brodee's solar.

"If ye were anyone else under my command, Will, I'd seriously consider cutting out yer tongue for insubordination."

William lowered the goblet, pressed to his lips together, and then grinned. "Well, I'm nae anyone else, and I ken what others dunnae."

God above knew that was true. They knew things about each other that no one else did. Instead of asking what he meant, which Brodee knew William was waiting for him to do, Brodee poured himself a goblet of wine, found a seat, crossed his legs at the ankles, and took a long drink, allowing the liquid to slide down his throat to his belly, in hopes it would move along to other parts of his body and dampen the lust Patience had awoken in him.

He'd had women in the years since Arabel had died, and it wasn't that he hadn't wanted them, but it had been more like a scratch that needed to be itched just so the uncomfortableness would go away. The kiss he'd shared with

Patience, however, had elicited a storm of yearning. He'd not planned on kissing to end the wedding ceremony, and he wasn't quite sure how his lips had ended up on hers. Frankly, his good sense had left him when she'd blurted out that she had hoped never to speak wedding vows again and then implied with her silence that it was because of her dishonorable dead husband.

Why? Why had that bothered him? He'd spent years training himself not to need or care if someone denied him or found him lacking in some way, and he wasn't even convinced Patience had loved Kincaide. *That was it!* It was because he suspected she *hadn't* loved the man that it felt personal that she did not want him at all.

"Am I going to have to wait all night for ye to ask me what I ken that others dunnae?" William inquired, drawing Brodee's attention to his friend once more.

Brodee decided to play William's little game, if only to draw his thought away from Patience. "What do ye ken about me that others dunnae?"

"Finally!" William said. "Ye dunnae dispute yer reputation when others mention it, though it's false." He gave Brodee a long look. "Letting yer enemies believe ye to be savage keeps them scairt and those who'd try to get close to ye at a distance."

"My reputation ensures that many a fool who would oppose us dunnae, and that spares lives," Brodee replied, correcting William.

"As I said." William winked. "It keeps yer enemies scairt and those who'd try to get close to ye at a distance."

Brodee leveled William with a scowl. "I did nae say a word about keeping anyone at a distance."

William took another swig of wine and shrugged. "Ye did nae have to. I ken ye. I already kenned yer aim was to spare lives." He took a seat in the chair across from Brodee and leaned forward, as if he was about to reveal a secret. "Ye forget I've been fighting by yer side for over a year."

"I did nae forget," Brodee responded, leaning forward to reveal a few of the secrets he kept of William's. He saw what William was trying to do. Make Brodee analyze himself, and he didn't want to any more than William did. Mutual ignorance of the past was one of the things that had bonded them as friends. "Ye forget I ken what drove ye to seek out the Dark Riders to train ye."

William's face darkened. "We are nae talking about me."

"We will be, if ye push me to talk about myself."

William frowned at Brodee. "All I was going to say is I've watched ye for a year in the battles, and ye did all ye could to avoid killing other men, even enemies who were determined to kill ye. And I watched ye after battles, too. Ye rarely took women to yer bed, and when ye did, ye chose carefully. Ye picked women who did nae want more from ye than a night of pleasure."

Brodee's temple began to pulse with annoyance. "Ye waste yer time watching me so closely, Will," he said, hoping it would end the conversation.

"Nay." William shook his head. "I watch ye to pattern myself after ye."

"What?" He could not have heard correctly.

"Ye have respect," William said. "Of the men who fight under ye, of the king, of lairds and commoners alike. Hell, even of yer enemies when they come to see how honorable ye are. I want respect. I want to wipe away the dark cloud that hangs over me. I see how the men, even the king, eye me. As if I may one day betray them as my brother did. I want them to look at me with trust and respect as they do ye. So I watch ye." William let out a long sigh and set his wine goblet on the floor by his feet before threading his fingers together. "I watch ye to learn, to emulate, so that I can be the sort of man people look to for guidance."

Brodee felt his mouth drop open. Growing up, he'd struggled to gain even his father's esteem. He had always made Brodee feel not good enough. Not purposely, Brodee knew that now, but that did not wipe away how his father had made him feel. Then he'd struggled to gain the respect of his clan, who'd feared him more than respected him, unsure in their hearts whether he was a murderer or not. The memory made his fists clench, recalling how people had thought he'd possibly killed Arabel, whom he'd loved, and Lenora, whom he'd not loved but was supposed to wed to keep the peace between their clans. When the truth had finally come out years later, that a man who'd long hated his family had killed the women, he'd expected to feel differently, to feel as if his clan now respected him, but he'd felt the same. So he'd left.

Brodee ran a hand through his hair, feeling a new burden, the heavy one of William's admiration. It wasn't unwelcome, just surprising. "I did nae expect to be curious about her," he said low, admitting a truth, feeling compelled to, given what William had just shared.

William nodded. "I figured as much. But ye *are* curious?" William hitched up his dark brows.

Brodee gave a reluctant nod.

"Ye look so forlorn about it," William said with a chuckle.

"'Tis the God's truth, it makes me feel forlorn," Brodee said honestly.

The smile that had been on William's face quickly faded. "Why? Because of Arabel?"

"Will." The one word was a warning.

William held up his hands. "I'll nae attempt to discuss yer past."

"Excellent," Brodee replied. "'Tis a sound way to ensure ye keep yer tongue."

A derisive sound came from William, and then he said, "I think if ye were nae intrigued by yer new wife, that would be the bigger concern."

"Oh aye? Why is that?" Brodee asked, finishing the wine in his goblet and setting it down.

William held up his fist and popped out a finger. "She's quite bonny."

Her image filled Brodee's head. The same that had several times. Patience with her arm's spread wide, skirts tied to expose her shapely legs, and her head thrown back as she twirled under the moonlight with shadows cast by the fire dancing across her face. "Aye," he replied, not saying more. He had no wish to reveal just how enticing he thought Patience was.

William held up a second finger. "She's pretending to be touched in the head."

"Aye," Brodee agreed. "How did ye ken that she was feigning it?"

"She has too many logical moments," he replied and popped up another finger. "She's intriguing. A bonny lass who blurts her thoughts without realizing but purposely is pretending to be cracked? Is it because she dunnae wish ye to touch her or bed her because her dead husband has her heart?" Brodee took a breath to speak, but William kept talking. "Or it is because she fears ye since she only kens ye as the Savage Slayer? Or is it neither? She's intriguing."

"Aye," Brodee reluctantly agreed a third time. "But I dunnae wish to be intrigued."

William let out a bark of laughter. "I dunnae believe ye have much control over that."

"I can control it," Brodee said, willing it to be so.

"Ye think 'tis so easy to control how a woman makes ye feel?"

"Aye, I do. I've nae wanted a woman in my life for many years, so I've nae allowed myself to feel for one."

William shook his head at Brodee and gave him a look that implied he had no sense. "Ye are a daft fool. Ye've nae had the complication of a woman who meant anything to ye because ye had nae yet met a woman who truly intrigued ye. And now, my friend," he said, standing up and stretching, "ye are wed for life to a woman who intrigues ye."

Brodee didn't like how logical William's point was. He would *not* care for Patience. He had no desire to ever open himself up again to the pain that went along with loving someone and losing them. It was misery.

William clapped him on the shoulder, bringing Brodee's attention back to his friend. "If ye need guidance in discerning Patience's true character, I'm happy to aid ye," he offered with a wink.

Brodee frowned. "What the devil do ye ken about women?"

"Nae much myself," William said with a shrug, "but I've watched verra carefully how a woman can lead a man to the Heavens or to Hell. And from what I've observed, men that protest the most, fall the hardest. I saw it happen with my brother."

Brodee gave a tilt of his head in acknowledgment. He knew William's brother, Bram, had betrayed the king and his laird for the love of a woman who had led him astray.

"I've compiled a list of qualities to be wary of in a woman," he went on.

Brodee raised a brow. "Such as?"

"She's cruel to animals and children. She complains a great deal. She's lazy. She steals. She is nae true to ye."

The mere idea of Patience bedding another man made Brodee's fingers reflexively curl into a fist. The vows had been spoken. He would not have made himself hers voluntarily, but that had nothing to do with her. She was the bonniest creature he'd ever beheld, and aside from pretending she was cracked, she seemed lovely. And now he was hers and she was his. He would never take another woman to his bed, and he expected her to never take another man to hers.

"She sneaks off," William continued, oblivious to Brodee's inner thoughts. "Especially at night. Oh, ye catch her in a lie that endangers yer life." William pointed a finger at Brodee. "That one is especially important."

Brodee laughed. "So 'tis fine if I catch Patience in a lie as long as it dunnae endanger my life?"

"Exactly," William pronounced. "She may say things such as she's nae angry when ye ken damn well that she's vexed. 'Tis annoying but harmless. Now imagine that she feigns her own kidnapping, for instance, and when ye go to rescue her, ye realize it was a ploy to get ye in front of the king's enemy. For the love of Christ, dunnae join with the enemy for her and betray the king."

Brodee knew well that William spoke of Bram's plight. William's face twisted with shame.

Brodee clasped William on the shoulder. "Yer brother's shame is nae yers."

William's gaze locked with Brodee's. "'Tis why I pledged myself to ye, Blackswell. Ye honestly believe that, whereas most men believe the opposite. But we are nae here to discuss me. Since ye are nae going to care for yer wife's feelings, I suppose ye will permit a public bedding tonight? After all, what does it matter if she's shamed when we all watch ye join with her?"

"I ken what ye are trying to do," Brodee said, "and there's nae a need for ye to try to protect *my* wife."

William grinned. "Ye're verra possessive for a man with plans nae to care—"

"Will," Brodee warned again.

"All right, all right," William said and held his hands in the sign of peace, his palms facing Brodee. "What shall I tell the men? Ask for the public bedding or nay?"

"Nay," Brodee replied, seeing William fight a relieved smile. "I detest the practice, as well."

"I had hoped ye might," William said.

"I dunnae have any intention of allowing it, and I'd already planned on telling the men at the conclusion of the wedding feast nae to call for it."

"Excellent. I'll give them yer orders."

Brodee nodded as he stood. "I've another assignment for ye, too," he said, his mind turning over all he had discovered in his short time at the castle.

"Aye, what's that?"

"I want ye to take the next few days to discover— *quietly*—what ye can about Patience."

William frowned. "Do ye fear she's going to spy on ye for her father?"

"Nay." He thought of what she'd said about her father when she'd not even realized she was speaking aloud. *As if he has ever given me a choice or even cared.* No, he did not think Patience was spying on him for her father. "I want ye to discern what people think of her, beyond them believing her *ban-druidh*, thanks to Father Bisby. And what do they ken of that? Discover if she's hated or liked, and if hated, is it more than the rumors surrounding her? How long was she wed to Silas? How long has she lived here?"

"I can do it, but 'tis interesting to me that ye wish me to discern things about a woman ye dunnae want to truly be part of yer life."

Just because he did not believe her to be a spy did not mean he knew who she was. "I would ken all I can of anyone I'm to sleep next to," he said.

"'Tis a well-made point," William said, heading for the door. "I'll start now. That lass Kinsey is verra fetching, and I'm certain with a little persuasion, I can get her to talk."

"Careful with that one," Brodee said. "Something about her makes me distrustful."

William flashed a wolfish grin. "I can handle one wee lass. I'll see ye at supper."

"Aye," Brodee agreed. He departed the solar after William but headed to the loch for a swim before the festivities. For once, old memories did not drive him to the icy waters for the oblivion the numbness offered.

Desire hastened his steps. He wanted to be in complete control of his yearning for Patience before tonight. There would not be a public bedding, but he would take his wife that night, as much for her protection—men *would* know she was the wife of the Savage Slayer and fear hurting her— as for the lust that had flared to life within him.

⚜

Patience sank into the tub of warm water with a weary sigh. Her hands and back ached from carrying all the heavy buckets of water necessary to fill the tub for the bath Brodee had ordered her to take. Not that she minded washing—she didn't. But she hated being ordered about as though she did not have any intelligence, and she detested swallowing how she really felt out of fear of what would happen if she spoke the words aloud.

Water sluiced over her skin and began to ease the tension that had built up from today. She spread her fingers under the water and swished them through the liquid, reveling in the instant soothing of the raw blisters she'd gotten from trudging up and down the back stairs, the ones only the servants took. It would have been faster to take the main stairwell, but she'd been afraid to chance Brodee, or any of his men—especially William, who seemed nearly as observant as Brodee—seeing her.

The servants had never actually served her, except Jane occasionally in the last few weeks, and that was simply because Silas was dead and Kinsey had instructed Jane to do so. Mostly Jane just left the goblets of wine Patience didn't drink. Thoughts of the wine conjured recollections of her father. He always drank wine, and too much of it. It made him crueler than he naturally was, which was already terribly so.

The other servants had either ignored, feared, or belittled Patience since the day she'd arrived at the castle, and Silas had made it clear they were free to act that way. Still, she'd thought perhaps they might aid her with the water buckets today, out of fear of angering Brodee. Yet each person she'd asked had snickered at her, and she'd been unable to find Jane.

The heat rising from the water made sleep tug at her, sleep she could not relent to when she had to present herself in the great hall soon. Panic swiftly choked her at the thought of the public bedding she'd likely have to endure. She squeezed her eyes shut and inhaled a long breath, trying to stave off the rising tide of terror. Blood roared in her ears, and her throat closed.

"Patience?"

She jerked at the voice and opened her eyes, crossing her arms over her chest as she twisted around to glance toward the voice. Kinsey stood behind her, looking down with an intense look on her face. Contemplation, perhaps? Then the expression gave way to one of concern, and she held a goblet toward Patience. "Wine?"

When had the woman come in? And what was she even doing in here?

Patience shook her head. "I dunnae drink wine."

"So Jane tells me."

Patience frowned. "Jane? Why would Jane tell ye that?"

"She was fretting that ye were nae pleased with the way she was serving ye."

Patience made a note to herself to ensure Jane knew she was glad to have her as a lady's maid. "What are ye doing in here?" she asked as she reached for the wrapper that was on the floor by the tub.

Kinsey set the wine goblet down, bent over, scooped up the wrapper, and held it out to Patience. "I came to apologize."

"What for?"

As Patience reached for the wrapper, Kinsey grabbed her hand. "I'm ashamed to say I believed Silas when he said ye were *ban-druidh*, which is why I kept my distance. And 'tis why, I, well, I—" Kinsey bit her lip. "I told Blackswell about it. I'm verra sorry."

Patience stared open-mouthed at the apology. Kinsey had barely spoken to her in the months since Patience had come here. She had suspected Silas's claims were why, but she had wondered sometimes if it were more, if there was something inherently unworthy about her that made people simply dislike her.

She tugged her hand free from Kinsey and stood, careful to cover herself as she did. She stepped out of the tub while wrapping herself in the drying cloth. "Ye dunnae need to apologize. Ye apparently believed it. Besides, ye telling Brodee about it is why Father Bisby was sent away, and that is a blessing. The man was horrid."

"Aye, it seems so. I did nae have any notion of the things he'd done to ye. Of course, I kenned he cleansed yer soul, but I did nae ken what it entailed. Did ye ken ye were to be wed to Blackswell?" The question had an odd undercurrent to it. Perhaps Kinsey felt it was disloyal to Silas's memory for Patience to be wed so soon to another.

"I only just found out this morning when I received a missive from my father," Patience said, sidestepping Kinsey and walking to the bed where her gown was laid out. She slipped it over her head, then let the drying cloth fall once the gown was covering her. She turned to Kinsey, who now stood by the window. The woman's back was to her, her arms hugging her waist. Her long blond hair hung in a heavy braid down her back. The light color was the exact shade Silas's had been. Patience found herself clenching her teeth on memories of him looming over her, his hair hanging on either side of his face as he took her quickly and without tenderness. Patience squeezed her eyes shut for a moment, trying to battle the memories, and when she opened them, Kinsey was watching her.

Patience could not fathom why Kinsey was not yet wed. She was several years older than Patience and a beautiful woman. She was clearly competent at running castles, too, as she ran this one. All the servants stopped immediately to do her bidding, unlike how they treated Patience. Perhaps since Kinsey did not seem to fear her anymore, she would aid Patience in swaying the castle staff to accept her. She could dearly use a friend in plotting how to drive her husband away from her, as well. Patience would love to know how Kinsey really felt about her brother, but she could not just bluntly ask, so instead she said, "Thank ye for the apology," for lack of anything better to say.

Kinsey surprised her by walking toward her and grabbing her hand. "I want to do more for ye to atone for nae aiding ye sooner. I suspected that Silas was unkind to ye, and I did nae do anything to help. I was already feeling guilty for not interfering on yer behalf, and I'm ashamed to admit I first sent Jane to ye to spy on ye."

Patience nodded. She'd suspected as much.

"I'll tell her nae to do so anymore," Kinsey offered.

"I'd appreciate that," Patience replied. "Did ye nae aid me because ye were afraid of me?" It was a leading question, one she hoped would earn her a response about how Kinsey felt about Silas so Patience could judge the woman. Patience held her breath as she waited.

Kinsey bit her lip. "That was some of it, but mostly, I did nae interfere because I was afraid of Silas."

"I see," Patience said, her mind turning over all she was discovering. "Is that why ye showed me support earlier when I said I spoke with yer brother's ghost?"

"Aye," Kinsey admitted, eyeing Patience. "Did ye truly?"

Patience shook her head.

Kinsey smirked. "I suspected ye did nae."

"Why?" Patience asked, concerned that if Kinsey had seen through Patience's charade, then Brodee surely had, too.

"Because Silas was a cruel, evil man," Kinsey said, her

gaze seeming to bore into Patience as if she was waiting to see Patience's reaction. But she just stood in silence. She'd learned the wisdom of keeping her opinions to herself a long time ago.

Kinsey waved a hand in front of her face as if she'd lost where she had been going with her thought, but then she said, "I could nae fathom that he'd be trying to aid someone other than himself, even as a ghost."

Patience could hardly believe Kinsey had just said that, and she was even more shocked when Kinsey smiled, then linked her arm with Patience's. She led her to the bed and pulled her down to sit beside her. "I imagine ye dunnae wish to be wed to a man kenned as the Savage Slayer, do ye?" Kinsey asked.

"Ye imagine correctly, but I'm wed now. So…" She trailed off, not sure how much she should trust Kinsey, if at all.

"So ye want to make Blackswell think ye cracked so he will leave ye be? So he will nae bother with ye or harm ye as my brother did?"

"Aye," Patience admitted. "Ye think it a terrible plan?"

"Nay." The woman gave a secretive smile. "I think it's an excellent plan to make the man think ye have gone mad. If we are verra clever, he will nae take ye to his bed. Then the marriage would nae be valid, and he could cast ye—" Kinsey gave Patience an apologetic look. "I mean, ye could be free of him. Sent home when he realizes he simply kinnae tolerate being wed to ye. Of course—" the woman tapped a finger to her lips "—that could take a bit of time." Kinsey moved her mouth back and forth. "It will do."

Patience frowned. She got the feeling Kinsey was not talking to her so much as thinking aloud, but she appreciated the aid. Yet uneasiness did stir within her. While she certainly did not want to be wed, being sent home to her father was not a good alternative. He'd likely kill her if she mucked up the marriage or he would hurt Duff.

Do or die, Patience.

No, she could not go home. Until Duff came to rescue he—if he came at all—she wanted her husband to stay away from her, not *send* her away. "I…" She swallowed, ashamed to admit her predicament, so instead, thinking upon the moments with her new husband in which he'd not seemed savage, she said, "What if his reputation is exaggerated or untrue?"

Kinsey gave her an annoyed look. "Dunnae be a fool. 'Tis nae exaggerated. I overheard his warriors boasting earlier about how merciless he is. He apparently slaughters his enemies even if they surrender."

Patience tried to imagine the man who had kissed her so passionately being so heartless, and she simply could not, but that was naive and foolish, as Kinsey had just pointed out, rudely but likely justifiably.

"This is what ye need to do," Kinsey said. "Continue to act touched in the head. If he tries to touch ye in any way, mayhap ye could pretend it scares ye." Patience shifted, uncomfortable with how close to the truth that was.

Except, she realized with a start, she'd not felt scared at the end of Brodee's kiss. She'd felt warm, tingly, and full of want. She hissed in a breath, and Kinsey patted her on the hand again. "Be braw, and remember, dunnae allow him to consummate the marriage." Her voice had grown harsh. "If ye do join with him, he kinnae ask the king to dismiss the vows, so ye must nae allow it."

But if Brodee asked the king to dissolve the marriage, she'd be sent home. God above!

The supper horn sounded, and Kinsey stood so fast that

Patience blinked in surprise. "I'll go ahead of ye to the great hall and try to aid yer cause in ensuring Blackswell leaves ye alone. Wait awhile before coming, and ye can claim ye were talking to Silas and lost track of time."

"Oh!" Patience exclaimed. "That's an excellent idea."

Kinsey's eyes gleamed with triumph that made Patience laugh. It was so good to finally have a friend.

Kinsey's lips twisted into a wicked smile. "I'm full of excellent ideas, Patience. *Have faith.*"

Seven

"*I* think if ye make the men wait any longer for the bride, ye may have a riot." William's tone was light, but his face was serious from where he sat to Brodee's right upon the dais.

Brodee nodded, stood, and held up his hands for silence. It took a moment for the cacophony in the great hall to subside, but when it finally did, he could have heard a sigh, or a door creaking open, which is exactly what happened.

He looked toward the entrance more swiftly than he wished he had. The anticipation in his gut to see Patience was undeniable and irksome, but the disappointment that immediately consumed him was shocking. And more than troubling. He should not care where she was as long as she was safe. Except he'd told her to be in attendance, and if he could not command obedience from his wife, the men would note that and think they could disobey him, as well. And then he'd have a problem. He preferred to avoid problems that would cause him to punish people. Yet, as Kinsey Kincaide entered the hall and strolled toward them, he found himself hoping she was coming to tell him of Patience's whereabouts.

"Laird," the blond-haired, blue-eyed woman said as she curtsied. "Might I join ye at the dais?"

He was tempted to say no, but he'd learned from his

time working for the king, that sometimes it was best to keep close those you were not sure you could trust.

"Let the celebration begin!" he said to the waiting clanspeople, and then he motioned to the empty seat to his left where Patience should be sitting. "It seems I'm minus one bride, so by all means..."

Once Kinsey was settled into her seat, she leaned close to him, as if what she had to say were secret. That or she simply wanted to press her breasts against his arm. He suspected it was the latter based on the flirtatious look upon her face, and based on William behind her shaking his head and wagging his finger. Brodee scowled at William. The man should know he'd never take up with the sister of the man he'd killed—or any woman, for that matter. He'd told William he intended to be loyal to Patience, and he meant it.

"I'm dismayed to tell ye that Patience may nae come to the supper," Kinsey said.

He arched his eyebrows at the revelation. "Is my wife ill?" he asked, his chest tightening at the word *wife*. Would he ever feel settled with the new state of his life?

Kinsey placed her hand on his bicep, a smile curving her lips even as her fingers tightened upon him. It was a seemingly innocent gesture, but a warning went off in his head. Yet, when he looked at her, he saw nothing concerning in her gaze. The woman let out a long sigh, too exaggerated to be believable, and said, "I dunnae wish to speak ill of her..." She glanced expectantly at him from under her now-lowered lashes, giving him a prodding look.

Behind her, William rolled his eyes, and Brodee found he wished he could do the same. Except of course, he'd play whatever game she was currently involved in until he learned her rules and defeated her. It would be simpler to wed her away, but he had no liking for forced weddings. Mayhap she had someone in mind, though.

"Of course ye dunnae," he said, picking up the stick she dangled in front of him. "But I must insist, if ye ken something that will guide me in dealing with Patience, then I wish to hear it."

"Well," Kinsey said, quirking her mouth, "she was always most difficult for my brother. Nae ever wishing to do as he commanded. It seems she will continue to be that way with ye. I heard," she whispered, "that she was verra difficult with her first husband, as well."

"She was wed before yer brother?" Brodee asked, surprised. The king had not told him that.

She tilted her head at him. "Aye. Did ye nae ken it?"

"Nay," he admitted. "To whom was she wed?"

"Ivan Sutherland."

Brodee had known Ivan. He'd crossed paths with the laird at many tournaments. The man had been sadistic and had a penchant for beating women and boys who he was supposed to be training. An uneasy feeling flared in his chest. "How long was she wed to Sutherland?"

"Three months," Kinsey said. "He simply dropped dead. Some say she killed him."

"He probably deserved it," Brodee announced, pleased he kept his tone neutral even as he gripped his wine goblet so hard his fingers pulsed. William spat out the wine he'd just drank onto his trencher and laughed.

Kinsey frowned, looking back and forth between William and Brodee. "Laird, surely ye dunnae mean that."

"He likely does," William said, scooting forward so that his chin was almost resting on Kinsey's shoulder.

A look of pure annoyance swept across her face. "Do ye mind?"

"I do, as a matter of fact," William replied with a grin. "We both kenned Sutherland, and I've nae a doubt that if Lady Blackswell killed the man, he had it coming."

"Do ye have proof that she killed him?" Brodee asked, his mind turning. He thought he recalled someone mentioning that Sutherland had been wed earlier this year. That had to be to Patience, which meant Brodee's marriage to her made the third in a year. He had an unwelcome suspicion the first two marriages had not been pleasant.

"Well, n-nay," Kinsey sputtered.

He'd not thought she had. Still, the confirmation was welcome. "Then dunnae accuse someone of murder," Brodee replied.

"Blackswell dunnae take kindly to accusations of murder, having been accused of it twice himself," William announced in his characteristically blunt, unthinking manner. Brodee would have cheerfully throttled William in that moment for revealing things he wished to remain private.

"Oh," Kinsey said, her eyes not showing the fear he would have expected at such news. She seemed strangely unaffected by the announcement that people had accused him of murder. Maybe his gut was wrong about her. Maybe she was a better person than he had thought. She shrugged. "I did nae have any notion. I'm verra sorry, laird." She squeezed his arm, and his fingers twitched with the need to smack her hand away. "Obviously, ye were nae guilty of the deeds, as ye are sitting here now."

"I appreciate yer willingness to judge my character for yerself," he said, meaning it.

Her gaze meandered slowly down him, and he got the feeling again that there was more to Kinsey Kincaide than she was revealing. She brought her eyes to his. "I ask that ye do the same for me."

It felt as if she somehow knew he'd had an almost immediate wariness of her. He didn't like being read; he preferred to be the one doing the reading. "Of course," he replied. "I dunnae ever decide upon a person's character without learning them."

This time, a look came to her eyes that he did recognize: desire. It was gone so fast, he could almost believe he'd imagined it, except her hand, still curled on his bicep, now gripped him tighter. He knew many married men took lemans, but he wanted no part of that. If he'd been certain that was what she was thinking, he would have made it clear right then that it was not something that would ever happen, yet he was not sure so he kept his silence.

Instead, he stood abruptly to put distance between them and to find Patience, who should have already appeared for dinner. The door swung open, and as if conjured by his thoughts, his bride stood on the threshold dressed in—He blinked, and then his lips parted in shock. His new ghost-talking, supposedly cracked wife was dressed in her very transparent léine with her hair unbound and her feet bare. Positioned strategically across her chest was a Blackswell plaid, tied in the strangest knot he'd ever seen. Lust mingled with humor. He was hard as a stone and grinning, he was certain, like a fool. The effort she'd gone to in order to continue her ruse of being mad was quite impressive, except a person truly not in touch with the real world would not have given a damn if her breasts could be seen underneath the thin material of her léine.

He swept his gaze lower and he groaned. The outline of her slender legs was just as clear as her breasts, and an image of those legs wrapped around him as he took her filled his head. And if that image was filling his head, what was in the thoughts of the other men in this room? A primal possession gripped him and sent him flying down the stairs and striding down the center of the great hall toward Patience. But as he stalked toward her and he noted all the lust-filled gazes of both the Blackswell and Kincaide warriors clinging to his new wife's sin-evoking body, irritation gave way to anger.

He jerked to a halt in front of Ulric Kincaide, who had been captain of the Kincaide guards and looked to be undressing Patience with his eyes. Brodee reached out and yanked the man toward him. "If ye wish to live, ye will quit gaping at my wife as if she is a morsel ye intend to eat."

The man's eyes widened in surprise. "Are we to respect her, then?"

"Are ye to respect her?" Brodee repeated, frowning. The implication that this man, who should have given his life to protect her, may not have even given her the respect she deserved had him curling his hands into fists. And he sent his fists right into the man's nose. Bone crunched, which was satisfying, but not satisfying enough. He aimed another punch straight into the man's stomach, and the Kincaide warrior fell to his knees.

"What are ye doing?" Patience cried out from beside him.

He flicked his gaze to her, noting her bloodless lips and colorless face. "What a husband should—protecting his wife." He kneeled down as the man swiped a hand across his bloody nose and looked at him. The great hall was once again silent as Brodee brought his face a hairsbreadth from the warrior's. "Ye will nae want to see how angry I become if ye ever fail to show my wife respect again. Do ye ken me?"

The man nodded, his angry gaze locking with Brodee's.

"I ken ye, *laird.*"

It was obvious the man was not pleased to have Brodee as his new laird, but he'd be a lot less pleased in a breath. "Hear me now," he said to the people gathered in the great hall, as well as Ulric. "Whatever positions ye held in the previous guard, ye dunnae hold them any longer."

Angry words filled the great hall, but Brodee held up his hands for silence. He'd been thinking about how to appoint the warriors to different leadership positions, and he thought he knew the best way to be fair. "In a fortnight, we will have a small, informal tourney amongst ourselves. Any man who wishes for a leadership position in my guard may compete. Until then, ye will all train with me. We will train upon the rocks by the shore after the nooning meal and finish before supper every day."

Brodee met Ulric's gaze as the man stood, then refocused on the men in the great hall. "I am the only leader of ye men now, and the only way to earn and keep a position in my guard is to be the best at what ye do and to give respect to yer comrades, to me, and to the women." Brodee turned his head and bore his gaze into Ulric. "Disrespect will nae be tolerated from this moment forward." He shoved his finger into Ulric's chest, even as the man openly glared at him. "Consider this a warning—and the only second chance I will ever give ye."

The man jerked his head in a nod.

Brodee turned to Patience, and took her by the elbow, careful not to hold her too tightly. "Come with me."

"Why?" she asked. "I only just arrived."

He clenched his teeth. He would not chastise her in front of the others for questioning him. He did not want to embarrass her. He leaned close and whispered in her ear. "Ye will come with me because I told ye to do so."

Her head turned toward him, so close that their lips almost brushed. She let out a little gasp, and damned if his lust did not grow even stronger. When she licked her rosy lips, it was all he could do not to press his mouth to hers and taste her once more. Her upper teeth sunk into her lower lip for a moment, and then she whispered, "And do I, too, nae wish to see how angry ye can become?" She lifted her chin in an impressive show of defiance, but the wobble in her voice revealed her uncertainty about doing so.

He sighed. He was caught in a trap. If he told her she did not need to be afraid of him, even if she defied him, then perhaps she'd do just that. He could not have her refusing to obey his orders. "I suppose ye dunnae, but nae because I would ever hurt ye." The disbelief was apparent on her face. "I vow it to ye," he added.

She blew out a long breath, her mouth quirking. *As if I have a choice.*

"There is always a choice, Patience." Before she could respond, he turned her toward the door, glad she let him, and guided her out of the great hall. When the door closed behind them, the noise resumed almost instantaneously.

Anger and confusion swirled within him as he faced her and raked his gaze over her thin léine and his clan's plaid.

Mine. The word rang in his head.

He had not wanted a wife, but now he had one. And she was interesting. And tempting. He suspected there was a great deal to this woman that she was trying to hide. He'd planned not to get involved with her. He nearly laughed at that as he drew his gaze back up to her face and to her eyes, dark, unfathomable, and locked on him.

Impossible. It would be impossible not to be entangled with her somewhat. He'd been a fool. She was his to protect. The surety of that thought squeezed his chest, hard.

Things he'd not felt for a woman in years, things he'd never wanted to suffer again clamored inside him, demanding freedom. He gritted his teeth, determined to keep that part of him trapped within the cage he'd put it in.

He noted the rapid pulse at her neck, trying to decide the best way to start this conversation. "Why were ye late to our wedding celebration?"

"I was talking to Silas," she said, her cheeks coloring with her attempt to lie.

"Oh aye?" he said, and she nodded, her lashes lowering. For a moment, Brodee considered how to proceed. "He's quite an attentive ghost," he started. "Was he verra attentive as a husband?"

"When he wanted to be," she said, the words sounding mumbled as she stared down at her feet.

He hooked a finger under her chin and gently tilted it until he was looking in her eyes once more. Twin pools of temptation—that's what her dark eyes framed by her long, thick lashes were like. "And when did he want to be, Patience?" She flinched and then attempted to hide it with a shrug. The suspicion within him grew tenfold. "Did ye hit ye? Is that how he got obedience from ye?"

"Is hitting yer men how ye get obedience from them?" she demanded, nicely avoiding his question.

"Nay," he said, thinking immediately of his loss of temper moments ago. Normally he was a very controlled man, but then his normal had changed drastically in the last few hours.

She stepped away from him and crossed her arms in front of her chest. "Why did ye hit Ulric?"

"Because he did nae seem to ken that he should respect ye."

She quickly averted her gaze but not before he noted

the vivid scarlet that had blossomed on her cheeks. "He'll be verra vexed that ye demoted him as captain of the guards."

Brodee nodded. "I ken it. But if he's the best, he will earn his position back—as long as he follows my rules."

"He is the best fighter," she admitted, talking to the wall more than to him. "He was also Silas's friend."

Brodee quirked an eyebrow. "Ye dunnae believe he will follow my rules?"

"I believe he will challenge them," she said. "They are verra different from what he has kenned. Do ye wish him to respect me because it shows a disrespect for ye and yer dominance if he dunnae show regard for me, yer property?"

It seemed to be a simple question, yet his gut told him it was anything but. "Aye," he said, watching her shoulders droop. "But ye deserve respect in yer own right."

Her head whipped toward him, her brow furrowed. "What sort of game are ye playing with me?" Anger was hot in her voice.

He could have told her he wasn't playing one, but she'd not believe him. "What sort of game are *ye* playing with *me*, Patience?"

"I'm nae playing at anything..."

He heard the *but* at the end of her sentence as clearly as if she'd said it. "Nay?"

She bit her lip but shook her head.

"Did Silas's ghost tell ye to wear yer léine to the wedding feast?"

"The voices in my head did," she said, matter-of-fact.

"'Tis awfully noisy in there, I imagine, between the voices and yer dead husband's ghost."

"Ye kinnae begin to conceive," she muttered.

But he could. For years he'd lived with whispers of doubt about his own worth and the guilt of failing to protect the woman he'd loved and the woman he'd been told he would wed. "I can," he assured her, hoping his eyes conveyed what he'd never admit with words. To do that would be like inviting her in when he wanted to keep her out.

"Should we nae go in?" she asked, shifting from foot to foot, showing her nervousness.

"We should," he agreed, reaching his arms around her.

"What are ye doing?" The alarm in her voice made him frown. What was her experience with men that the simplest movement, the most innocent of touches, elicited such fear?

"I'm going to unwrap the Blackswell plaid because ye have it fashioned incorrectly," he explained.

"I was...I was..."

"Covering yer breasts since the voices told ye to wear only this thin léine?" He could not keep the amusement from his voice. He was gifted with the loveliest smile, but it was gone so quickly he could have believed he'd imagined it if the moment of levity had not lightened her eyes. "Ye have the most enticing dimples." He wanted to run his finger over them.

He felt just as shocked as she looked. That one brief glimpse of her dimples had seared them into his brain.

"I—" An odd expectant look settled on her face as she stared at him. Did she want another compliment?

Before he knew it, he was giving her one. "Yer dimples dunnae compare to yer eyes when yer smile reaches them and lights them, though. They go from twin pools of beckoning darkness to the likes of loch water with the moon shimmering down on them."

Where the devil had that come from? Who was the daft one now?

"I...I...I'm sorry." She shook her head.

"Ye're sorry for being beautiful?"

"Aye?" The look she gave him was one of utter uncertainty, as if she could not trust his compliment, as if something horrible might happen next. He wasn't sure what to say, and before he could decide upon the right words, she spoke again. "I can retie the plaid." She immediately looked away from him and set to work. He suspected she'd done it purposely to avoid any more conversation.

He watched as she undid the plaid while darting looks at him. When she drew the folds of cloth away from her body, the full outline of her loveliness stole his breath. She was all curves and shadows under her léine, and the desire to explore what was hidden there was almost unbearable. If he'd not had a pressing need to gain loyalty and obedience from the Kincaides and bring the clan under his own, he would have skipped the tradition of the wedding feast. But there was a necessity to celebrate this new beginning with the men and women of their combined clan. Joining with his wife would have to wait until later that night.

Patience darted several long looks at him, almost as if she were studying him, and then she started to tie the plaid. Again, she did so completely wrong. It was as if she'd never worn one before. "Did yer lady's maid always put yer plaid on for ye?"

Patience stilled, her gaze flying to him. "Nay. I—"

"Ye've nae ever fashioned a plaid before, have ye, lass?" He softened his voice, hoping to ease some of the embarrassment that was skittering across her face.

Her shoulders slumped as she shook her head. "Nay, I did nae ever have the opportunity to."

He frowned. "Did ye nae wear yer father's plaid, or either of yer husbands'?"

She bit her lip. It was a response he was coming to understand showed she was unsure just how truthful to be. "My father forbade me to wear a plaid, and my first husband—"

"Ivan Sutherland?"

"Aye," she said, grasping a long strand of her unbound, glistening hair and winding it furiously around her finger. "He—" She sucked in a long breath. "Well, he—" She turned her face away then, and with her free hand, she swiped at her cheeks. Was she crying?

Brodee's chest squeezed tight. What the devil had Sutherland done to her? And how the devil had her father treated her? Every indication was that she'd been abused mentally, possibly physically, by her father and husbands. It sickened and enraged him. "Lass?"

The great hall door swung open with a swish, and William stood there. He looked between both of them for a moment, his eyes widening just a bit as he took in Patience's near-naked state. William jerked his gaze to Brodee. "If ye intend to show solidarity between ye and the lass, the two of ye need to actually be at yer wedding celebration."

Brodee gave a quick nod. The desire to ask Patience how Sutherland and her father had treated her and why she'd never had the opportunity to fashion a plaid nearly singed his tongue, but he bit the question back. If there was any hope of her telling him, he doubted she'd do so in front of William, if at all. He stepped toward her, and she flinched. Motioning to the plaid, he said, "May I? I'm verra quick with it. I'm certain ye can make a plaid look much better than I can, but we should return to the great hall."

Intense astonishment touched her face, and her mouth dropped open. Then she gave him a look of such gratitude that he was stilled by his own shock at what her appreciation evoked in him. Triumph swelled in his chest. This was not part of his plan. He should turn from her now. And yet she was like a Siren, and he a sailor on a ship sailing unstoppably toward her.

His blood rushed through his veins in acute awareness of her as he stepped close. When he inhaled, the scent of wild flowers and rain filled his nose. God's teeth, who smelled like that? Like the promise of renewal and freedom? He made quick work of setting the plaid to rights, and then backed away and assessed her, to ensure he'd done a good job. She looked as if she'd been born to wear that plaid. The thought brought him a moment of pleasure, which irritated the devil out of him. "Where did ye get the plaid?" he asked, realizing he did not know. He would have given her one of his tonight.

"I left it in her bedchamber," William said from behind Brodee. "I went to look for her, and I noticed the Kincaide plaid on her floor had been torn to shreds."

The play of emotions across Patience's face—surprise, embarrassment, and then trepidation—fascinated Brodee. "We'll be right behind ye, Will," Brodee said as a hint to William to leave, which he took with a nod.

The door swished shut, leaving Patience and Brodee standing face-to-face once more with no one around and nothing between them but air. He wanted to kiss her with every fiber of his being. Instead, he swallowed the desire and said, "When we are alone, I'll teach ye how to put on my plaid."

She nodded, her gaze watchful and wary. "Why did ye keep my secret?"

"Ye are my wife," he said. "'Tis my duty to protect ye, and that dunnae just include from physical harm. I will nae give others a reason to taunt ye or belittle ye. Will ye trust me?" he asked, holding out his hand to her. He could not say why exactly, but hearing her say now that she would trust him meant a great deal to him suddenly.

"For this moment, I will. Beyond that, I kinnae promise anything."

Again, an overwhelming sense of triumph filled him. Little battles—that's what he would wage with his new wife. And eventually that would lead to his winning the war. "Then I'll take this gift and hope for more."

He started to turn, sure she would not take his hand, but when her fingers caught his and she gave him the sweetest shy smile he'd ever seen, he wrapped his hand around hers, and stilled himself against the chains on his soft emotions that rattled. He kept hold of her hand, determined to protect her and protect himself, too. He opened the great hall door with his free hand, and a sea of noise flowed out on the air. When Patience tensed under his touch, he ran a soothing finger over her palm, but he frowned at the rough spot on the inside of her hand.

It wasn't that he minded a callus. It bespoke of a woman who did not shy away from work, yet he'd have expected a woman in Patience's position not to do much manual labor. He released the open door and turned toward her once more to catch her other hand with his before she could think to protest.

Nervousness skittered across her face. "What is it?"

He refrained from answering, unsure she'd give him an honest response. Instead, he turned her hands so her palms faced up, and he glanced down. "What in God's teeth happened to ye?"

She closed her hands into fists and tried to pull them away. "'Tis nae anything for ye to be concerned over."

"Ye are my wife, so yer injuries are a thing for me to be

concerned over. How did ye do this?" Heat swept through him as he thought about someone hurting her.

"I did it to myself," she said, trying to tug her wrists from his grasp.

"Explain," he commanded, and because he definitely needed to know if there was someone at this castle he needed to protect her from, he added, "with the whole truth."

When she stole a glance at him from under her lashes, he leveled her with the look he reserved for his men who were not doing as he wished. Her nostrils flared, and she went rigid before his eyes. He hated to be the cause of such a reaction, but he had to ensure she was safe.

"Ye ordered me to bathe, and I needed water for the tub," she said with a seemingly nonchalant shrug, but her pained expression belied the gesture.

"Why did ye nae simply ask the servants to fetch the water for ye?" he asked, wondering how many trips it had taken her from the kitchens to her bedchamber to carry up enough water needed for a bath.

"I—" Her gaze shot down to her feet. He'd have to remember her feet were particularly interesting to her when she was trying to hide something. It was not the first time that she'd studied them as if her slippers had precious stones embedded in them. Then her hand went to her hair, and she began to wind a long, ebony lock between her thumb and forefinger. Another telling sign that she wished to conceal a truth but was nervous about it. "I did nae wish to bother them."

He cupped her chin and brought her face up so he could read the truth in her eyes. "Did ye ask them?"

"What's that?" She cupped her hand to her ear. "Oh! Silas says we really must go in now." And then she whipped around faster than he'd known she could move, dashed around him, and bolted through the great hall door.

He wanted to scowl at her obstinacy, but he grinned. Like a clot-heid. Like a man who might care. He forced the grin away by pressing his lips together and stared at the door. He should have stopped her. He could have, yet he had restrained himself. Why? Simple, he decided immediately. He did not want a simpering wife, and she'd shown bravery. There was no other reason he'd been so soft with her. *Absolutely none.* Any thought that there might be was savagely blocked. He took a deep breath. Tomorrow would be time enough to get to the bottom of what was occurring with Patience.

Eight

*P*atience stole a sideways glance at her new husband as
he gave a full belly laugh at the tale the bard was
spinning in the center of the great hall. For a man called the
Savage Slayer, he seemed anything but savage currently,
and in honesty, at many more times as well since she'd met
him. Oh, he looked savage enough, in an incredibly rugged,
handsome way. She'd wager he could kill a man with his
bare hands. He had more muscle than she'd ever seen on a
man, and when he was angry, well, it *had* frightened her.
Yet the only time he'd become angry since arriving was on
her behalf.

No one had ever acted protective of her in the way
Brodee had. She ran through the times he'd come to her
defense today: He'd ensured she was safe when he was
about to raid the castle. He'd punished Father Bisby when
he'd discovered what the priest had done to her. He'd
punched Ulric when Ulric had shown her the disrespect that
Silas had always encouraged. And Brodee had hidden her
secret of not knowing how to fashion a plaid because she'd
never had the chance to learn.

He'd not even known why, yet he'd kept her secret so
she'd not be embarrassed. And she had a suspicion he saw
through her ruse of being mad, yet he was allowing her to
continue with it. Was it conceivable that he truly was a

good man? Was there a chance his reputation was wrong? Possibility and tentative hope sprang in her as she studied him from under her lashes, yet she was not so foolish as to let down her guard. Not yet. Maybe not ever.

Her memories of her past husbands were much stronger than any new memories of one single day. He could turn to cruelty in the blink of an eye, she knew. Silas had done so the moment the door had been closed on them. Every time the door had been closed, really. But to others, he had made it seem as if he cared for her, was concerned for her. And Ivan, he'd praise her beauty in one breath, and then be flogging her the next for supposedly purposely tempting his men.

"Patience?"

She blinked and raised her gaze from her hands, which rested on her empty trencher, to find Brodee staring at her and the kitchen servant Mari standing in front of them. Mari had her faded-blue eyes narrowed on Patience. The woman's silver eyebrows were arched and her lips were twisted in a scowl that made the fine lines around her mouth more pronounced than usual. The woman was head of the kitchens and disliked Patience with an obvious intensity, which Patience suspected was likely Silas's doing. No telling what he'd said to Mari about her.

Heat warmed Patience's cheeks as she realized everyone at the dais had been served but her. Had Mari spoken to her, perhaps asked her to move her hands so she could put cuts of meat on her trencher? "I'm sorry," Patience said and quickly moved her hands, letting out a relieved breath when William asked Brodee something, and he turned away from her.

"Aye, ye are," Mari responded, her tone derisive and low. Patience's nostrils flared at the disgusted look the woman gave her. "Ye'd nae last a day doing my chores, but ye dunnae care, do ye?"

"I'm certain my wife cares a great deal about the rigors of yer chores, as she is yer mistress and has yer welfare in mind," Brodee said, his tone a gentle reprimand.

Mari's eyes widened, and she pressed her lips into a thin line. After a long, awkward silent moment, she finally said, "If ye say so, laird."

"I do, but better than my words, Patience will come to the kitchens tomorrow so ye can lodge yer complaints of yer duties with her and show her what is too taxing."

"Do ye ken how to find the kitchens?" Mari asked in a falsely sweet voice. Patience wanted to hate the woman for being so wretched to her, except she understood the older woman's anger.

Devil take Silas for refusing to allow Patience to see to her duties as mistress. She'd wanted to, but he'd told her no one wanted her there, so he'd forbidden her to go there. She'd attempted to once, and he'd sent her off to Father Bisby for a particularly painful round of soul cleansing.

"I ken how," she said, finding it hard to choke the words past her mortification. She stole a glance at Brodee's face and found his jaw tense and his eyes lit with obvious anger. Whether at her or Mari was the question. Patience bit her lip. She didn't want to incur his anger, but she did not want his vexation turned upon Mari, so she would hide the truth and take the blame. "I'm terribly sorry I have nae been a better mistress. I will rectify that now."

Mari gave her a doubtful look but nodded and placed a few pieces of meat on Patience's platter before moving on, leaving Patience under Brodee's intense scrutiny.

"Why did ye nae ever go to the kitchens?" he asked.

"I could nae," she said, hoping to God he'd not question

her more in front of William, Father Murdock, and Kinsey, all of whom sat at the dais.

"She had better things to do." Kinsey popped up from the end of the dais by Father Murdock where Brodee had instructed the woman to move when he and Patience had come into the great hall.

Brodee frowned. "Such as?"

What could she say? "I... I..."

"She dunnae care for the duties of mistress," Kinsey said, to which Patience stilled with disbelief. Was Kinsey on her side or not? "She's too many voices in her head, and all the chatter in the kitchens makes it worse. Is that nae right, Patience?"

She understood now that Kinsey was trying to help her, trying to make her seem crazy so that Brodee would leave her be, yet Patience was not as sure as she had been that making Brodee think she was mad was the right course. "I'll manage," she finally said.

She turned her attention to her food, attacking it as if she had not eaten in years. Honestly, she was too embarrassed to look up. Conversation around her flowed, and then Kinsey excused herself, but Patience kept her focus on her trencher. Suddenly, she became aware of a low chant.

She looked to the center of the great hall, and her breath caught in her lungs. Two lines of Kincaide warriors had formed down the center of the room all the way to doors. The men were chanting, "Bedding," and then Cul, one of the youngest Kincaide guards, started stomping his feet. The other warriors soon followed. Patience noticed Kinsey behind Cul, whispering something in his ear, and then the woman blended back into the gathered crowd. Had she been trying to intervene on her behalf? Is that why she'd left the dais? To get Cul to stop rallying the men to call for a public bedding?

Patience began to shake as fearful images of her past public consummations built in her mind. The louder the chanting grew, the harder she trembled, when suddenly Brodee's hand, warm and solid, settled on top of hers.

When she glanced at him, she sucked in a breath at the determined set of his jaw and the tic of irritation by his right eye. "Will?" Brodee asked, looking to the man.

William frowned. "I told them, Blackswell. I vow it."

Brodee nodded, squeezed her hand, and stood. He held up his hands for silence, and within moments, it fell. All Patience could hear was the loud thumping of her heart as she waited for Brodee to speak. She did not have to wait more than one fearful breath. "I dunnae hold with the practice of a public bedding."

Patience let out a relieved breath. Brodee did not look at her, but his fingertips came to rest on her shoulder, and to her utter astonishment, she did not flinch from his touch.

"What?" Cul cried out to Brodee's announcement. "We would ken the marriage is true between yerself and our mistress."

Brodee's eyes grew hard and filled with dislike. "Ye will have my word, and ye must satisfy yerself with that."

"What is yer word to us?" Cul demanded.

Patience wanted to curse Cul.

"My word is law, unless ye care to challenge me here and now for the lairdship."

A gasp swept through the room, and she found herself grasping his fingers in sudden worry for Cul. The lad was young and foolish, and she did not want Brodee to become too angry with him. "Brodee," she whispered, but he kept his gaze on Cul.

"I accept the challenge," Cul said. "If I win, ye will give

us the public bedding."

Patience wanted to shrink from the possibility.

"Dunnae fear, Wife," Brodee said, his gaze suddenly boring into her. "I will nae lose. I vowed to protect ye, and I dunnae ever break a vow." To Cul, he said, "If I win, ye will bend the knee and pledge eternal fealty."

"If ye can best me, I'll do it with pleasure," Cul replied.

She couldn't watch.

No. I have to.

Patience clenched her teeth and fisted her hands at her sides as she forced herself to stare straight ahead into the center of the circle formed by the Blackswell and Kincaide warriors who surrounded Brodee and Cul in the courtyard. Both men had stripped down to only their braies, and Patience stared openmouthed at her husband and the picture of raw power he presented. He was all hard planes, dips, and swells. And where his braies clung to his hips, his abdomen rippled to a *V* between his hip bones.

She trailed her gaze upward once more, the odd marking on his right shoulder catching her eye. It appeared to have a circle with a dagger through it inked on his shoulder. She could not help wondering what it stood for. *A battle won? An enemy defeated?*

Her belly tightened looking at him. Neither of her former husbands could have compared to Brodee. They'd been warriors, but Brodee was a different breed of man. He'd been born, and she was almost certain bred, to fight. He moved with the grace of a trained hunter—lithe, fast, lethal. He circled Cul once, twice, then darted forward, planting a hit on the man's nose that jerked his head backward and sent the sound of broken bone echoing through the captive audience.

A breath later, cheers erupted from the Blackswell warriors, and the men stomped their boots, making the ground beneath her feet vibrate. A cool wind gusted suddenly, sending the flames of the torches up higher and casting a dark shadow over Brodee as he danced backward for a step.

She thought perhaps he would consider his next move, but he sprang forth again, emerging into the orange glow cast from the flames, and he looked ferocious. Her breath caught in her chest when he delivered a blow to Cul's stomach as the youth righted himself from the last hit to his nose. Cul doubled over once more, and Brodee swung his hand down, like a blade to the back of Cul's neck, to send the warrior sprawling to the ground.

"Finish him!" came a cry from Ulric, who was clearly not pleased that one of his warriors had lost. For one suspended breath, when Brodee held his hand out for his sword that William had possession of, and then her husband brought his sword forward, she feared Brodee might "finish" Cul by killing him. Maybe her new husband had no tolerance for weakness. Ivan and Silas had both been that way.

"Nay!" she screamed, over the jeers and cheers from the men.

No one seemed to notice her, except her husband. His eyebrows arched in obvious surprise, and then he brought the tip of his gleaming sword to the ground near Cul's hands. The man was struggling to get to his knees, but when he finally managed it and raised his bloodied face to Brodee's, Brodee spoke. "Pledge yer fealty, respect, and protection now and forever *to my wife* or leave my home."

She froze as her head swam with disbelief. He'd fought

Cul not to gain respect for himself but for her. He'd done it to get a pledge of *loyalty to her*. A vow of protection *to her*. She rushed to Brodee, driven by a wave of gratitude and awe, and she touched her hand to his arm.

A twinkle of moonlight caught his eyes as he glanced to her, and she could have sworn she saw tenderness there. "Thank ye," she whispered.

He nodded, then brushed a thumb against her cheek and smiled. "Ye're welcome, Wife."

His voice slid over her like silk and made her shiver. The hope that had blossomed grew just a bit more, but once the pledge had been given to her and Brodee took her hand to lead her inside to their bedchamber, her stomach roiled and gooseflesh swept her skin. She knew he intended to join with her, and all she knew of bedding was humiliation and pain.

With each step she took up the stairs, her nervousness grew, so that by the time he stopped outside of what was now his bedchamber—what had been Silas's not so long ago—she froze. He opened the door and motioned for her to enter, but all she could do was stand there. When he raised his hand, she flinched, suddenly certain he would slap her as Ivan used to do, but a feather-light touch grazed her cheek.

He trailed his hands to both her shoulders where he settled his warm palms. "Are ye so frightened of me that it makes ye tremble, Patience?"

She swallowed, unable to form words. All she could do was look at her new husband as he stared down at her with sharp, assessing eyes. She suddenly wanted to run and hide, find the shadows she'd grown accustom to dwelling in and return there. If she stayed too long in the light, he'd see her for who she really was. He'd discover her shameful secrets.

She could not feel passion in joining; she never had. His kiss came to mind and how it had made her feel so alive, unlike anything she'd ever experienced.

Maybe 'tis nae me?

"What?" Brodee asked, a crease appearing in his brow. His finger curled a tad firmer, but just enough that she was catapulted away from him and to Ivan. Ivan had been rough. Mostly slapping her, sometimes whipping her as he'd done the night they had wed. And when the whipping had been finished, he'd gripped her neck and taken her. She'd thought she would die because she could not breathe, and then later, she'd wished for death.

She groaned. She'd not meant to speak out loud. She clenched her fists and squeezed her eyes shut, desperate to get Ivan out of her head. Maybe Brodee was not a bad man. It seemed he was good. She wanted something good and true in her life. She opened her eyes.

"Patience, what is it?"

Ye're worthless, said Silas's voice.

Was that true? Blood pumped hard through her veins and roared in her ears, and her palms and scalp became hot and tingly.

Ye're a cold fish. Ye dunnae have any passion in ye. 'Tis a chore to bed ye.

"Stop it!" she said and pressed her hands to her ears, but Silas's voice grew louder.

Yer arms are too thin. Yer hips too narrow. Yer breasts too small.

"Leave me be!"

"Patience!"

She jerked her eyes open, shocked they had been closed.

Worry etched the lines of Brodee's face. "Is it Silas?" he asked, his voice low.

She didn't even realize she was crying until warm tears slid down her cheeks. She wanted to trust him, to tell him of her past, but she just couldn't. Not yet. Maybe never. Perhaps she was a fool for even considering trusting him. "Aye," she croaked, finally answering him.

His eyes hardened before her, and the change made a physical ache blossom in her chest. It was Silas. And Ivan. And her father. And her. She had pretended to be broken, but perhaps it was the truth. "I'm sorry," she said with a shake of her head.

"Come," he replied and released his hold on her shoulders to catch her fingers. He turned and walked her across the hall to her bedchamber, and a desperate laugh escaped her. Did he think a simple change of bedchamber could fix her? God, she wished it could. She wished she would feel something when he touched her. She wished he was tender and kind, and would grow to love her as she had once dreamed of being loved, back when her mother would tell her bedtime stories so very long ago.

She clamped her jaw tight, not daring to say any of this aloud. He turned to her, cupped her face in his large palms, and when he leaned in, her breath escaped on a startled hiss. He pressed a kiss to her forehead, then her nose, and ever so briefly her lips, so quick and light was the touch that later she would wonder if she'd imagined it.

"Rest easy, Patience. I'll be across the hall if ye need to battle Silas."

She was too surprised by his words to do more than nod. He leaned past her, opened her door, and gave her a gentle push into her bedchamber. Darkness consumed her. The fire had not been lit. She made her way to her bed, sat, and fell backward to stare up at the ceiling and the way the moonlight made odd shapes there.

Alone. She was alone on her wedding night. She'd set out to ensure Brodee wanted nothing to do with her, and it seemed she'd been successful. Why did she not feel happier? Why did she feel as if she might have made a mistake.

Ye're worthless, Silas whispered in her ear.

"Ye're dead," she whispered back.

The knock at the door did not wake Brodee. It merely interrupted the continuous questions running through his mind about his wife. As he rose from the bed, the questions resumed again. Why did some of the men not show her respect? Why did Patience not seem to know her own worth? Why was she so frightened of him? Was it his reputation or something else? Had she been beaten by Sutherland or Kincaide or possibly both men?

He opened the door to find William standing there.

"I'm sorry to interrupt yer wedding night—"

"Ye've nae interrupted anything."

William peered around Brodee into the empty bed-chamber. "Where's yer wife?"

Brodee pointed to Patience's bedchamber door across the hall.

"I'd nae have taken ye for a man who is so verra quick with the bedding," William said.

"And ye should nae," Brodee replied, trying to make light of a situation that was anything but amusing.

William nodded. "I see. Is this about barriers, then?"

"What barriers?"

"The ones ye have built around ye?"

Brodee jerked William through the doorway to his bedchamber and slammed the door. "Dunnae think to offer me lectures or well-meaning advice this night, Will. I'm nae in the mood."

Understanding lit William's eyes, and then he grinned at Brodee. "Ye did nae bed yer wife."

"I did nae," Brodee confirmed. William was the only person he'd ever have this sort of discussion with other than his brother, Broch.

"Dare I ask—"

"She's afraid," Brodee supplied, turning and stalking to the washstand. He poured some wine. When he turned back to William, he found his friend studying him.

"Of ye?" William asked.

Brodee shrugged. "Perhaps. Actually, likely so, but I dunnae believe it's simply because of my reputation." He sat in a chair by the window and kicked his legs out in front of him, thinking on the events of the last day. "When we got to the bedchamber tonight she was violently trembling, and then she started talking to Kincaide's ghost."

William sat in the chair next to Brodee and cocked his eyebrows. "Another ruse? To avoid the bedding, perhaps?"

Brodee shook his head. "Nay. 'Twas obvious she did nae even realize she was talking to Kincaide's ghost."

"Maybe she really is crazy. Maybe we misjudged it, and—"

"Nay. 'Twas nae like that. He's in her head, but I vow it's because of things he did to her. And things perhaps Sutherland did to her. And her father."

"Her father?" William arched an eyebrow.

"I think he was cruel to her, perhaps. Did ye find out anything yet?"

"Nae much. I could nae find Kinsey to get her alone and attempt to persuade her."

"What do ye mean ye could nae find her?" Brodee

asked.

"She was nae anywhere in the castle ye'd expect. Nae her bedchamber, the great hall, the kitchens, or the courtyard. I asked around, and the Kincaide who I questioned about her whereabouts did nae ken where she might be. I did have a little chat with a Mari, the woman who is head of the kitchens."

"And?"

"Patience was wed to Kincaide four months ago and has lived here that long. According to Mari, Patience has nae ever stepped foot in the kitchens, as a good mistress would do—Mari's words, nae mine. Mari says Patience has nae ever taken an interest in any of her duties as mistress and threatened to put a spell on Kincaide if he tried to force her to do so."

Brodee laughed at that ridiculous notion. "Let me guess, Kincaide is the one who conveyed all this to Mari."

"Aye, but 'tis widely believed by all the lasses in the kitchens, and I imagine by everyone in the castle. They think yer new wife thinks herself above them, is lazy, and basically likes to keep to herself. And they thought her *bandruidh* before ye dispelled that belief."

Brodee could not reconcile any of those things with the woman he had just met, granted he *had* just met her. "Did any of them mention seeing Patience treated harshly by Kincaide? Perhaps they saw him hit her?"

"I did ask that, but nay. Though Mari did mention that since poor, beleaguered Kincaide did nae have a recourse to force his wife to do her duties, he'd informed the servants they were nae obligated to serve or aid Patience in any way, and they were to consider Kinsey the lady of the castle."

Brodee thought immediately of Patience's raw, rough hands from carrying her water buckets for a bath without aid.

"It also seems that he did nae punish men for being disrespectful to her, but rather encouraged the behavior by laughing when they leered at her or grabbed her or made a disrespectful comment to her. Mari, nor the other lasses gathered in the kitchens who were listening as I spoke to Mari, cared for Kincaide allowing that, but they also seemed to agree that Patience had caused her own problems by being so cold, conceited, and wicked."

"Damn Kincaide." Brodee's fingers curled in a reflexive desire to throttle the dead man. "He was clever."

"Aye," William agreed.

"He purposely made her an outcast among his people while making sure he looked like he was a good husband. Why?"

"I dunnae, but I would think mayhap Kinsey does. Yet somehow I doubt the woman would tell ye."

"Aye," Brodee agreed.

"What are ye going to do about yer wife?" William asked.

Brodee wanted Patience. Fiercely. But that was lust, and he would control his lust rather than compel her to join with him when it was obvious she did not want to. He had no interest in bedding the lass for his own pleasure when she'd gain nothing from it. Hopefully, she'd soon see beyond the moniker people had given him and come to realize he would not hurt her and, instead, wanted to bring her pleasure. He felt almost certain she'd enjoyed their kiss. He'd build on that, little by little, until desire for him stirred in her.

"I'm going to remove the obstacles holding her back from being a real member of this clan," Brodee explained. "And then I will see her true character, as will everyone else."

"And what if ye dunnae like what ye see? What if she's as cold and conceited as they believe?"

"She's nae. I'd wager my life on it."

William grinned. "Ye certainly are willing to risk a great deal for a woman ye dunnae have any intention of caring about."

William was right, and Brodee hated to admit it, so he glared at him instead. William responded with a chuckle, and then he said, "Do ye ken what I think?"

"Could I stop ye from telling me even I dunnae wish to hear it?"

"Nay," William replied with a wink. He leaned over, grabbed Brodee's goblet, and finished the wine that was in it. He set the goblet on the floor by his feet with a *thunk*. "I think ye will find it verra hard nae to care about yer wife if she proves to be the woman ye are defending and nae the woman the Kincaides think she is."

"And I think I need sleep and so do ye. I want ye to train the men with me tomorrow after the nooning meal until supper."

William nodded and stood. "What do ye wish me to do in the morning?"

"Find and follow Kinsey. I've an odd feeling about her, and I wish to have answers."

William parted with a wave of his hand, and Brodee took to his bed, but this time sleep claimed him quickly. Yet his sleep was not restful. His dreams were filled with his past and his present. He dreamed over and over of the day he found Arabel dead, except every time he turned her over to see her face, it was Patience's face. He awoke before dawn in a sweat and filled with a sense of dread. It had been a long time since he'd worried about a woman, and he did not like it one bit. He barely knew the lass. How the devil would it be when he knew truly who she was? The thought made him groan.

"Again," Brodee demanded the next morning of Cul as they faced each other on the rocky shore that encompassed the west side of Crag Donnon Castle. The sun had just risen in the sky, making the sweat that dripped off Cul visible. He would give this to the man: he'd been here before dawn, just as Brodee had told him to be, he'd not complained once, and he'd worked hard in his training. He was actually a fairly good fighter, and with training he could be great. He was simply young, only twenty-two summers.

"Keep yer sword up," Brodee commanded swinging his own blade high above his head in an arc to make a slash at Cul from the left. The man met the incoming hit and managed to push Brodee's sword back, but when Brodee came immediately from the left, Cul was not ready. Steel met steel, the vibrations of the hit tingling down Brodee's arm, but he pushed through the feelings and forced the sword from the younger man's hands. It went flying and landed with a loud *whack* against the rocks. "Again," Brodee commanded, sweat now dripping from his own forehead. He swiped it away with the back of his hand as Cul moved to fetch his sword.

When Cul turned toward him, Brodee said simply, "Again."

They came together once more, and Brodee once again knocked Cul's sword from his hands. Brodee repeated the lesson until Cul fell to his knees with fatigue and wretched up the supper left in his stomach from the night before.

Brodee kneeled down by Cul as the young man swiped a hand across his mouth. "Why did ye imagine ye could beat me?" Brodee asked, not to taunt the younger man or out of a sense of his own merit as a fighter, but out of curiosity.

Cul's face reddened. "Kinsey convinced me I could."

"Kinsey?" Brodee asked with a frown.

"Aye," Cul said and kicked at a pebble as the blush reached his neck and made it splotchy. "She whispered in my ear that I should challenge ye, that I could best ye. That it would please her and turn her eye to me. I... It was foolish."

"Ye like her?" Brodee asked, not voicing the other questions in his head. Was Kinsey plotting something or had she simply been goading Cul to see if he would do her bidding?

The man's blush deepened to a shade Brodee had not known possible, and Cul nodded. "Aye, but 'twas nae until verra recently that she has shown that she even kens I'm alive. And I'm nae the only one."

"Who else?"

"Ulric. She flirts with us both. One night she'll dance with me, and the next she'll be in Ulric's arms."

Ah. Likely the lass was toying with the men. "Has Ulric trained ye?" Brodee asked.

"Aye. Personally. Which is another reason why I thought I could best ye."

Ulric had clearly, deliberately not trained the younger man well, and he said as much to Cul. "He has nae given ye proper training, and I fear it was purposeful."

"I'll deal with Ulric," Brodee said. "As to Kinsey, I think ye'd be better served pursuing a lass who only has eyes for ye."

"I'm thinking ye're right. Have ye appointed a personal

guard for Lady Kincaide?"

Brodee smiled at Cul's eagerness. He remembered a time when he was very eager to please his father and serve him, and his father made him feel worthless for a very long time. He'd vowed never to do that to another. "I've nae appointed her guard yet. Are ye asking for the position?"

"Aye, though I ken if ye dunnae wish to give it to me after last night in the hall and my performance today in battle with ye."

"Last night is forgotten. Ye gave yer pledge of fealty to my wife, and I consider that a binding lifetime pledge. I'm certain ye realize to ever betray that pledge would be a forfeit of yer life."

"Aye, laird. I'll nae ever betray it."

The man's voice resounded with sincerity. "Then consider yerself my wife's personal guard." He'd also appoint one of his men to shadow them until Cul became a much better fighter. He knew the perfect man, too—Fergus Blackswell. He was a huge man, who looked frightening and fought like the devil himself, but he was a gentle giant. Fergus had been devoted to Brodee ever since, at the age of ten, Brodee had saved him from the men who'd been torturing him.

"Truly?" Cul asked, his grin showing his youth.

"Truly," Brodee assured him, "but on one condition."

"Anything."

"Ye will train here every morning with me before dawn until I say ye have mastered all ye need to ken."

"Gladly, laird."

Brodee stood, and Cul followed suit. "This will nae excuse ye from the afternoon training."

"Nay, laird."

"And if anyone should challenge ye for the position at

the tourney in a fortnight, ye'll have to best them to keep the position. But if ye train hard, ye should be able to do so."

"I will train harder than any man ever has."

Cul's sentiments echoed a familiar one Brodee had once said to his father, to prove to him that he was not worthless just because he was not the firstborn son. "Then go find my wife, and tell her I've appointed ye as her guard." It occurred to him that he could also use Cul to discover information about Patience. "And while ye are with her, keep note of what she does and how she interacts with the rest of the clan. I'll be calling the clan to the courtyard shortly for an announcement. Bring Patience there when the bell rings." If things went as he planned, Patience would get an opportunity to prove herself to the clan, and he'd get a chance to discover who his new wife really was.

Nine

Guard, indeed! Patience trudged toward the courtyard as the bell rang. Or rather, she was guided along by Cul. She had no notion how he'd come to be appointed as her personal guard, given Brodee had been so angry with the young man last night. But she was fairly sure that Cul had been given the duty because Brodee thought her truly mad after her bout of talking to Silas at her bedchamber door.

After many sleepless hours, she had come to the conclusion that she was not truly touched in the head, nor was Silas's ghost talking to her. Her dead husband's voice was certainly in her head, but that was of her own doing. She knew that. Just as she knew that she was more afraid of her past memories of Ivan and Silas than she was of Brodee. At least at the moment.

There were too many instances since she'd met him where he'd shown that he was not a savage man for her to dismiss them. She would proceed prudently until she learned more of his character. Caution and hope. They were both there—no point in trying to deny it. If he was good, a world of possibilities would be dangling in front of her. Ones she'd not dared to allow herself to dream about.

Restrain eagerness, Patience.

"My lady?" Cul said from behind her.

Blast, she had to get a firm grasp on her loose tongue.

She waved a dismissive hand, praying Cul would follow her lead. "I was simply reminding myself to take a care on the stairs."

Suddenly, Cul was beside her, gripping her arm to aid her down the stairs. The consideration startled her so greatly that she paused and was certain she was gaping at him, because when she inhaled, the cool air of the afternoon made her teeth ache. The temperature had dropped considerably overnight, which was a sure sign that fall was coming to an end and winter would soon be here.

She allowed Cul to lead her down the stairs, though she was perfectly capable of walking down them herself. She noted the way he stood taller and pride seemed to shine from him. Distant observation had revealed to her some time ago that the young warrior was not a favorite of Ulric's; therefore, he'd struggled to find a place in the guard.

"Tell me, Cul," she said, as they left the stairs for the long corridor that led to the main entrance. "How did ye come to be appointed as my personal guard?" As they made the turn, she noted a man was following them—one she was certain was a Blackswell warrior.

Cul did not appear to notice. "Laird Blackswell gave me the honor this morning."

The honor? The man thought it an honor to guard her? She felt her mouth pull into a smile.

"The position is mine unless someone challenges me for it in the tournament and bests me. Then I'll have to cede the position to them," he went on. "But Laird Blackswell offered to personally train me every day to ensure my skills are superior."

She imagined Brodee had a great many pressing things he'd have to see to every day until he had the men completely under his command and the castle running the way he wished, yet he was going to take the time to train Cul? Why? Had he seen potential in him and wanted to aid him? The thought of being married to a man who would do such a caring thing filled her with warmth.

As if Cul had heard her silent thoughts, he said, "Yer husband is a verra fair man."

"Is he?" she asked, hoping Cul would provide more insight.

He stopped and faced her, his dark eyes friendly and warm. "Aye. I vow it. I ken ye must have heard all the same things I have about him being the Savage Slayer and all that his reputation entails."

She shrugged in an attempt to appear nonchalant.

"Despite my foolishness in the great hall last night, my lady, he told me this morning that it was forgotten by him."

Not lies. He did not forget or forgive those. He'd said it himself. Would he forgive her if he knew for certain she'd lied?

She bit her lip. Was she truly considering being completely honest with a man she'd known one day based off the opinion of a young warrior who was clearly in awe of her husband?

"May I speak bluntly, my lady?" Cul asked, his voice slightly hesitant.

The earnest look he gave her tugged on her heart. She nodded.

"Laird Kincaide was nae a forgiving man," he admitted. "He would remind me daily of my faults and mistakes."

"Ye are nae the only one," she murmured, then turned her head quickly away, horrified she'd revealed that much. She got another glimpse of the man following them, and she pulled to a stop. "Ye go ahead to the courtyard. I dropped a ribbon. I'll be right along."

"I'll get it for ye," Cul offered.

"Nonsense," she said, trying to make her tone sound as unbending as Brodee's had yesterday. "I dunnae need a guard in this passage, and I'm perfectly capable of retrieving a dropped ribbon."

"But, my lady—"

"I order ye to go," she cut in, quite sure he'd simply ignore her order. So when he inclined his head and did as she had bidden, she grinned, barely resisting the urge to shout her happiness. Not that she took pleasure in ordering Cul about, but it was so unexpected to have someone listen to her as if she mattered.

Once he was out the door to the courtyard, she turned and looked down the corridor. "Ye can come out," she called. When the man who she was quite sure had been following her did not show himself, she said, "That's fine. Stay in the shadows. I'll simply tell my husband someone is following me and my guard."

"He ordered me to," a voice called, and then a big, burly man stepped into the light.

She waved him toward her, momentarily astounded by her sudden bravery. The man's heavy footfalls came toward her, but then he stopped a respectable distance away. He was a giant of a man, easily as tall as Brodee and twice as wide, and a patch was fastened over his left eye. "What's yer name?"

"Fergus Blackswell," he said, regarding her warily.

So he *was* a Blackswell warrior. She offered him a proper curtsy, and when she righted herself, he was gaping at her. "What is it?" she asked.

"I've nae ever had a lady curtsy for me except Lady Katreine. Gentle creatures are usually scairt of me," he said, waving at the patch on his face.

"I dunnae ken why they'd be scairt of a patch."

"Dunnae it make me look menacing?" the big bear of a man asked, wiggling his bushy eyebrows.

She laughed at that. "Hardly. What happened to ye?"

"Some men thought to torture me because they wanted information I did nae feel inclined to give, since it would mean the death of many innocents who were in hiding." He shrugged. "They cut out my eye in an effort to get me to talk."

She winced, and her hand fluttered to her own left eye. "That must have hurt horridly."

"It did sting a bit. Luckily, Brodee saved my other boll— Beg pardon, my lady. It just occurred to me that this is nae a polite conversation."

She waved a dismissive hand at him. "Dunnae fash yerself. Was Brodee with ye when they were torturing ye?"

"Nae. But he stumbled upon us and rescued me. He's had my loyalty ever since."

She tucked the information away, and asked, because he'd mentioned the name, "Who is Lady Katreine?"

Surely, if Brodee had been wed before, she would know or have heard. What a foolish notion. Of course he could have been wed; she did not know him.

"She's Laird Blackswell's wife. She's verra pretty, but so are ye."

Her eyes felt as if they might explode out of her head. "How many wives does Brodee have?" she asked, unable to keep the shrillness from her tone.

"Dunnae fash yerself, lass," came Brodee's deep, rumbling reply from behind her. The effect of that smooth voice was instantaneous. A current raced through her. "I assure ye," he continued, "ye are my only wife."

She turned toward Brodee, her stomach tightening in

awareness of his presence, but even before she was fully facing him, Fergus said, "He speaks the truth. Brodee has nae ever been wed, though—"

"That will be enough, Fergus," Brodee interrupted. Patience would have given anything to know what Fergus had been about to say.

The warrior nodded. "Aye, laird. Shall I go to the court-yard?"

"Aye," Brodee said, not taking his gaze off Patience to answer Fergus. His gaze did not even so much as flicker from her when Fergus passed by them.

He peered at her intently, and the very air around her seemed electrified, like when lightning lit the sky. And her heart! Heaven above, it pounded as loud as thunder and pushed blood through her veins so that it roared in her ears. The man affected her so oddly. She was not scared in this moment; she was utterly and completely intrigued.

"Ye sent yer guard away." He did not sound happy.

"I-I'm sorry," she said, irritated that she had so quickly reverted to a groveling woman tingling with fear.

"Ye dunnae need to be sorry. I simply want to ken why."

Her brow furrowed. She was not used to a husband who was not immediately angry at her and asked her *why* she did something. "I saw Fergus shadowing us, and I wished to learn who he was and why he was trailing us."

Brodee nodded, crossed his arms, and leaned against the stone wall. He looked so at ease that he made her relaxed, as well. "That makes sense, lass, and I'm pleased ye showed such awareness."

"Ye are?" She felt like grinning, but she managed to keep it controlled.

"Aye. The more alert ye are, the more likely ye are to

stay out of danger. However, ye did nae ken for certain that whoever was following ye was nae dangerous, so ye should have told Cul. He was made yer guard to watch ye. I've already spoken to him about leaving ye unprotected—"

"It was not his fault," she hurriedly explained. "I ordered him to leave. If ye wish to punish someone, punish me."

"I dunnae wish to punish anyone, Patience. I only wish to keep ye safe."

His words wrapped around her like a warm blanket. She nodded. "I'll nae send him away again."

"He'd nae leave ye even if ye did."

"Let me guess," she said, smiling shyly at Brodee, "ye threatened to cut off his hands if he ever obeyed me again?" She meant to tease, but she found herself holding her breath, wondering if Brodee had stripped her of all power before she'd ever really had any.

"Nay, Wife." He moved closer to her so fast so didn't have time to flinch, and he cupped her face in his large hands, stealing her breath. "I threatened to gouge out his eyes if he ever failed in his guarding of ye again. And I told him to obey ye in all things, unless he truly believed yer command would put ye in danger. Can ye live with that?"

"Aye," she said, her pulse skittering alarmingly at the gentle slide of his fingers across her cheekbone. Yet it was not so very alarming that she pulled away. It was not like last night at all, when she had been terrified. He leaned in, the heat of him enveloping her, the scent of toil and sun surrounding her, and he slid a rough pad across her lips. She closed her eyes as his fingers hooked under her chin.

He was going to kiss her! He was, and she wished him to. She wished to know if the feeling he stirred before could be stirred again.

His face came beside hers, the whiskers of his several-days-old beard growth tickling her cheek, and then he spoke, his breath fanning her ear and sending delicious shivers down her spine. "Is the ghost quiet today?"

She sucked in a sharp breath and tilted her head so that she could see his eyes, but discerning what he was thinking was like trying to see to the bottom of a murky river. "So far," she murmured.

"Good." He pulled away from her then, and she felt the loss of him in every part of her, as if she'd almost grasped a prize except it had slipped through her hands. But then he caught her fingers and threaded them with his, as though it was the most natural thing in the world. She'd never held hands with her other husbands, and as she fell into step beside Brodee, she found that this gesture, this innocent gesture, awoke a longing in her she'd given up on many years ago and awoke a desire she'd had no notion she was capable of feeling.

Her simple plan to drive this man away had just become more complicated.

As Brodee led Patience to the courtyard, her small hand in his, he could not help but glance at their intertwined hands. It had been years since he'd held a woman's hand. Some feeling he did not wish to define coursed within him. Abruptly, he turned his thoughts to the exchange he'd overheard between his wife and Fergus. She'd curtsied to Fergus, a man who was to serve her as Brodee's wife. She'd showed humbleness and a generosity of spirit, and she'd displayed kindness.

Her fingers twitched, tightening around his hand as they

stepped out into the courtyard. It was packed with Kincaide clanspeople and Blackswell warriors, with Ulric standing in front of them all as if it was his rightful place. Brodee glanced swiftly at Patience. Her lip was tucked under her lower teeth as she looked to Ulric. That knowledge that she feared the man made Brodee want to simply cast him from the clan, but he needed to be careful. Casting out Ulric might make him a martyr to Kincaide men who would otherwise be won over. But making Ulric want to go on his own, well, now, that would be fine.

Brodee led Patience to the center of the crowd with him and released her hand to hold his own up for silence. Once the people settled, he spoke. "I've called ye here for several reasons. For those of ye who were nae present in the great hall last night, I want ye all to hear that in a fortnight, we will have a tournament for all the Blackswell men and Kincaide men who wish to participate. If there is a position that ye wish to have in the guard, ye may put yer name in for it, and then ye will show me yer skill in the tournament." Many of the clanspeople nodded. "I will use the tournament to help me decide yer assignments, but I will also be watching ye men these next couple of weeks. I wish honorable, hard-working men to be the leaders of our clan, nae simply men who are good fighters."

A murmur of approval arose from the crowd, men and women alike. "I have also decided to create a council to sit beside me and share their opinions on the matter. In the end, the council will be made up equally of three Blackswell warriors and three Kincaide warriors, but until the tournament, and until I come to ken ye Kincaide men better, the council will include William MacLean, Fergus Blackswell, and Cul Kincaide."

"Cul?" Ulric repeated, the words more snarled than

spoken. "Cul is nae half the warrior I am." He banged a fist to his chest.

Brodee closed the distance between himself and Ulric in one stride. They stood face-to-face and Brodee spoke, making sure it was loud enough that all could hear and take heed. "And ye are nae half the *man* that Cul is. He's already shown me his willingness to work hard and his forthrightness. Ye," he said, poking the man in the chest, "were personally responsible for training Cul, we're ye nae?"

Ulric's face turned deep red, and his eyes narrowed. "Aye."

"Then 'tis yer fault he is nae yet the warrior he should be. Ye are nae fit to command at this point in time. Mayhap nae ever. Ye will need to show much change."

"And how do ye wish me to prove myself?" Ulric growled.

"Ye can start by shoveling horse dung from out of the stables," Brodee said, matter-of-fact. Ulric's glare, and lack of contrition, confirmed what Brodee already suspected. The man would never make a good leader. "That is yer job for now: mover of the dung."

When snickers started to trickle though the crowd, Brodee held up a silencing hand.

Ulric shoved away from Brodee. "Ye expect me to shovel horse dung?"

"Aye," he said plainly. "Or ye can leave the clan. Those are yer choices."

"I'll be leaving!" Ulric said, his hand moving toward his sword, but before his fingers ever grazed the hilt, Brodee had his sword out, as well as half his guard. The steel sang in the air. "Ye'll leave under guard on two feet or carried away dead. 'Tis yer choice." Brodee brought the point of his sword up to Ulric's chest. "Make it quickly. I dunnae have more time to waste on ye."

"I will be back for the tournament," Ulric snarled.

"I look forward to it," Brodee replied, then motioned two of his men over. They immediately came to either side of Ulric. "Take him off my land, but let him collect his things."

The guards nodded and fell in beside Ulric, who stormed away.

Kinsey rushed into the inner circle. "Ulric is stubborn and angry." She turned all of her attention to Brodee. "I'll go speak with him."

That same distrustfulness of her intentions filled him, but he pushed it down. William had followed her this morning and Kinsey had done nothing more than perform all the duties the lady of the castle should perform. And she seemed happy to do the work, according to William. Maybe this time Brodee's gut was wrong. It wouldn't surprise him overly much, given how distracted he was by his new wife. Mayhap the lass developed a tender for Ulric. "He kinnae stay now that he's made his choice, but ye can say yer goodbyes to him."

With a hasty nod, Kinsey departed, and once the murmurings of the clan died down, Brodee spoke again. "The women of the clan will maintain their positions, but henceforth, ye will take yer orders from Lady Patience." He glanced behind him to see that Patience's jaw had dropped.

"She dunnae ken anything about this castle!" one of the women objected.

He went to Patience's side and took her hand in his. He gave it a squeeze and was gratified, too gratified, when she moved close to his side. It was a sign of trust, and he seemed to relish it, which bothered him. "She will learn."

"She dunnae care to," Mari said.

"That's nae true!" Patience protested. "I will prove it to ye."

"Then ye can start immediately," Mari said, a mocking lilt to her tone. "The nooning meal needs to be prepared, meals for the sick need to be delivered, and someone needs to gather herbs in the woods. Are ye too good or gentle to help with these chores?"

"It would be my pleasure," Patience replied, and the woman's eyes widened. Around Mari, the men and women nodded respectfully at Patience.

A swell of unexpected pride twisted in Brodee's chest. Patience could have chastised Mari for speaking so rudely to her. She could have even punished her. But what she'd done was showed her kindness.

"Wife," he said, his breath snagging in his throat when she looked up at him and smiled. It was like the sun had come out from behind a dark cloud. "I'd like to speak to ye for a moment before ye make yer way to the kitchens."

She nodded, and after he bade the men to prepare for afternoon training, he led her from the courtyard to the garden. Once they were out of sight of the others, he turned toward her and captured her hands. The overwhelming desire to kiss her again rushed through him, but he would not. Not yet. He needed to learn what had made her so fearful last night, so he could banish that fear. Until then, he would restrain himself. Instead, he slowly raised one of her hands to his lips and brushed a gentle kiss upon her silken skin.

She let out a little sigh he did not think even she was aware of, and she leaned in toward him. It took every ounce of willpower he had not to give in to his yearning. "Ye made me verra proud in the courtyard."

Her lips parted and then she grinned. "I did?"

"Aye. Ye will gain the respect of the women once ye show them ye are willing to lead and aid them." He wanted to ask her why she'd never taken up her duties as mistress, but he was almost certain it was Silas's doing. Besides, he'd rather have her share the reason willingly, which he did not think she was ready to do.

She shifted restlessly before him, and then her gaze dropped to her feet. Shame. It struck him like a bolt of lightning. She tended to look down when she felt shamed. "I did nae wish to neglect my duties," she said, her voice drifting to barely a whisper. "But Silas, well, he…he…"

"Forbade ye from offering help in the castle?" Brodee asked.

She looked up, her face clouded with uneasiness, but she nodded. "Aye. He said that they did nae want me around." She started to look down again, but he caught her chin lightly with his fingers.

"Ye dunnae need to feel shamed. Tell me."

He watched as something flickered far back in her beautiful, beguiling eyes. "He said I did nae have any knowledge to offer. He said that it made me worse than worthless; it made me a hindrance."

"It's too bad he's dead," Brodee said, rage coursing through him on her behalf. "I would gladly have taught him a lesson in how to treat a woman, one he'd nae ever forget."

"I'm glad he's dead," she said, taking a deep, shuddering breath. "I suppose that makes me sinful."

"Nay, lass," he replied, pulling her into the protection of his embrace. She may not have felt she had anyone watching over her before—maybe ever—but he would ensure she understood she did now. He'd felt alone and inadequate just as she had, and it was a gut-twisting thing.

He thought she might pull away, as she had stiffened at

first, but after a moment, she rested her head against his chest. "Do ye ken Greek mythology?" she asked.

"Aye."

She tilted her head back and studied him. "Ye're nae like Dolus, are ye?"

He laughed at her asking him if she was like the Greek god of trickery. "Nay, I'm nae a master of deception."

"They call ye the Savage Slayer. Ye did nae come by that name for naught. There have been moments since ye came here that ye seem anything but savage, though. Almost tender."

"Och, lass. Dunnae ever call a man tender. 'Tis the worst criticism."

"'Tis nae a criticism," she protested. "'Tis a compliment."

"Nae to a warrior."

She smiled. "I'll remember that. So, did ye truly earn the name 'the Savage Slayer'?"

He held her gaze. "Some would say I have."

She arched her eyebrows. "What would others say? Those who truly ken ye."

"There are few people who truly ken me, Patience."

"Me either," she said glumly. "Only one. My brother."

"And where was yer brother when ye needed protecting from Kincaide?" he asked, his tone hotter than he'd intended. Devil take it, why did her brother not protect her as he should have? He knew her father, and the man only had his gain in mind, despite what the king hoped.

Her brows dipped together. "He has tried. Is trying."

"He's a little late if his intent was to stop this marriage."

"Aye," she said, a blush coloring her cheeks once more.

"I ken ye did nae wish to wed me." It was not a question, but a recounting of what she had said earlier. "I did nae wish to wed ye, either," he said.

She glared at him. "Oh, yer pretty compliments do make me want to swoon." The flash of inner fire his wife possessed but had buried deep made him grin. "Why are ye grinning at me?" she demanded.

"Because ye are nae scairt of me in this moment."

"I'm nae," she said, her voice full of her amazement. "What's to be done? We did nae wish to wed each other, and we are nae certain we can trust each other."

"We are wed, and ye will learn to trust me," he said, almost as if he was commanding it.

"What of ye? Will ye nae learn to trust me?"

"That depends," he said, teasing her now.

"On what?"

"Would ye say ye are like the Greek goddess Apate?"

She smirked at him. "I'm nae deceitful." The moment the words left her mouth her blush turned crimson. "I do sometimes hear Silas's voice," she said, giving Brodee a worried look.

"We all hear the voices of those that hurt us the most," he said to her, forcing himself nae to say more. He'd become entangled enough, much more than he'd meant to.

"In that case," she replied, "I should be hearing my first husband Ivan's voice, as well. And my father's. His lack of care stung the most. I am his daughter, but he cares only for how he can use me."

The pain in her voice gutted him, and it rang so similar to the pain his own father's callousness had caused him that he winced. He could tell her. He could tell her they shared a common past, but that would intertwine them more. So instead, he simply said, "One day his voice will disappear." It was a truth he knew from his own experience, but he would not reveal that. He could not. He went on, the desire to share his secrets suddenly clawing at him. "I need to get to training and ye need to go to the kitchens. Come." And before she could share more, he was tugging her back the way they had come.

Ten

*P*atience made her way to the kitchens with a smile on her face and the memory of Brodee's kiss singed upon her hand. It still tingled where his lips had grazed her bare skin. As she walked across the courtyard, weaving through the men gathered there, she could swear she felt Brodee's gaze upon her back. On impulse, she turned, and he stood in the center of the courtyard watching her. It wasn't like Silas used to watch her: with assessing eyes, waiting for a chance to belittle her. Nor was it how Ivan used to watch her: to pounce on the best time to "punish" her, as he liked to call it when he hit her. The look upon Brodee's face was one of concern, and unless he had skills of deceit like Dolus, the god she'd teased him about, she was inclined to believe his concern was genuine. She lifted her hand in a final wave, and he did the same before turning to speak to one of his men.

She continued across the courtyard, then entered the door to the kitchens, which was outside the main keep above the entrance, and she climbed the stone steps, thinking. He'd practically told her he did not believe her truly mad, and she was fairly certain that he'd been hurt greatly, too, though by whom, she didn't know. Her husband hid behind a mask cleverer than the one she'd tried to hide behind. His was rooted in legends born from his skill as a fighter and deeds for the king as his right hand.

He could be hard, it was true, but there was also a tenderness there that she had never dreamed possible. She couldn't help but wonder what sort of passions he concealed. The only thing she'd known of the passion of a man was that it was accompanied by pain, both physical and mental, and left her feeling empty. She could not imagine that a man as Brodee, who had kissed her so gently, would next cause her pain.

She climbed the stairs to the kitchens and paused outside the door, listening to the laughter of the women who were friends, the chattering talk about the clan, their men, and families. She wanted that. All of it. Desperately. Did she dare try to find it with Brodee? Would he even wish to try with her? He'd admitted that he'd not wanted this marriage, either, yet he'd pointed out that they were wed and had declared she'd learn to trust him. She ought to be irritated that he thought to order her to trust him, but she was grinning. She could feel the wideness of it on her face and the joy of it in her heart. His command had not been threatening or frightening; it had been more of a fact he'd stated, as if he would never consider that she might *not* grow to trust him. But she thought she wanted to. She really did.

Not once had it occurred to her that this marriage might be good, but now that the possibility was dangling before her, she wanted to grasp it. All she had to do was silence the voices in her head, lock her horrible memories away, and conquer her fear of the bedding. She snorted. An impossible list, but perhaps she was up for the impossible, if he was.

With a deep breath, she opened the door to the kitchens, and the smell of fresh baked bread wafted out, making her mouth water. As she stepped into the room, all eyes turned to her, and all the happy chatter stopped. Doubt pricked her immediately, and Silas's voice whispered in her ear, *Ye're worthless*.

She forced a smile, though her stomach twisted with nerves. She would prove to these women, and to Brodee, that she had worth. "I dunnae ken a thing about the kitchens or have any notion where to begin," she admitted in one breath.

Mari, who Patience knew all the women looked up to and admired, weaved her way through the women gaping at Patience. The older woman arched her eyebrows at Patience and crossed her arms over her chest. "Then why are ye here?" she demanded, her tone unfriendly.

Patience suspected they did not like her because Silas had made it seem she did not wish to help, not that he'd not let her. She was their mistress, but simply demanding they allow her to learn and then listen to her would not gain her friends or loyalty. Maybe honesty would. "I want to learn how to be a good mistress of the castle, and no one kens the inner workings of this castle better than ye ladies."

"Why did ye nae come here before?" someone questioned from the crowd. Patience glanced around to locate the person who asked the question, and a woman lifted her hand to indicate it had been her. She was a tiny thing with big green eyes.

Patience took a deep breath. "I did nae come here before because Silas forbade me to do so."

"'Tis nae what Laird Kincaide told us," Mari piped up.

"Laird Kincaide was a liar," Patience replied, her hands coming to fists at Silas's ability to wreak havoc in her life from beyond the grave.

"Well, how are we supposed to ken who to believe?"

Mari demanded, to which there were many grunts and words of agreement.

"All I ask is that ye give me the opportunity to show ye," Patience said. "I ken Brodee told ye all to get yer assignments from me, but I also ken I dunnae have the first idea of how to run a castle, so I will need all of ye to help me, to teach me. I vow to ye I will be as fair as possible and work right alongside ye daily."

Murmurs of approval rose from many women in the crowd, but Mari gave Patience a doubtful look, but it was better than the narrow-eyed one from moments ago. "Ye're the daughter of a laird, and ye've been wed thrice now," Mari said, "so why do ye nae ken how to run a castle? If ye claim Laird Kincaide was nae truthful about why ye did nae help us, what *is* the truth?"

"Aye," one of the women said, "we deserve to hear it if we're to welcome ye in now."

Humiliation burned Patience's cheeks. It grew even hotter when the kitchen door creaked open, sunlight flooded the room, and Cul stepped into the kitchen. He inclined his head to her, and she cleared her throat, wishing desperately he had come in a few minutes later. She was not surprised he was here, of course, but she'd rather not reveal her humiliating past with him standing there. There did not seem to be a choice, however. She turned so that her back was to him, and she directly faced the women. "When I was much younger, my father married again after my mother passed, and his new wife did nae care for me. She told me I was too stupid to learn how to run a castle."

"Was she jealous?" the same petite woman with large green eyes asked.

"Jealous? Of me?" Patience asked, astonished at the question.

"Well, aye," the woman said. "If she was young, especially if she was close to yer age, she may have simply wanted to establish dominance over ye by ruling the castle without yer aid."

"Well, she *was* close to my age," Patience said, her mind turning. "I did nae ever think of that. I, well, I did nae ever really have anyone to talk to about it."

"I'm Ada," the petite woman said. She came forward and curtsied. "Ye can talk to me."

Patience smiled. "Thank ye, Ada."

"What of when ye were wed before?" Mari asked. "Laird Sutherland was yer first husband, aye?" She gave Patience another suspicious look.

"Aye." Patience shifted from foot to foot, half wishing the floor would swallow her up. Sharing the secrets she'd long kept was a terrifying prospect, but perhaps holding on to them was what continued to give the past power over her. "I stayed mostly to my chambers when I was wed to Laird Sutherland." She prayed the women would leave it at that.

"Why?" Mari asked.

"There are some truths," Patience said, her voice wobbling, her hand fluttering to her neck in memory of Ivan trying to choke her, of the bruises she had stayed in her chamber to hide, "too terrible to speak aloud."

Mari's eyes widened, and her mouth formed an *O*. She moved closer to Patience, surprising her when she took Patience by the hands and pressed her mouth close to Patience's ear. Behind Patience, she felt Cul step closer, as if he feared he might need to protect her from Mari. "Did the truth involve yer husband's fists?"

Patience sucked in a breath and turned her head, meeting Mari's assessing gaze. "How did ye ken?"

The distrustful expression she'd worn when looking at Patience for the months she had been here softened, and the woman's thin lips turned down into a sad smile. "Because I've been that woman. A hider of bruises. Fearful to leave my room. My husband died years ago, thankfully. I am sorry for ye, truly." A tear trickled down Patience's cheek and she quickly swiped it away. "Did Laird Kincaide hit ye, as well?" Mari questioned.

Patience shook her head. "His cruelty was of a different nature."

"Ah, lass," Mari said, pulling Patience into her embrace. Mari was soft as only an older woman could be, in that way that spoke of comfort given by a mother to a child. And she smelled like bread, which felt comforting and safe somehow. "If ye ever wish to talk, find me."

Patience nodded, and then Mari pulled away and turned to the women who were as silent as if they'd all been put under a temporary spell. "Lady Blackswell shares my past and Jane's present," she announced.

Patience started at the news of Jane. She felt immediate kinship to the woman and sorrow for her, and she could not help but wonder if she could somehow aid Jane, as she'd wished someone would have helped her.

She cast a furtive glance over her shoulder, her eyes meeting Cul's assessing gaze. Would he tell Brodee what she'd revealed? Before she could ponder that, mutterings of outrage filled the room from the women. Then, to Patience's complete and utter shock, the women poured forth introducing themselves and some even hugging her and offering sympathy, their own stories of abuse from men, some husbands and some not. Never had she felt so much a part of something, so much like she had found a home, a place to belong.

And it was because Brodee had given her this opportunity.

She wanted to go to him and to thank him, but she
knew he was training. *Later,* she told herself. *And mayhap...*
Well, mayhap they'd even share another kiss. Her belly
tightened, and her cheeks heated at the thought.

"Come," Mari said, motioning to the door. "I'll show ye
where we get our herbs and how to pick them, and then we
will teach ye all about the kitchens."

Patience turned and was face-to-face with Cul. Now his
expression held a mixture of anger and sorrow. He touched
his fist to his heart, and she frowned, not understanding.
"What does that mean?" she asked him.

"'Tis the motto of Laird Blackswell's branch of the
clan," Cul said. "It means 'the strong shall nae break.'"

It was perfect. She nodded, touched her fist to her heart,
and followed Mari outside to the herb garden.

Mari spent the better part of the early afternoon teaching
Patience about the herbs and what they were used for. "Jane
normally gathers the herbs for the kitchens every morning,"
Mari said as they collected the herbs to take inside to the
ladies who were busily cooking.

The mention of Jane's name brought Mari's earlier
comment regarding their shared experiences. Patience
thought of the woman whom she really did not know. Jane
was timid. Patience had thought it was because Jane had
feared her, but it seemed it was more than that. "Mari,"
Patience said, putting her hand on the woman's arm to stop
her progress into the kitchens, so they could have a private
word—or as private as it could get with Cul standing at the

kitchen door within hearing distance. "Is Jane's husband cruel to her?"

"Aye. He hits her all the time," the older woman replied, disgust in her voice. "Jane has made us vow to keep her secret because he threatened to kill her if she told anyone, though I do think she confessed the truth to Kinsey, which is how Jane came to work in the kitchens and work as yer lady's maid. I think Lady Kinsey was trying to aid Jane as best she could without putting her in more danger. Normally, Jane would work in the sheep field with her husband all day, and every little thing set him off and made him hit her, but now that she works with us and for ye, she dunnae get hit nearly as much." Mari shook her head. "If only she had someone to take her in who could protect her. Lady Kinsey promised to ask Laird Kincaide—" Patience scoffed at the notion of Silas aiding Jane, to which Mari nodded. "I did nae ken he was cruel to ye. Anyway, Laird Kincaide died before Lady Kinsey could speak with him."

"She was likely waiting for a time the devil would possibly be generous," Patience said, "but that could have been a lifetime." Patience nibbled on her lip, thinking. Brodee had given her the power to make decisions for the women. She was mistress of this castle, and as mistress, it was her duty to protect her clan just as much as her husband's. The notion of having the power to help Jane, someone abused like Patience had been, filled Patience with a sense of purpose. "Where is Jane?" Patience asked. She wanted to talk to the woman, and after she spoke with her, if Jane was agreeable, Patience would ask Brodee if he would aid Jane.

Mari frowned. "I dunnae actually. She is normally here in the kitchens in the mornings, but she did nae come today."

"Do ye ken where her cottage is?"

"Oh, aye. 'Tis to the west near the edge of the woods."

"I'm going to go see her," Patience said, determined to aid the woman. She'd never had anyone to help her, and she wanted and needed to do this for Jane.

"Ye kinnae go there!" Mari announced so loudly that Cul, who had been distracted by one of the kitchen women who'd come outside to flirt with him, looked over to where Patience was.

"Ye kinnae go anywhere without me," Cul announced, striding toward them.

Patience opened her mouth to order Cul to remain here, but then she clamped her jaw shut and nodded. She doubted Cul would listen in this case, and if Jane's husband was violent with Jane, it would be wise to have Cul come along, just in case. "I'm going to visit Jane to speak of womanly matters," she said in an effort to keep the intimate details of Jane's secret until Jane said it was all right to reveal it. When I speak with her, unless ye wish to hear of womanly problems, I suggest ye keep yer distance."

He looked distinctly uncomfortable. "Gladly."

It took longer to get to Jane's cottage than Patience had expected. The sun was setting in the sky, casting burgeoning shadows in the woods as the cottage came into view.

"We'll be late for supper," Cul said, a note of disquiet in his voice.

"I'm certain there will be food left for us," Patience assured him.

Cul laughed at that. "'Tis nae food that vexes me, my lady. 'Tis the laird."

Patience's brow furrowed. "Brodee? Why?"

"He'll be distressed, I'd think, when we dunnae appear for the meal. I should have told him before we came here."

"If he's concerned," she said, "I'm certain he will ask around, and Mari will tell him where we've gone." It was so foreign to think that someone might be worried about her whereabouts that she had not even considered Brodee. Yet, if his behavior so far was any indication, he would be alarmed when they did not appear for supper, and the happiness she felt at that idea made her warm and content.

"My lady, ye're grinning."

"Am I?" She pressed her hands to her cheeks as they approached the cottage, but then a desperate scream rent the air and fear stopped her in her tracks.

"Stay here!" Cul hissed, his sword singing in the moment of silence as he withdrew it.

Cul's command was not hard for Patience to follow because she was frozen in place with terror. Her heart beat viciously as she watched Cul pound on the door. Another scream cut through the forest, and then the door banged open and a man came out swinging a gleaming sword.

Eleven

"*Y*er new wife is making a habit of holding up supper," William said with a grin.

Brodee was not amused. "I dunnae ken where she could be," he said, thinking out loud. "She worked alongside the other women in the kitchens all day." And they were all present.

"She did?" Kinsey asked, a note of irritation in her voice.

"Were ye nae in the kitchens with them?" Brodee replied.

"Nay. I had to tend to a sick clan member," she said easily. "It's fallen to me to act as lady of castle since Patience is nae able."

Her comment sparked irritation within him. "She *is* able. Yer brother made it *seem* she was unable and unwilling."

"Of course," Kinsey said, her jaw tensing noticeably, but she did offer a smile, albeit a slightly brittle one. He was certain she was unhappy with what he'd just told her.

"I've made it clear that she should be treated in her rightful place as lady of the castle," he reiterated.

"As she should be," Kinsey agreed, biting her lip. "But are ye certain she is capable, though, given, well—" She tapped her head, indicating Patience's mental state.

He knew damned well Patience was not crazy, and he

thought they'd mostly gotten past her trying to pretend she was. But if that was the case, either she'd not told Kinsey yet, who it seemed Patience must have actually enlisted to aid her in driving him away, or he'd been wrong that he and Patience had made progress.

"Mayhap, she is simply nae capable of fulfilling her duties as yer *wife*," Kinsey suggested softly.

He frowned at the woman, unsure if she was working with Patience or against her. He preferred it to be the latter, and he could quickly deal with Kinsey. But perhaps he leaned toward that option because somewhere between yesterday and today, his pride had become involved.

God help me.

"Whether she is capable or nae," he said, rising and stepping away from the hand Kinsey had just placed on his arm, "we are wed, therefore she will become capable."

He started to move away from the dais, glaring down at William, who was watching him and Kinsey with open amusement, but as he did, Kinsey jumped up and grabbed his forearm. "Aye," she said on a rush of breath, "but we both ken"—her voice dropped to barely above a conspiratorial whisper—"that if the marriage has nae been consummated, it is nae a true marriage, and therefore can be set aside. That would save a tiresome time."

A powerful surge of denial at the suggestion of setting his marriage aside, setting Patience aside, whooshed through him and left him shocked for a moment. His feelings for his wife were quickly becoming a confused mess. The wife he'd vowed to feel nothing for. The wife he'd known for two days and been wed to for only one. The turn of events did not bode well for what was to come.

Flashes of painful memories lit within his mind. Arabel dead. The dark, consuming guilt that he'd failed to protect her. The doubt of his worth. He gave himself a little shake. He would not go down that path again. He'd loved and lost. He'd learned his lesson. Hadn't he? Why could he not seem to stop how he was beginning to feel for Patience? He didn't want these emotions, but what he wanted and what was occurring were not the same thing. "Our marriage will nae be set aside," he said, not bothering to look at Kinsey when he answered.

He pulled his arm out of her grasp, made his way off the dais, stalked toward the door that led to the passage to the kitchens, but as he was opening it, Mari appeared holding jugs of wine.

"Where is Patience?" he demanded by way of greeting. His temper had now snapped like a twig under his boot.

The older woman's eyes widened. "I assumed she was in here, my laird. Has she nae come to supper at all?"

He shook his head, a familiar sense of unease, one that had kept him alive in many battles, rising.

"Is Cul in here?"

"Nay," he said. He'd looked for Cul repeatedly since he was to be guarding her. "Was she with Cul?"

"Aye. They left hours ago to make their way to the edge of the woods to see Patience's lady's maid, Jane."

Another kitchen lass, a small thing with blond hair and green eyes stopped in the doorway and gaped at Brodee and Mari. "They did nae return?" the woman asked on a gasp.

His uneasiness gave way to hot worry. "Who are ye?"

"Ada." She dipped a curtsy, but he impatiently waved her up. She bit her lip, then launched into a rambling story about how she had thought it a bad idea for them to go, but after twenty sentences she'd not explained why. All Brodee could feel was the pounding of fear within him for Patience's safety.

"Enough," he said, trying not to bark the word, but he knew he'd failed when the woman Ada's body jerked, and then her lower lip tucked between her teeth. "Tell me what I need to ken about Jane and why ye did nae believe it a good idea for Patience to go."

"'Tis nae Jane," Ada said, to which Mari nodded.

"'Tis her husband," Mari went on. "He beats Jane."

"He has a horrid temper," Ada supplied.

"Jane did nae appear in the kitchens today," Mari said, and she and Ada exchanged a long look. "Lady Blackswell wished to help. She felt the wish keenly, too, given her and Jane's shared past."

"Shared past?" he asked, confused.

The women exchanged another look, this one distinctly uneasy.

"Get on with the telling now," he commanded, not sorry in the least for how cold he sounded. Patience could be in danger.

"Well, Lady Blackswell was beaten—"

It was spoken as if he should have known. Of course, he *should* if he and Patience were not practically strangers. If they'd not been forced to wed. If he'd not decided to keep her at arm's length. He would never forgive himself if she was injured—or worse.

The thought lodged a knot in his throat. "By Kincaide?" White-hot rage, seared him from the inside and broke him out in an instant sweat.

"Nay, Laird. By her first husband. Laird Kincaide hurt her in other ways, to which I fear left scars as painful as any fist."

"I kinnae believe this," he muttered, fiercely angry with himself that these women had only spoken with his wife today and knew more about her than he did. He was a stubborn clot-heid.

"'Tis true!" Mari insisted, clearly incensed on Patience's behalf. "I'd be able to tell if she was lying, and—"

"I did nae mean I dunnae believe what she told ye," he said, to which both women looked relieved. He turned toward the dais, waved a hand until he got William's attention, then motioned his friend to come to him.

William was there in a breath, looking at Brodee expectantly.

"We're going hunting."

William frowned. "For what?"

"A woman beater," Brodee growled, "and my wife."

⚜

The going was slow from the castle to the woods with night having descended. And Brodee's worry grew every moment that passed. As they approached the cottage, the first thing he noted was the absence of any voices. Only the sounds of the forest frogs and owls filled the night. The cottage was dark, and the door was open.

Something was wrong.

He withdrew his sword, and beside him, William did the same. They crept forward together, their motions in sync, their responsiveness to each other heightened as only two people who had performed dangerous approaches together countless times would move.

Brodee went in first, much to William's obvious irritation, but the man had to obey, given he was currently under Brodee's command. A moan of pain, a man's, whispered across his awareness, and he located the sound coming from a corner.

He cut across the room, shoving turned over furniture

out of his way and kneeled, seeing the outline of Cul, feeling something warm and sticky on Cul's chest. "Cul," Brodee said, not whispering. The man was here alone. Brodee knew it as certainly as he knew the seasons. "What happened?"

As he asked the question, he felt along the man's chest. It was a bloody mess. Brodee jerked off his plaid. "William, help me." William was there in a flash, and together they lifted Cul and wound the plaid around the man's upper chest to stop the bleeding.

"I'm sorry," Cul said. "I failed ye."

Jesus. Did that mean…

"Where is Patience?" Brodee asked, forcing the words past his constricted throat.

"She ran with Jane. Loskie pursuing."

"Jane's husband?"

"Aye." The word was weak. Cul was fast fading. "I had him, but then he took his wife. Knife to her neck. He would have—" A coughing spell wracked Cul, and the words died. After a moment, he gasped in a breath. "He would have killed her." The words were no more than a whisper now. Brodee had to lean close to hear. "I had to put my sword down to save her."

Brodee ground his teeth together on the desire to roar his fury. "Dunnae ever put yer sword down unless ye have a dagger to throw. When ye are better, we'll practice the scenario." He squeezed the man's shoulder and turned to William in the darkness. "Take him back to the castle. I'm certain they have a healer. See that he lives."

"Aye. I'll send men to ye."

"Hopefully, I'll nae need them." But he would not decline William's offer.

Brodee rose, moving swiftly now in time with his rushing blood and rapid breathing. Somewhere out there was his wife. It was true they were strangers, but she was his responsibility, and he would rather die than see injury come to her. The cool night air swept over him as he stepped outside. He paused and crouched, patting his hands over the forest floor, grazing wet, soft lichen and scratchy, tangled moss. He noted the dips where feet had stepped and followed the clues to a path tangled with roots and brambles and littered with fallen limbs, rocks, and a thousand other things that could trip his wife and give her pursuer time to overtake and kill her. Anger he could no longer contain seared him. He let out a bellow of rage, both for the past and for how it was trying to repeat itself.

"I ken ye're in here."

The voice was clear above the hum of the waterfall Patience and Jane stood behind. Spray from water soaked Patience's clothes and face.

"I'm coming for ye. Both of ye," Loskie called out.

Patience's scalp tingled. Loskie was closer. And calm. Too calm. Like someone who was certain they'd be victorious. Patience shuddered as she clutched Jane's hand and plastered herself against the wet, jagged rock. In front of her, the water came down deafening from the rocks above that rose toward the sky. Patience's heartbeat thudded in her ears. She curled her left hand tighter around the dagger she'd grabbed from the table in Jane's cottage as they had raced out.

"We're going to die!" Jane cried.

"Shh," Patience said. "I refuse to die today." She didn't know where her bravery was coming from. All she knew was that one of them had to be brave, and she was in much better condition to try than Jane, who had been beaten badly.

The images of her battered state flashed behind Patience's eyelids, awakening her own past. She had to suck in her cheeks and bite the inside of them to keep from screaming her anger. Busted lips. Swollen eyes. Aches that took weeks to subside. Breathing was hard. Movement impossible.

That was then, not now. In this moment, her body was alert and ready. Shadows protected them, but not for long. Soon, he would come upon them, traveling as he was on the same ledge they stood upon. He'd come from her right. She stared hard into the dark, seeing nothing.

All she had to do was plunge the dagger into his chest where his heart was. Nausea roiled in her stomach. She didn't want to do it, but she would. Her brother had once shown her how to wield a dagger, and she prayed she remembered. Her fingertips pulsed around the hilt of the weapon.

"Which one of ye should I kill first?" Loskie taunted.

Jane whimpered and Patience elbowed her. Jane immediately fell silent. Patience bit her lip against her own desire to whimper until the metallic taste of blood touched her tongue. Was he ten steps away? Nine? Jane suddenly pressed herself even closer to Patience, the violent trembling of her body making Patience's memories rattle louder. She pushed back against the tide of fear and squeezed Jane's hand to try to offer reassurance. She wanted to run, but there was nowhere to go. There never had been anywhere to go. No home. No safety. Her whole life had been blocked by men and now she was trapped by rock, too. They were the same. Immovable.

No more, no more, no more.

Rock crunched from her right just audible beneath the hum of the waterfall. Turning toward the noise, she released Jane's hand in the same instant and stepped toward the sound, hoping to block Loskie from reaching Jane.

Almost. Almost.

Blood pumped from her heart, down her arm to her fingers, and a shriek split her ears.

God's teeth! Had that been her?

A bellow came next. Then a hand grasped her arm. Without thought, she brought the dagger up and thrust it forward into flesh. A grunt resounded, and suddenly, she was jerked off the ledge, falling with Loskie to the dark water below. She hit hard, her breath gushing out as rock met her head and the blackness consumed her.

⚜

There was no time for thought or fear, only action and determination. As Patience fell, gripped by Loskie, Brodee dove into the water far below, hoping he ended up close to where the shaft of moonlight they'd fallen through indicated. Rock sliced his shoulder as his body cut through the water, ripping his skin open and leaving a blazing trail of fire. It didn't even touch the pain in his chest with the thought of Patience dying.

He broke the surface with a roar, dagger in hand. Loskie attacked immediately. Fist flying and landing with a crunch against Brodee's nose, then his lip. Desperation and rage drove Brodee to fight back like a possessed man. Or maybe he was possessed.

The next punch that came at him did not land. He grabbed Loskie's fist, both of them going under, and Brodee gripped the hand in his until the man's bones broke. Even underwater, he thought he heard the howl of pain. He drove the dagger forward into the man's chest, next to the one he only just realized was already there, protruding and potentially fatal if it had not been just off the mark. His dagger hit its target, and Loskie instantly stilled, all the fight and evil in the man silenced forever.

Brodee kicked him away and swam for the surface. He sucked in air and gulps of water as he broke the surface once more, only to be hit by the sharp sting of the water coming from the rocks above.

Where was she? He swished his hands through the water like blades turning this way and that, the desperation in him coiling tighter and tighter, and then his fingers tangled in something silky. Her hair! He gripped her with one hand and turned her over from where she floated facedown in the water. Sliding his arm across her stomach, he brought her to him as he flipped onto his back and laid her against his chest while he kicked toward what he prayed to God was the jagged embankment.

Sharp rock met his hand in moments, and he gripped the rocks, finding purchase. His bicep burned as he pulled himself up, his skin sliding over the rough edges, protecting her as best he could. With a grunt, he straightened his free arm and pulled her up until she was against his side once more. Her head lolled, and his heart seemed to do the same. Then he was fully on the rocks, scrambling to his knees, and bringing her up to lean her against his chest as he smacked a hand against her back as he'd once seen the healer at his childhood home do when someone had been underwater for too long. When he got no response, he repeated the movement, despair rising, but then she coughed and coughed again. He trembled like a newborn as he drew her away from him just enough to glimpse the outline of her face.

He brought his hands to her face and roamed them over the slope of her silky skin to her lips, and then he pressed his mouth to hers, not in lust but in desperate relief.

Her hands came to his shoulders, and he broke the gentle kiss to cup her face. He could not stop the tremors that coursed through him. He'd almost lost her. He'd almost lost her, and the crazed feeling that brought to him was all too familiar. And unwanted. He should release her, and yet, and yet he could not. Not yet.

"Tomorrow," he said, hugging her to him, reveling for this moment of allowed weakness in her breath on his cheek, her warm skin against his, her tiny hands clutching him, "I will teach ye how to properly aim a dagger, Wife, so if ye ever have need, ye will kill who ye intend."

She buried her head in his chest. "I...I stabbed him. I kinnae believe I did such a thing."

He lifted her chin so he could look into her eyes. Regret and guilt shimmered there, and he wanted to wipe both away for her. "Would ye have preferred ye die?" Before she could answer, he asked, "Would ye have preferred he killed Jane?"

She shook her head.

"Then ye did what ye must. Dunnae ever feel guilt for doing what ye must to defend yerself or those ye love."

"So ye have nae ever felt guilt after ye killed someone?" Her gaze searched his.

He should not answer. He should not reveal a piece of his soul. Yet he could not resist doing so. No man alive would have been able to resist his wife in this moment. She was temptation incarnate with her sweetness, her vulnerability interwoven with her strength, her caring nature.

"Guilt, nay. Sorrow, aye. Bone deep. I see their faces

many times when I close my eyes—the faces of the men who stood against the king, men I begged to put down their arms but who refused, men I had to cut down so they'd nae cut me down, kill my men, or worse, kill women or children."

Her lips parted on an exhalation. "Ye've killed women and children?"

"Nay. But I've killed their husbands, their fathers. And when ye take the life of someone that another loves, the person left alive dies a bit. Oh, they are still breathing, but a part of them is dead."

She lowered her head to his chest and pressed her lips to his heart. He stared down at her in shock and wonder. He had never felt as connected to anyone, not even Arabel, as he did to Patience in that moment.

"Ye speak from personal experience." Her voice was but a whisper between them.

He could have denied what she stated, what she'd keenly ascertained, but he found he did not want to. If he was taking this one instance to let her in, he would gorge on the moment. It was the only one he could allow. "I do," he said.

She turned her head and set her ear against his heart.

He stilled, thinking she'd say something, but when she did not, he asked, "What are ye doing?"

She looked up at him with eyes full of undeniable hope. "I'm listening to see if the part of ye that's dead can be revived."

Her words sent a shaft of longing through his heart and straight into the depths of his soul. As he drank her in, a Siren with the heart of an angel, he knew without a doubt that no adversary he had ever faced had been as dangerous to him as his wife was now. He was at war with himself, and in this moment, he was losing. So he did what any savage slayer would do: he made a plan to avoid defeat.

Twelve

Something shifted between Patience and Brodee in the following week, or possibly they were beginning to take form as two people bound together for life. She caught glimpses of what they could maybe be if they could trust each other. Hope glimmered like sunshine slanting through a crack to fill a dark hole. Patience wanted that warm light. She hoped maybe Brodee did too. She could not forget their conversation after he'd rescued her when he'd admitted a part of him had died. Nor could she forget that he'd not responded to her saying she was listening to his heart to see if the part of him that had died could be revived. Yet she took hope that he'd not simply said no.

It could well be foolish hope, given she'd seen him very little since that night. Well, technically, she'd seen him every day since then, but their time together was brief. She saw him in the morning after she broke her fast and he came in from training his men. They would meet in the courtyard, and he'd instruct her on how to defend herself. William was there every day, and she half wondered if Brodee had not asked William to be present so they would not be alone again, and so she'd not try to talk to him anymore about the things he'd revealed. It was strange. She'd initially wanted to push him away, but now she didn't think she wanted that at all. He seemed determined, however, to keep a barrier between them.

She saw him at night in the great hall for supper, as well, but there would be no talking of private matters there. They sat at the dais with William, Father Murdock, Fergus—who was her personal guard while Cul recovered from his injuries—and Kinsey, who had been so touchingly relieved that Patience had survived her fall. She did not see Brodee after supper, though. He'd not come to her bedchamber or even hinted that he wished to consummate their marriage once since the night of her fall.

So at night, she was left with only her thoughts for company. She thought upon stabbing Loskie some, but she tried not to allow herself to linger upon it. It had been done in self-defense, yet she did not think she'd ever forget it, and those instances when she did recall it, it made her realize even more so than his admission had the heavy burden Brodee carried considering what his duties had called for him to do as the king's right hand. Though she knew he had done all in his power to spare the lives of the men whose castles the king had him take back, she also knew the pain it cost him for those who would not allow him to spare them.

When she was not in bed thinking upon that, she considered how it seemed almost a dream the way her life had changed so drastically since Brodee had arrived at Crag Donnon. She had a husband who did not scare her, though the idea of the joining still left her frozen, not because she was frightened he'd purposely hurt her or be callous with her but because she feared she would disappoint him. She could not, though she was content, entirely silence the self-doubt that Silas had instilled in her, nor could she forget the pain and lack of passion she'd found in joining with her previous husbands. But when she thought about what Brodee had revealed, she knew him to be good. And when she recalled how gentle Brodee's daily touches were, or how his kisses made her feel so deliciously wonderful, she almost believed it would be different with him. *She* would be different with him.

She was determined today to get some time alone with him so they could learn each other a bit. First she went to get herbs from Mari for the wound on Cul's chest. It turned out Mari was not only head of the kitchens but she was the castle healer, as well. After Patience tended to Cul, she made her way to the west bank of the castle, where she had discovered yesterday, by happenstance, that William trained alone every morning for a bit before he joined her and Brodee in the courtyard.

She wanted to ask William not to come to the courtyard this morning, so she and Brodee could be alone. She was so preoccupied with her thoughts on what she even wanted to say to Brodee that she did not see Kinsey until the woman seemed to appear from nowhere and was before her.

Patience let out a yelp of surprise and then laughed. "Ye scairt me."

"I'm sorry," Kinsey said. "I called to ye, but ye did nae seem to hear me."

Patience frowned, detecting a slight censure in Kinsey's tone, one that reminded her of the way Silas used to speak to her.

"Are ye vexed with me?" Patience asked, amazed that she had asked such a blunt question. A week ago she would have never been so brave, but she was changing.

"Of course nae. Just fashed for ye," Kinsey replied and slipped her arm through Patience's. "I wager ye were thinking upon yer husband," she said, a hint of disapproval—or was that mockery?—in her voice.

It occurred to Patience suddenly that though Kinsey had told her she thought her brother evil, she may have still loved him as a sister would a brother, and it may be hurting her that Patience seemed to now be setting him, and the bad memories he'd left her with, aside. "I was," she said slowly. "I'm sorry if that hurts ye because of Silas."

"Why would that hurt me?" Kinsey asked. "I wish ye to forget my brother just as much as ye desire to."

"Oh," Patience said, unsure if she truly believed her. "Ye dunnae have to say that just so our friendship will nae feel strained."

"I'm nae," Kinsey replied. "I vow it to ye." Her words sounded completely genuine now, so Patience nodded. Kinsey gave her a squeeze. "I've just come from speaking with one of the Blackswell warriors, and I've heard something disturbing about yer husband."

Patience sighed. For the last four days, Kinsey had re-layed things she considered disturbing about Brodee. Patience knew she meant well, but it was becoming irritating. She'd listened to her and even asked around about the things Kinsey had passed along to her. According to Kinsey, Brodee had hit a child during training. In fact, he had—*accidentally*—when he'd swung around and a boy had walked up to him to offer him some mead. Then Kinsey had offered that Brodee had yelled at one of the kitchen lasses. When Patience had asked the women in the kitchens, they'd said that Brodee had yelled at one of the kitchen lasses because she had been walking with a large trencher and she could not see the path in front of her when there was a limb that could trip her. So he'd yelled to aid her since he was across the way from her in the great hall.

Kinsey had also grumbled that Brodee trained all the men until they were nearly about to drop. He did. It was true. Patience had watched from afar, but anything he asked of his men, he did, as well, and she'd heard the men, both Blackswells and Kincaides alike, talking in the great hall of their training with awe and admiration in their voices for Brodee. He inspired them to want to be their best, which was a good thing. Not only did they have to defend this castle, but she'd heard William and Brodee talking at supper, and that the time was fast approaching that Brodee would have to leave to continue his work as the king's right hand. If she'd overheard correctly, he was to join forces with her father to seize Laird Gordon's castle since the man supported the Steward.

Patience still had a hard time believing her father had changed allegiances from the king's nephew to the king, but knowing her father, he'd undoubtedly done it because it served his interests. For once in her life, she was glad her father was so greedy for power and wealth, because if he'd not been, she'd not now be wed to Brodee. Her father had used her, given her in marriage to a man whom he thought was his enemy's ruthless right hand. He'd done it without a care for her, only himself. He'd done it so the king would accept it as his pledge of faith. He'd made it seem she was precious to him, and he was entrusting her care to Brodee.

Such lies! Yet she found her anger at her father had subsided. Not because he was deserving of forgiveness, but, in the end, her father had done her a good turn by wedding her to Brodee, and that was something that would likely vex her father to no end to discover, which made her grin.

"Do ye nae wish to hear what I learned?" Kinsey's irritated tone jerked Patience out of her musings.

Between Kinsey's needlessly cross attitude and her refusal to see that Brodee was a good man, Patience's temper flared. She'd had enough, even if Kinsey did have well-meaning intentions, something Patience suddenly began to question. Wouldn't a friend trying to keep another safe cease the effort when they realized there was no danger? She bit her lip. Truthfully, she wasn't certain, as she'd never had a close friend. If it had been Kinsey who had been wed to a man Patience feared was horrid, how much proof of his honorable nature would she need before she quit trying to protect her friend? Again, she was not entirely sure, but her gut told her that by now, in light of all the good Brodee had done, if she were Kinsey, Patience would have allowed for the possibility that she might be wrong about Brodee, so that, she decided, was what she would say. "I think ye must allow for the possibility that Brodee is a good man," she said, deciding mincing words was useless.

"Well, I would have—honestly, I would have—but I heard just today that Brodee is a murderer," Kinsey stated, sounding more triumphant than regretful about her announcement.

Patience inhaled a long breath for, well, *patience*. She'd found in the last day that what she normally possessed in abundance seemed to have all but disappeared. "I dunnae believe defending yerself—"

"Nay," Kinsey interrupted. "He has killed two women, and neither had anything to do with his duty."

"Who told ye this?" Patience demanded.

"I overheard some of his men speaking about it," she replied. "One said it was rumored he killed his leman, and the other mentioned a rumor that he'd killed a woman he was betrothed to but whom he did nae wish to wed." Kinsey squeezed Patience's arm. "Ye could be the next woman he kills!"

"That's enough!" Patience said. She could not imagine the protective man she'd come to know in the last week and a half killing any woman, let alone one he was joining with and whom he was to wed. But it did bother her that she knew nothing about this rumor—or him. It was precisely why she wanted to be alone with him. She pulled her arm from Kinsey's grasp. It was time to put an end to this. "If Brodee were going to kill me, he could have already done so," she said not curbing her blunt tone. Kinsey opened her mouth to speak, but Patience held up her hand to silence her. "Ye are nae going to convince me he's a killer of women, so dunnae bother with any more arguments."

Kinsey's mouth set in a line of distinct annoyance.

Patience's brow furrowed as she stared at her friend. "Is this about Brodee, or is this about Silas? Perhaps both men?" It was a half guess, but half suspicion, that Kinsey had not been fully honest moments ago. Despite Silas being horrible to Patience, she'd not once seen him be anything but kind to his sister. As she thought about it now, Silas had been protective of Kinsey. In fact, Patience had wished that Silas would treat her with the same regard he had treated Kinsey.

"Ye miss Silas, dunnae ye?" Patience asked, gentling her tone. "Ye said my moving on from him did nae bother ye, but it does truly, dunnae it?"

Kinsey visibly stiffened at the question, but then her shoulders drooped and a bleak look swept her face. She dropped her gaze from Patience to the floor. "Aye. I do. I'm sorry I do. I ken he was a horrid person," she said, her voice tight. "I ken he was nae good to ye, but he was my brother, and I...I..."

"Ye loved him," Patience finished.

Kinsey's head jerked up, and a startled gaze settled on Patience. Patience quickly patted Kinsey's arm. "It's all right. He was yer brother. It's natural that ye loved him, despite the things he did to me. He was nae that way to ye."

Kinsey opened and shut her mouth, and a pained expression crossed her face. "Nay," she said in a choked whisper. "He was good to me."

Impulsively, Patience hugged the woman to her. "I am sorry for yer loss, and I do understand ye're feeling as if I'm going to replace Silas with Brodee, but ye must stop this now." She could not say she was sorry for the loss of Silas, because it was simply not true.

Kinsey pulled away from Patience and swiped at the tears that trickled down her face. Patience felt horrible. Had she been too harsh, too blunt with her words? Finally, the woman said, "Ye are right, Patience. Please forgive me. I'm horrid. I ken Silas was nae good. I ken he did evil things, and I ken yer husband only killed him in defense when Silas tried to kill him. I dunnae harbor hatred over that. I just," she quirked her mouth as if looking for the words to explain herself, "I'm already forgetting him," she finished in a near whisper.

"Nae anyone else here seems to wish to remember him. Nae even the warriors who were supposed to be loyal to him. They have a new laird now, so they dunnae even speak of Silas. And I just thought, well I just thought—" She pressed her fingers to her temples as her tears trickled. Patience's heart squeezed for Kinsey's sorrow. Silas did not deserve Kinsey's tears, but that did nae mean the woman did not feel true sorrow. "I dunnae what I thought. Her voice was resigned. Heavy and filled with regret. Her gaze met Patience's. "I suppose deep within I did nae want Blackswell to have ye since ye had been Silas's wife, even though, even though—" She lifted her shoulders in a helpless gesture. "Even though 'twas nae fair to ye. I understand if ye need to tell Blackswell. I imagine he'll send me away."

Kinsey had done no real harm, other than passing on whispers she'd heard and exaggerating things she'd seen, and Patience did understand what had driven her. After all, she loved her own brother Duff, and she suspected it would be hard for her to see him easily forgotten and replaced. "No harm has been done," Patience said. "This can stay between us." Patience squeezed Kinsey's shoulder. "I dunnae expect ye to forget Silas, but I would ask that ye give Brodee a chance."

"I will!" Kinsey said, and pulled Patience close for a hug. "I vow it." The woman pulled away and offered Patience a wobbly smile. "I think I'll go lie down. I've a pain in my head."

Patience nodded. She suspected Kinsey wanted to simply be alone, and she understood that. "I'll see ye later."

Kinsey nodded and strolled away, and Patience stood there, processing all that had just happened. More than ever, she wanted to go find Brodee and really discover who her new husband was. She whirled around to find William approaching her.

She smiled. "I was just coming to find ye."

He grinned back, two dimples appearing. "Well, I was sent to find ye. Brodee is quite irritated with ye."

She thought she knew why. She had slipped away from Fergus earlier. "I dunnae need a shadow in the castle."

William arched his eyebrows. "Ye're changing."

She nodded and tried to stop the smile, but it was hopeless.

He chuckled. "I'm glad to see it. A man like Blackswell needs a lass with a spine of steel."

"Ye think I'm strong?" she asked, astonished.

"Aye. Ye would have to be to survive what ye have."

She tilted her head. "Do ye mean Jane's husband?"

William shifted from foot to foot, and an uncomfortable look crossing his face. "Well, aye, but nae just that man. I'm speaking of yer past."

Patience's cheeks grew hot. "What do ye ken of my past?"

"I ken yer first husband beat ye, and Kincaide, well..." William shrugged. "All I ken is that he was cruel to ye in a different way, though. I dunnae ken what that was exactly, but I can imagine."

Cul. It had to have been Cul who told William since Cul had been in the kitchens when she'd spoken of her past. And if he'd told William, had he told Brodee? "Does Brodee ken this, as well?"

"Aye." She pressed her lips together on her annoyance. She wasn't really irritated with Cul. He'd likely thought he was helping her. She was vexed by the fact that almost everything she and Brodee knew of each other had come from someone else revealing it. That was not the sort of marriage she wanted nor did she think she and Brodee could truly come to know each other that way.

"I think it's time my husband and I come to ken each other," she said, half contemplating if Brodee had been avoiding being alone with her because of what he'd learned.

A slow smile curved William's lips. "I could nae agree more. He's in the courtyard fighting his demons."

She had to wonder if those demons had to do with the women he supposedly killed.

"Go to him," William said.

She paused a moment. "Have ye kenned him a long time, William?"

He shook his head. "Nay. I was sent on a mission last year with his brother, Broch. 'Tis a long story, and one ye need to hear from Brodee, nae me, but I met him during that mission, and after I left and did nae reappear where I was supposed to, the king ordered Blackswell to come find me. He saved me. Ye dunnae need to fear him. He is ruthless, but only when it is called for. And mostly to himself... Would ye like a piece of advice?"

She nodded.

"Dunnae lie to him," he counseled. "He values honesty above all. His father lied to him for years, and it caused a great deal of pain for him."

"I'll remember that," she promised, glad she had all but admitted she was not crazy.

Thirteen

Where the devil were William and Patience? Brodee wiped the sweat from his eyes. He tried to stifle the rising tide of worry within him, but it was near hopeless. He still couldn't believe she'd slipped Fergus's guard. His mouth tugged into a smile of genuine appreciation at her clever tactic of having Mari distract Fergus while Patience fled the kitchens unnoticed.

He glanced to the castle door again, which remained closed. He definitely should have gone to search for her himself. But then they'd be alone, which was something he had taken great pains to avoid since the night in the woods when he'd realized how weak his resolve to keep his wife at a distance had become. She'd awakened feelings and longings he'd locked away after the pain of Arabel's death. He was a man of control, but Patience seemed to rob him of it. He couldn't allow that. Control kept the possibility of more pain away. And until he could gain back control, he had to keep distance. Space. Someone with them at all times, so he did not reveal things about himself, nor ask her about herself, about the things he'd learned. Each fact they could share was like a string that would bind them together, and the more he learned, the tighter they would be bound. And then what if he lost her?

He wanted to simply protect her and be good to her

without caring too much. It was too late for not caring at all.

Suddenly she was coming through the castle door, a vision in green with her dark hair flowing around her shoulders and a flower tucked behind her ear. His heart tugged, and he groaned. She strode toward him, purposeful, proud, like a warrior queen. His little wife had changed in the blink of an eye, and for her, he was glad of it. For himself, he was afraid of it. She was even more enticing in her new boldness.

"Where's William?" he asked as she approached.

"I asked him nae to come with me," she replied, not looking apologetic in the least.

"I wish ye would nae have done that. And I wish ye would nae have slipped away from Fergus."

"He's nae in trouble for that, is he?" she asked, looking and sounding suddenly worried. "It was nae his fault; it's mine. If ye must punish someone—"

"I told ye before I dunnae have a propensity to punish." The fact that she was more concerned for Fergus than herself was a fresh reminder of why he was having such a hard time keeping his guard up around her. She was kind, gentle, and fragile. Yet she had a strength she did not even realize. He wanted to tell her that. But he could not, there were too many strings—the kind that bind, the kind that only a woman could tie around a man. Those kinds of strings could kill a man when he lost the woman who had tied the knots.

Brodee inhaled deeply, trying to clear the jumble of thoughts that were normally so orderly, but that this slip of a lass in front of him set into chaos every time she was near.

She set her hands on her hips and glanced up at him. "Are ye scairt to be alone with me?"

"Dunnae be nonsensical," he said. "I'm the Savage Slayer."

She arched her eyebrows. "From what I've observed, ye're more tender than savage."

"I told ye that ye dunnae call warriors tender," he grumbled. "I'm nae tender."

She held up her hand. "Ye punished Father Bisby for me. Ye punched Ulric for me. Ye fought Cul for me. Ye *killed* a man for *me*." She frowned as she glanced from her four fingers to him. "Oh. Ye *are* savage. But only when ye have to be, and always to protect *me*."

Devil take the lass. The tiny bit of control he felt he'd gained in the last week was fast slipping away. She reached out and touched his arm, the feel of her fingertips like a feast for the part of him that hungered for her. "I want to ken ye, Brodee, and I have nae ever been able to say that about a man I've been wed to before."

Christ, she was cleverer than any warrior he'd ever encountered. She seemed to know his weakness, though he'd been certain he hid it. She cleared her throat, revealing her nervousness, and the protectiveness inside him rose. How was he to protect her when he was trying to shield himself from the hurt only she could cause?

"I was wed to a man who beat me," she said. The words were the most blunt she'd ever spoken to him, and his gut twisted with her raw revelation. He'd known, of course, since the night in the woods, but to hear her say it so matter-of-factly brought all the rage he'd initially felt on her behalf storming to the forefront.

"I was then wed to a man who belittled me, who made me think I'm worthless." Her voice had dropped to a suffocated whisper, and he knew then that she still doubted herself. He understood it far too well. Her eyes bore into his, searching, he realized, for a sign from him.

"Ye make me feel I can hope," she said.

He was at once high and low. He wanted to give her hope, and yet she would not stop with that. He knew it. "Hope another person fills ye with is dangerous," he replied after a beat, feeling like a complete beast for the way her shoulders fell with his words, but he pressed on. He had to. "When they are gone, so is it, and all ye are left with is guilt and regret."

She notched her chin up, his beautiful warrior wife. "I would rather have that than never experience the happiness I can taste when ye're near."

God's teeth. There was no resisting the desire she ignited. He wanted to take her. Make her his. Claim her body. He trembled with the need to do so. That's all he would do. No sharing of his soul, only his body. He would stay in control. His heartbeat roared in his ears, and his blood pumped through him like it did before battle. He reached for her then, and when his fingers grazed her silken skin, he knew he was lost.

*   *   *

She couldn't even say how they got to the bedchamber. All she could remember was her entire being filling with yearning, anticipation, and a surety that he would refuse her. Then something seemed to flare within him and he'd touched her, making her her body grow tight with wanting. Then he'd pulled her against his chest to wrap her in his embrace.

His mouth, hot and searching, had covered hers, and all she could recall was the slide of his tongue along hers, the graze of his hand down her back, over her bottom, and under her legs. The feeling of being feather light as he carried her up the stairs. And then they were at the bedchamber door, and she became aware of everything at once. Her heart pounded so hard that her chest hurt. Her ears roared with her rushing blood, and fear and expectation fought for dominance inside her.

His lips touched her ear, causing swirling sensations of painful desire. "I surrender," he said, his hot breath gliding over her sensitive skin as triumph flared bright within her. Then, to her utter astonishment, he reared back and kicked open the door to the bedchamber. It opened with a slam against the wall, and he carried her into the room, pausing only long enough to kick the door shut behind them.

A look of raw hunger came to his face as he bent his head to her and parted her mouth for a kiss. Urgent need gripped her as his warm, velvet kiss stole all her fear and replaced it with heart-pounding curiosity of what was to come. His tongue tangled with hers and sent her senses reeling and pushed her toward reckless abandon. He broke the kiss, making her moan her despair, but then his lips came upon her once more to trace a fiery path down her neck to her breasts. It was divine ecstasy. It was going to make her truly mad with how needful it made her feel to have his lips everywhere on every part of her. Parts no lady should even dream of having a man's lips, but she was going to do more than dream. She would take, and very soon, if he did not kiss her all over.

"Brodee," she moaned, praying that he understood without the need for her to say it. Suddenly, his hands glided to her breasts, and he freed one, as if the gown she wore did not even exist. She cried out with pleasure as he took her nipple in his scorching mouth to suckle the sensitive bud.

The way he worked his mouth upon her skin was magical and maddening at once. Long pulls and tiny nips caused a pulsing that started in her belly and moved between her legs to her core. She needed more. "More," she said between pants, bringing her hands to his broad back to give him a not so gentle nudge. When he continued to tease her with a wicked chuckle, she dug her nails into his skin, and he released a sound of guttural pleasure that made her feel she could conquer anything.

He paused in his lovely feasting upon her nipple to say, "Ye want more?"

"Aye. Please," she shamelessly begged.

He rolled off her as he took her by the waist to swing her over his hips. Her gown creeped up her legs as she straddled him on the bed, and his hand slipped under her clothing to skim her hips and higher. And then he stilled, fingers hovering, then tracing the rough scar Ivan had left on her right thigh after he'd lashed her so badly that he'd cut her flesh wide open.

"What's this?" Brodee asked. The single question reminded her of Silas, of his shaming her and listing her flaws, including the scars Ivan had left on her body. Doubt invaded her desire. If this continued, he would see all the things that made her so imperfect. And maybe she would prove to be just as broken as Silas had claimed, just as unresponsive to the actual act of joining and only feel the pain, not the pleasure, only experience loathing and not wanting.

She tugged up her gown and pushed away from him, her hand against a chest that may as well have been carved of stone. She didn't even get her palm off the hard surface of his hot flesh before his fingers circled her wrist. "I kinnae," she said, trying to scoot back, but his free hand slid behind her back and pressed against her tailbone. She felt his desire in the hardness that she had unleashed, had practically demanded he release.

"What is it?" His gaze burned into hers. "Tell me the fears Kincaide instilled in yer heart, and I'll destroy them. Tell me why ye hear his voice, and I'll silence it."

It was now or never. She could live a life of fear or she could release herself from the chains. She reached her free, trembling hand to the edge of her gown and pulled it up to the scar Ivan had left on her leg. Then she pointed. "This is but one scar Ivan left with me. There are more, and they are ugly. Silas reminded me of it every time he viewed me without clothes."

Brodee's hands immediately came to her waist, and he set her off him in one fluid motion. She blinked as he towered above her, and then her heart twisted painfully. He was disgusted. But then he bent toward her, set his hands to her ankles, and tugged her gently to the edge of the bed.

"What are ye doing?" she asked, the weaker her trying to resurface.

The look of tenderness that he gave her instantly calmed her, but when he kneeled between her legs and put his large palms to either of her knees, she tensed. "Lass, ye could have a thousand scars, and all I would see is the beauty in yer heart, which shines through in yer eyes, yer smile, in every gesture ye make."

"What gestures?" she asked, so intrigued that she forgot to keep her legs locked, and he eased them open, positioning himself between her thighs. She hissed in a breath, and he arched his eyebrows.

"The way ye stand up for others and are more concerned for their welfare than yer own." He bent his head and brushed his lips to her scar. She went immediately rigid, but there was no closing her thighs with him between them. When he came up, he had an assessing look on his face. "Ye've nae ever had a man intent upon ye between yer legs, have ye?"

Heat singed every part of her body, even parts she'd not realized could feel the flush of embarrassment. "Of course I have had a man between my legs," she said, her voice catching as his fingers traced a gentle path up and down her inner thighs. "I've been wed twice."

"Aye. To fools. One who beat ye and another who made ye feel utterly worthless. Whatever Kincaide convinced ye about yerself is a lie."

She shook her head. "Maybe some of it, but nae all of it. I dunnae feel passion," she said, "for the joining. I…I nae ever have. Nae with Ivan or Silas." Brodee watched her steadily, but he did not comment, so she continued, wanting to get the truth out there. She was tired of holding it in. "Mayhap the way they treated me was my fault. I failed as a wife."

"Ye dunnae believe that," he said, his voice strong and carrying a unique force, one that compelled her to look inward for a moment.

"Nae totally, but I'm scairt. What if something is wrong with me? What if I simply kinnae feel anything good during the joining? Ye would, ye would—"

"Dunnae fash, Patience. There is a difference between having a man between yer thighs and having a man who is *there for ye* between yer thighs. Though I dunnae wish ye the pain that has come with nae having the latter, I'd be a liar if I did nae admit that I'm glad I'll be the first and only man to introduce ye to pleasure and wipe away any doubt that ye can feel it and give it." He smiled at her, his gaze smolder-ing. "Lie back," he said in a gentle tone.

She nibbled on her lip, nervous. "Should we talk first? Ye have spent a week avoiding me, and I... Well, I did do my best to keep ye away."

He guided her back with care until she was staring at the ceiling, then to her complete and utter astonishment, he relieved her of her undergarments in one swift motion. She went to close her legs, but his firm hands stopped her. "What are ye doing?" she asked, her voice a breathy whisper. She tried to rise, but his hand whipped up to urge her to stay down.

"Ye will need to be lying back for what I intend to do to ye," he explained. "Ye'll be that weak when I'm done."

"Ye're verra certain of yerself," she chided.

"Aye, in this I am. Ye'll be glad of it, too, I vow it."

Her fingers found his shoulders, and she gripped him. "Did ye learn this by doing it to the woman ye were to wed?"

"*God's teeth*," he muttered.

She cringed. Why had she mentioned that? She should have left it alone until after they had joined, after he had made her weak. Every fiber of her being wanted to experience that weakness by his hands. But he loomed over her so fast her breath caught.

His legs came to either side of her hips to lock her in, and his hands rested by her arms, his muscles bulging just from bearing his weight. "I see we do actually need to talk first." He did not sound happy.

"I'm sorry," she said, both out of habit and because she truly was.

"Dunnae," he said, leaning down and gently brushing his lips to hers, "apologize. 'Tis I who should do so. Ye asked to talk to me, and to be honest, it's just about killed me to restrain my desire for ye this last week, so when I finally gave in, the last thing on my mind was talking about our pasts. But that was selfish, and ye have had yer fill of selfish men."

She stared at him in amazement. "Ye're verra surprising."

He chuckled. "I'm surprising myself, lass." He scrambled off her to settle beside her and motioned her toward the top of the bed. "If we're to talk, ye should scoot up to where ye are more comfortable."

Once they were both situated, sitting side by side, she turned to him, aware of the length of his muscled legs pressed against hers. His bright-blue eyes watched her with expectation. She'd never sat with a man like this. In fact, she'd never had a personal conversation with either of her other husbands. Suddenly, she wasn't even certain where to begin or what to ask. She twisted her fingers together, feeling foolish, and Brodee's hand came to rest on hers.

"I've been with many women," he said, his voice low and perhaps tinged with regret. "I think it best for both of us if we dunnae talk about where I discovered how to do things."

She nodded in full agreement.

He inhaled a long, slow breath, and she got the feeling he was trying to order his own thoughts. "I was to wed. 'Tis true. But I never joined with her, and I did nae… That is to say, I did nae…"

"Ye did nae care for her?" she guessed, wanting to help him out of what was clearly a miserable topic for him.

He frowned. "Nay. I did care for her, but as a friend. My father bade me to wed her. And I was prepared to do what I needed to for the good of the clan."

"What happened to her?" Patience asked, feeling a bit guilty for leading him to talk of it without revealing that

Kinsey had told her he'd killed this woman and his leman.

"She was murdered. But ye already ken that, dunnae ye?"

A hot flush singed her cheeks, and she nodded. "I'm sorry. I should have said. I just—"

"It dunnae matter." He gave her a long look. "I'm used to the whispers now, though my innocence was proven recently and the real murderer finally found."

It was interesting to her that he'd not mentioned the leman yet. It had to be the leman he'd been referring to that night he'd told her part of people died when they lost someone they loved. "Will ye tell me of it? I dunnae believe ye to be a murderer—"

Amusement lit his eyes. "If ye did, it would be quite foolish of ye to be sitting here beside me."

"Aye, it would. But I dunnae believe ye to have murdered two women." His eyes narrowed, and his mouth thinned. She bit her lip, wondering if she had pushed him too far. When he said nothing, she continued. "I would like to ken about yer past, though, given...given ye are my future. And I... Well, I see hope in that future." God above, she wanted to fan her face she was so embarrassed.

His eyebrows jerked sharply up at her words. "Ah, lass." His shoulders dropped as if he bore a heavy weight upon them. As if her words were almost more than he could take. He squeezed her hand. "I dunnae ken what ye heard, but I can imagine. When I was much younger, I got entangled with a lass my father did nae approve of. But I did nae care." His eyes broke their connection to hers, and he stared past her. "I did nae care for many reasons, but the two main ones were that my father made me feel much the way it seems Kincaide made ye feel." Brodee's gaze returned to her. "I was born the second son. My elder brother, Broch, was taken from my father by my mother when he was a newly born bairn. We were born just a few breaths apart, but those breaths made all the difference to my father, and he did nae let me forget my place in birth and his heart behind my brother. Nae ever. Nae for a minute."

Her heart ached for him. She reached for him, and he startled, as if surprised. He was very much caught up in his memories now.

"See this?" He pointed to the inking on his right shoulder that she'd noticed before. The ink of the circle was darker than the ink of the dagger that went through it.

"What does it mean?"

"It means I'm the second son. The lesser son." His tone was hard, but his pain radiated from him. She hated his father in that moment, because she could see clearly that he'd made Brodee feel second-best and it had caused him heartache. Was that why he was the king's right hand? Was that why he was so ruthless in battle? To feel the best somewhere?

"My father gave me this moments after I was born. He gave my brother one, too, but his is a circle with a sword through it. A sword is the first weapon a warrior would choose, just as the first son is the one my father would choose. But he was left with me, the dagger, when my mother took Broch away."

"Do ye...Do ye speak to yer father?" she asked, thinking of her own father, whom she'd not spoken to in over a year since he'd first wed her off. The next two times she learned of her fate by missives from him. He didn't even deem her worthy enough to tell her face-to-face.

"Aye." Brodee sighed and reached up to tug a hand through his hair. She could not help but watch in fascination at the way his body moved so fluidly, muscles rippling. "My father tried to make amends with me last year when my brother was sent to our home on a mission for the king. Broch did nae ken he was my brother, and we did nae at first, either. My mother died shortly after taking him and kept who he was a secret. She wanted to punish my father, I believe."

"Why did she nae take ye, too?" Patience asked softly.

"I think because I was ill." He shrugged. "I dunnae ken for certain."

"May I?" Patience asked, motioning to his tattoo.

He nodded. She traced her finger around the circle and then over the dagger. "This marking dunnae make ye less than yer brother."

Brodee caught her fingers and brought them to his lips to kiss the tips. Her belly tightened at the desire that shone in his eyes. "And the words of a fool dunnae make ye worthless."

Her breath caught. He was right, of course. She was beginning to see that, understand it. "Two fools," she corrected. "My father has always treated me just as poorly as Silas did. Ye should nae trust him. I heard talk that ye are to go on a mission with him so he can prove himself to the king."

"I dunnae trust him, Patience," Brodee said, brushing his fingers down her arm. She shivered at his touch and the wonderful feelings it evoked in her. "So dunnae fash yerself."

"What was the second reason that ye disregarded yer father's wishes about the woman ye got involved with?" she asked, unable to leave be her memory of what he'd told her. She wanted to know all about him.

"The lass herself," he said, breaking eye contact with Patience again but not before she saw the pain in his gaze.

She inhaled sharply, biting her lip so as not to attract his attention. He'd loved the woman. She knew it without a doubt. She studied his strong jaw, the reddish stubble sweeping his cheeks and chin, his full lips, thick lashes, and noble nose. What must it be like to have his heart? She could only imagine what he had been like to the woman he had loved when he was so tender with Patience, so protective of her, when she did not have his heart.

Jealousy gripped her so hard her stomach physically ached. Shame quickly followed: she was envious of a woman who was not even in his life. God's teeth, of a woman who might not even be alive.

She cleared her throat, dreading the question she was about to ask but knowing she had to ask it. "Was the other woman that ye were rumored to have killed yer leman? Is this the woman ye are speaking of?" *The woman ye spoke of indirectly previously.*

"Aye." His voice sounded strained. "I failed to guard her. I had enemies I did nae ken, and they took her from me, from this world." The confirmation was like a physical hit and made her wince.

"Is she why ye did nae wish to wed me?" His eyes came to her once more, and he gave her an almost imperceptible pleading look. Her heart clenched as the memory of his words echoed through her. *When ye take the life of someone that somebody else loves, the person left alive dies a bit.* She should have left it be, but she couldn't. "Do ye...Do ye love her still?"

"Ye dunnae quit feeling for someone ye once loved," he said on a sigh. He brought his hand to the back of his neck to rub it. "But it's nae the same as it once was. It's but a memory of a feeling that was as bright and warm as the sun." *And a part of you is dead. A part you never answered whether it could be revived.*

"If ye felt that way once, then maybe we could..." She was going to say they could forge a new path, a new future together, but she let the words fade with the look of discomfort that flittered across his face.

He shook his head. "I dunnae want those feelings again," he said, implacable determination shining in his eyes.

She was certainly no expert in feelings, but she did not think they could simply be stopped just because one did not want them. If they could, then she would never have felt worthless or afraid. And for a man who did not want to feel love, he certainly was thoughtful and kind. She vowed he was feeling *something*, whether he wanted to or not. But she was not about to point that out to Brodee, not now. He was afraid to love again. It was as clear as the ink on his shoulder.

If they were to have any chance, her gut told her that at least one of them had to conquer their fears. Her greatest fear was joining with him, allowing him to see her at her most vulnerable. If she could vanquish that fear, then maybe, in time, he could overcome his and they could have the life she had never dreamed would be hers to have. But she'd need to be clever. The more he thought she cared, the further she suspected he'd withdraw. Not that she cared that much yet. Certainly not. That would be foolish. And she was done being a fool.

Fourteen

$\mathcal{P}$atience did not move at all, but she might as well have. A cavern opened between them. They sat side by side, legs still touching, but he could feel the walls up around her once more. And he couldn't blame her. Far from it. He wished to God he could have simply lied to her, but he could not. He didn't want to feel so strongly for a woman again that if he lost her, a hole would open in his chest once more. Then the intense pain would start, and it was pain that did not dull for a long time. And even when it subsided, it left scars that numbed you so you could go on living.

No, he didn't want any more of the kind of pain that came from loving a woman.

Yet Patience was now his wife, and she had awoken something in him. He didn't even want to admit aloud what effect she was already having on him. If he didn't give the emotions a name, if he didn't acknowledge the strings that were binding them, maybe they would not grow stronger. Maybe they could be happy without the all-consuming emotions he'd once experienced. Except passion. He wanted all-consuming passion with her. God, did he. He glanced sideways at her, and she sat very still and very stiff. There would likely be no passion tonight, because he had not kept his clot-heid mouth shut.

"I'll walk ye to yer bedchamber," he said, starting to slide off the bed.

"I dunnae wish to retire to my bedchamber," she replied quietly.

He didn't want her to, either. It was galling how much he didn't want it. Even if he was not going to join with her this night, he'd like her by his side as he slept. That was exactly why she *should* go, but she would be safer by his side. "Would ye feel safer here?"

She gave him an odd look, as though he'd made an inane comment. "Well, aye, but I dunnae want to stay in yer bedchamber to sleep."

Her words were manna straight from God. He must have taken pity on Brodee, he thought wryly. "Ye dunnae?" he asked carefully, sure he was misunderstanding in his lust-filled state.

The shy look she gave him nearly sent him straight between her thighs, but he managed to restrain himself and stay at the edge of the bed.

"I'd like to experience what it's like to have a man between my thighs who is there to please me," she said.

His sweet wife's face turned scarlet, but it was the most beguiling thing he'd ever seen. He started toward her but then stilled, struck with a worry. "Patience, passion will nae sway my mind."

"Who said anything about yer mind?" she asked, almost flippantly.

He frowned. Why the devil did she not want to sway him? And why was he not simply glad of the fact that she did not want to do so? God's teeth, his head was a mess, and the lass before him was the cause.

She waved her hand dismissively. "I dunnae care if ye want *those* feelings again. I was going to say if ye felt that way once, then maybe we could live amicably. *Ye interrupted me.*"

"Ye were going to say we could 'live amicably'?" Disbelief filled his voice.

"Aye," she said, matter-of-fact. So matter-of-fact that he was inclined to believe her, and damned if he didn't feel irritated, but why he felt that way he did not exactly know. "Now, if ye care to introduce me to pleasure, I think I'm ready."

He studied her for a long moment. Her voice was full of bravado, but her pulse beat rapidly at her neck, making her vein rise and fall quickly, and she'd unknowingly dug her fingers into the bedcover. His wife was trying to pretend she was no longer scared to join with him. He had no notion why she had adopted this new pretense, but he'd not deny the gift. Still, he knew the care he must take with her, for he saw the fear she tried to hide.

"Scoot to the edge of the bed," he said.

Her eyes widened. "So ye can come between my thighs?"

His became instantly hard. "Nae yet, lass, nae yet."

This time, she did as he'd instructed, slowly moving to the edge as he scrambled off it to kneel before her. He set his hands on her legs and felt her trembling; he was surprised to find he was trembling a bit himself. It was if he was a green lad who'd never had a woman. Slowly, he parted her legs and positioned himself between her firm thighs. He ran his hands up her silken skin, imagining her legs wrapped tightly around him.

"So ye dunnae believe ye can feel pleasure?" he asked, his voice husky. It was a God-given miracle that he'd not simply tossed her skirts up already. She was the loveliest woman he'd ever beheld, and her heavenly smell enveloped him.

She nibbled her lip nervously. "I've nae ever felt it before."

"That was nae ye, lass," he assured her, wishing her two previous husbands were still alive so he could kill them himself. He skimmed his hand over her hips and then splayed his palm over her flat belly and slid it up between the valley of her breasts. He rose to hover over her and move his hands to her collarbone. He wanted to taste every bit of her, explore every part of her, and bring her sensations of absolute ecstasy in places she likely did not even realize she could feel such things. Anticipation became the beat of his heart.

"Ye dunnae have anything to fear," he whispered, wanting so much to wipe away her worry. It was such a natural thing, a thing that should be nothing but pleasure. "I would die before hurting ye," he vowed, running his fingers along her collarbone and then following the same path with his lips.

She watched him with those dark eyes that could look so fathomless. In this moment, though, they held concern with just a hint of anticipation. He pressed a kiss to her forehead, her nose, her chin, each of her cheeks, and finally, he claimed her mouth. He kissed her slowly, gently, massaging her lips to stir her desire. Once it burned hot enough, it would incinerate all other thoughts from her mind.

She parted her lips on a moan, and he slid his tongue inside her mouth, relishing the honeyed taste that was uniquely her. Her tongue tangled with his, and her hands came to his shoulders, her nails digging into his skin as she moaned again. Her desire was rising as he'd wanted, but so was his, fast and furious. He pulled his mouth from hers to trail kisses down her neck to her chest. With a gentle tug, he pulled down her bodice and released her breasts.

He sat up then, emotion he did not want to feel but could not stop rising inside him. "God, ye're beautiful," he murmured, his voice catching on the last word.

"I'm nae," she replied, moving to cover herself, but he caught her wrists and pulled her hands up above her head.

He held her gaze, willing her to believe what he saw. "Ye are perfection." He meant it. "Yer breasts are exquisitely formed." He moved both her wrists to one of his hands and trailed the other hand between her breasts. She shivered, and he smiled. He roamed his fingers to her buds, rosy and hard, straining to be touched. He grazed his fingers over one, and she whimpered, her body arching up toward him. "Yer buds are the loveliest shade, like the sun at dusk, and yer skin is the perfect complement." As he spoke, he circled her bud with his fingers, watching her body for guidance on what she liked. And she liked this. Her head moved back and forth, and he knew it was from the new feelings he was introducing to her. "The smallest touch," he said, leaning down and taking her nipple in his mouth to suckle it for a long, hard moment before releasing it, "when done right, can spark the most intense pleasure."

"Oh my God," she whispered.

Oh my God, was right. Desire had him in an unyielding grip. "Ye have the prettiest neck," he continued, tracing his tongue down the long, elegant column before he slid a hand under her back to lift her while his other hand deftly pulled her gown the rest of the way down her body until he tossed it aside.

"Brodee!" She started to cover herself again, but he caught her wrists once more.

"Dunnae," he said, bending down to plant kisses along

her stomach. Gooseflesh instantly covered her skin. "I love the way yer body dips and curves. The shadows. The smoothness. The slender, willowed make of ye."

"What of the scars?" she asked, her eyes searching his face.

"What scars?" he asked, meaning it. Oh, he knew they were there on some level. He'd felt them when he'd run his fingers over her skin, but when he looked at her, he truly saw perfection. "All I see is a beautiful, braw woman whom I want to possess."

The way Brodee looked at her with such awe, such yearning, gave her such hope and set her more at ease. "Then possess me," she whispered to him, praying her body would respond, praying it was pleasurable and not painful.

Complete and utter triumph flittered across his face, and then he stood and yanked off his plaid and his braies. She stared unabashedly at him. Even if she had wanted to turn away, which she didn't, she wasn't sure she could have. She was drawn to this man like Eve to the apple.

Please God let him not destroy me.

She had never truly looked at a man. With both husbands before him, she'd either squeezed her eyes shut or stared at the ceiling or the wall, depending on the situation. But with Brodee, she drank him in. Everything about him bespoke of power, from his broad shoulders to his Viking legs to his thick arms. And the scars. He had a few of his own. Jagged marks where she could imagine his flesh had met with the sword of his enemy.

His body was perfectly, beautifully proportioned, cut and chiseled by God's master hand, and in his face, looking reverently at her, held an inherent strength. Her heart squeezed painfully, even as her belly fluttered. He knelt before her and set his hands to her legs as he'd done previously, and as he spread her thighs, his gaze held hers. When she was bared to him, a devilish gleam came to his eyes.

"Dunnae be fearful," he whispered before his head dipped.

Then, to her utter astonishment, he parted her at her core and his tongue trailed up to graze her where at a spot, she had not known existed. She jerked, her heartbeat escalating with the unknown, but when he slid his tongue down her center, the trepidation melted away under a deluge of hot wanting. His tongue swirled deliciously over the throbbing spot, building something in her she'd never felt before. His hand splayed over her belly as his tongue moved faster, circling as his mouth sucked. Passion pounded her blood through her heart, chest, and head, and the room around her disappeared, leaving just her and Brodee, and a desperation she thought might splinter her.

She heard her moans and whimpers, unable to stop them, only able to grip his shoulders to try to ground herself, connect herself with touch to this man who was doing such wicked, wonderful, unmentionable things to her. The faster his tongue worked, the higher her level of pleasure rose. As did her impatience, which grew to an explosive proportion. She needed something. Now. But heaven help her, she did not know what.

"I need," she cried out. "Please, I, I—"

Suddenly, a finger slipped inside her, and she gasped, her body clenching around him, and just as she was growing accustomed to him, his thumb pressed on that same spot as before and then worked a magic that had to be bad because it was *so* good. Everything coiled, then let loose as wave after wave of ecstasy crashed into her and then left her feeling utterly spent, utterly languid. She could barely raise her hand, but she forced herself to do so. Their eyes met, and the pleasure she saw in his gaze, the joy that he'd been able to give her such a gift, nearly undid her. She was falling in love with him.

The thought froze her. She was falling in love with her husband. A tender man. A caring man, a man who'd just admitted he did not want to feel love again.

He was merely fulfilling a physical need with her, but with the gentle way he was doing it, he was taking her soul. If she was not careful, he could hurt her more than any hit, any cruel word ever had. Still, she had to take that chance. Fear had ruled her life for too long; she could not live that way knowing now what could await her without it.

"It was nae ye," he said, finally speaking as he climbed between her thighs, slid his hand under her buttocks, and lifted her hips to meet his straining body. "It was them." His voice was a velvet whisper. He slid into her then, a long, full stroke that filled her completely and left no room for past memories, no room for anything but him and her and this moment they shared.

"Ye are passionate," he told her, his voice low, as he withdrew almost to his tip, only to slide all the way back in until his pelvis pressed against the spot at her core he'd brought to life mere moments before.

Her body melted against his, and her world narrowed to only him. His whispers of her passion, his strokes in and out of her, his large hands gripping her bottom firmly to move her just so to spark her core to life once more. Again, the need consumed her, greater than even before. Her body hummed with it. Her blood rushed with it. Her veins felt as though they would burst with it.

She slid her hands from his shoulders to his hips, marveling at the way he knew precisely how to move his body to give her such pleasure. Emboldened when he grunted his own bliss, she trailed her fingers to his taut bottom, allowing them to roam over the hard muscle and then up to his back to explore the wide plane of muscle. His body was slick with sweat, and when she flattened her palms against his back, it was as if she absorbed the rhythm he had set. Together, they found a tempo that bound them as one until, once again, she felt she would splinter.

Yet she wanted him to have the same feeling. "Brodee?"

"Wrap yer legs around me," he answered immediately, his voice thick. She knew then that he'd been waiting for a cue from her, so she quickly complied. She secured her legs around his middle, and he lifted her up, plunging deep into her, touching something in her she'd never imagined existed.

Fiery sensations poured through her as involuntary tremors coursed, and the degree to which she responded stunned her. She arched toward him, clawing at his back, demanding he enter her harder and faster, and her words unleashed something he'd obviously been keeping restrained. He hoisted her up off the bed, and before she knew what was happening, her back was against the wall and Brodee was driving into her like a man bent on complete and utter possession. She wanted to be possessed by him. And with a scream that mingled with a bellow from Brodee, she yielded to the searing need that seemed to have been building for years. A hot tide of passion raged through them both, sweeping them away and fragmenting her thoughts as she abandoned herself to the whirl of sensations, to his masterful seduction, to him.

She could not say when she'd drifted to sleep, but she awoke to a darkness broken only by a slash of moonlight through the window. Brodee's hand lay protectively against her stomach, his leg over hers. His even breathing filled the room, a soft rise and fall of a man in the throes of exhausted sleep.

She'd worn out her warrior husband because she was so passionate. She grinned to herself at the thought as she stared at him, memorizing his face. He had such long, thick lashes for a man. She loved them. She loved his strong jaw, too. And the flecks of gold and brown in his red stubble. She loved how he held her, how he was wrapped around her, though his leg was heavy over hers. She felt safe, and she knew without a doubt that he'd wanted her to feel exactly that way.

She'd never awoken with a man beside her before, and she was desperately glad in that moment that despite the suffering she'd endured, neither of her other husbands had ever slept the night with her. It would never have been like this. Utter contentment. Complete peace. She stared at Brodee as she recalled every moment of what they had done together, of the pleasure he had made her feel.

Things she'd never allowed herself to dream of began to fill her mind. Long walks holding hands. Talks by the fire wrapped in each other's arms. Him combing her hair. Them dancing. Her bathing him and him bathing her. Sitting before the clan together resolving problems. Moonlight swims in the loch. Romps in the daylight in the forest. Their children surrounding them, God willing.

A dazzling future was dangling before them. She wanted to grab it. And she would—for both of them. She had to make him see he could love her, and when he did, she'd be free to love him in return. It needed to happen carefully, slowly, so he would not back away and close her out of his heart, because that, she felt certain, would be the greatest pain she could ever experience, a pain she did not think she could survive.

Fifteen

Brodee awoke with Patience in his arms. Her warm body was curled around his, her hand on his bicep, her head against his shoulder, and the feeling of complete satisfaction in his chest. It terrified him more than any enemy he'd ever faced. He carefully extracted himself from her sleeping form, dressed, and then started for the door. The sun was just beginning to rise, and a good bout of training with his sword would help clear his head.

But when Patience whimpered in her sleep and thrashed about, he rushed back to her, kneeling beside the bed. "Shh, lass," he whispered as he brushed her hair away from her face. She immediately quieted and stilled. He stayed by her side until her breathing became even once more and then made his way to the rocky shore to work through the knots she had unwittingly created within him.

A salty breeze blew over him as he went through the paces of a fight, swinging his sword in arcs, ducking, jabbing, slicing, and lunging, but his mind would not clear of Patience. He stabbed the point of his sword into the ground and sat to look out at the sea. Waves lapped the shore, and the sun glinted off the blue-green waters.

Memories of his joining with his wife came back to him in exact detail. Her eyelashes fluttering against her olive skin. The slope of her cheekbones and the long sleekness of her legs. Her moans and whimpers of pleasure, and the warmth of her thighs locked around him. The way they'd found perfect harmony in movement together, and the way he'd lost himself while inside her.

It was the last thought that caused him to curse. He had to do better at controlling how she made him feel or he would soon find himself consumed by her. Yet he didn't want to give up what they'd experienced last night, nor did he want to hurt her. She'd said she did not care if he gave her all of himself, but she had said it after he'd said he did not want soft emotions of love ever again.

His mind churned as he stood there. If he could be two different people—The thought stilled him. He could, in a sense. Why could he not give her passion and tenderness at night, but in the day, keep a distance? No hand-holding, no grazes of their fingers, no lingering looks. Respectfulness and protection, yes. Honor always. But he could draw a line that he would not cross, one by which he only allowed himself to feel for her at night. If he could control himself that way, he had no fear of falling into her, of her becoming the thing that could hurt him the most.

"Brodee?"

He started at Patience's voice, every nerve in his body singing to life. Unchecked joy rose in him at her soft, husky tone. His first instinct was to gain his feet, pull her into his arms, and kiss her senseless until they possibly—no, definitely—ended up back in his bedchamber. Uncontrolled happiness was not good. Intemperate responses were not for him. He would contain his emotions, and in doing so, he would control anything he might feel if he ever lost her.

"Aye," he answered.

He rose slowly and turned to her, her loveliness hitting him like a punch. It robbed him of breath and the ability to think for a moment. Her dark hair blew around her shoulders, strands of it whipping across her face. Her light gown molded to her breasts and contrasted her skin to perfection. Her eyes shone like two dark rocks polished to flawlessness. Her full, rosy lips were turned down. He wanted to kiss those lips. Instead, he clenched his teeth together and sent up a prayer.

Thoir neart dhomh.

"What do ye need strength for?" Patience asked, frowning at him.

He felt his lips part in shock. He'd spoken his thoughts aloud? His wife had passed on her tendency to blurt her most private thoughts. He went from clenching his teeth to grinding them. He'd have nothing but nubs left if he didn't gain needed control immediately.

"Brodee?"

"Strength to have tolerance to teach ye today," he snapped, then winced when she looked momentarily upset. But then his warrior wife's face grew angry. That was better. He didn't want her to be vexed with him, but it was preferable to her being hurt.

"If ye dunnae wish to work with me today—"

"'Tis nae that." He jerked a hand through his hair. What the devil could he say? *It's not you, but it is. You are too soft. Too warm. Too kind. Too lovely. Too enticing.* But most of all, she reminded him too much—dangerously so—of forgotten pleasures. Like how a smile from someone he cared for expanded his chest. How the simple act of holding hands with someone who meant something to him made his fingers twitch to curl tighter. How waking beside a person who had a piece of him could cause his breath to catch in his throat. How when he looked at her he could not help but hope that one day they had daughters who looked just like her and sons who would protect her and their sisters. He finally settled on, "I'm weary this morning, 'tis all."

Unmistakable relief touched her features. "How long have ye been awake?"

"Since before dawn."

"Ye did nae get much sleep. Tomorrow morning ye should stay abed longer."

God, he wanted to, but not to sleep. He inhaled a long, slow breath. Here was the perfect opportunity to show her how their relationship would be. "I'm nae going to become lax simply because ye are now my wife. I'm nae going to change."

She bit her lip but nodded. "Of course nae. I suppose ye should go to bed earlier, then."

The mention of bed brought images of her naked body to mind. The irritation he felt at himself nearly choked off his ability to speak, but he managed to spit out, "Are ye ready to train?"

Her response was to whip out her dagger from the sheath at her hip and point it at him. "Aye," she said with a grin.

They spent the better part of two hours working on her defensive skills, and Brodee was careful during that time to only touch Patience when it was absolutely necessary. And by the exasperated looks she gave him, he got the feeling she wanted his touch just as much as he wanted to give it. But he had drawn the line for himself and he damn well intended to stay on the right side of that line.

"Come," he said abruptly when they were done training.

Patience nodded and sheathed her dagger. "Where are we going? Would ye like to take a walk or go riding?"

He'd like to do both. More than he wanted to do anything else. More than he wanted to see to his duties, which was precisely why he would not do either.

"I'm laird, Patience. I dunnae have time for walks and riding." He hoped that would put an end to that. He did not want to hurt her.

"What *do* lairds have time for?" she asked. Gone was his mouse wife and in her place was a she-wolf. Very bold and worrisomely clever.

He paused and faced her. She was going to make him be more definitive, outline his battle position more clearly. Because it *was* a battle for him, for his self-preservation. "During the day, all I have time for—all I will ever have time for—are my duties to the clan."

When she looked as if he'd struck her, his chest ached, and he thought to soften the blow and bring the she-wolf, however worrisome, back. He started to reach for her face, to run his fingers down the slope of her cheek, but he drew his hand back when his fingers were but a hairsbreadth from her skin. "At night, though, when we are alone in our bedchambers, I will see to my duty to ye."

He expected to see relief on her face, but instead, her eyes narrowed. There was the she-wolf. "Ye think our time together a *duty*?"

He could have said no. Because it was the God's truth. He didn't think of it that way at all, but he needed to think of it that way. "Aye. Ye are my wife, and it is my duty to pleasure ye."

A flush tinged her cheeks, and her nostrils flared. "What are yer duties to me during the day?" she demanded, her tone now scathing.

He blew out a frustrated breath. This was going much worse than he'd imagined, but maybe it was best that she was angry now. She could accept how it was going to be, and then they could set into a pattern they both could live with. "To see to yer safety, train with ye, and to be here if ye need me to settle disputes for ye."

"I see," she bit out. "Well, ye can consider yerself relieved of those duties!"

"What? Ye kinnae relieve me of—"

"I can, and I did!" She poked him hard in the chest, then looked past him. "William!" she bellowed.

Brodee followed her gaze to the rocks where William was picking his way toward them. He looked back to his wife. "What are ye about, Patience?"

She pressed her lips into a thin line and did not say a word until William was nearly upon them. At that point, she arched her eyebrows at Brodee. "William can take me to the kitchens, so I dunnae need ye to see to my safety this day." Before Brodee could speak, Patience looked to William. "Do ye mind, William?"

William glanced to Brodee, and though he had the sudden urge to shake his head so William would decline, Brodee nodded, knowing it was for the best, even if it did not feel that way.

"Of course nae, my lady," William answered.

"See that Fergus goes to the kitchens to await Patience," Brodee instructed.

Patience set her hands on her hips as she scowled at him. "By the by, I dunnae need ye to train me anymore. William generously agreed yesterday."

"I did?" William asked, his mouth parting.

Brodee frowned. Jealousy slithered through him like a snake, despite how foolish it was. William had agreed to no such thing, Brodee was certain, and William would never lay a hand on Patience. Still, jealously warmed his blood and he found himself clenching his hands into fists. He forced himself to nod again, not arguing what she'd said. William was an excellent fighter, and he could train Patience well. It was perhaps best—again.

"Aye," Patience said, her attention on William. "Dunnae ye recall?"

A flick of William's eyes to Brodee and an imperceptible nod later, William cleared his throat. "Aye, I, er, just recalled the conversation."

Patience's shoulders drooped with obvious relief, but then she focused her gaze on Brodee once more. She drew herself up to her full height while shoving her shoulders back and lifting her chin. She was glorious. He wanted to lay her down, spread her thighs, and—*Christ*. She made him weak.

"There," she growled. "Two of yer duties are nae a concern of yers any longer. As to the third..." She poked him once more in the chest, to which William coughed and turned his head. "I have a mind of my own, and I can hold my own counsel. I dunnae need ye to settle disputes for me, unless ye insist on it, and then I will have to bow to yer command, as it seems I am again beset with a *lord and master*." She sighed and crossed her arms. And a beat later when she was looking beyond them, clearly done speaking came, "Never a partner. Never that."

William's gaze locked with Brodee's, and Brodee gave a slight shake of his head. He did not wish William to point out to Patience or even acknowledge that she had once again mumbled her thoughts aloud. His gut twisted that he'd hurt her, but he had to let things be as they were.

"I dunnae insist it," he said in a quiet voice. "Ye are an intelligent woman." She glared at him, and he sighed. "If ye need my counsel, ye have but to ask."

"I'll nae be asking," she snapped.

He acknowledged her comment with a tilt of his head. To William, he said, "Come find me at the west shore after ye have delivered Patience to the kitchens and fetched Fergus." To Patience, he said, "I will see ye at supper."

"I dunnae think I'll be hungry." She turned on her heel and stormed off toward the kitchens. William shot Brodee an annoyed look and then quickly followed Patience.

Brodee made his way down to the sea, thoughts of what had just happened haunting him with every step. On the one hand, he was glad Patience had asserted herself. It showed a level of trust in him that he'd never hurt her, even if she defied him, and it also showed she was discovering her inner strength, and he found that very alluring. He frowned. He did not want to be allured by her. At least not in the daytime. God, he was a clot-heid. His brow furrowed as he considered the exchange further. It was actually not entirely good that she felt the need to stand and assert herself because that meant he'd wounded her pride and that made him feel like a pure savage. He knew he'd hurt her, and that hurt him in turn. Between the desire she'd stirred in him earlier and his confusing emotions regarding what had just occurred, he wanted to dive into the sea and quiet his thoughts for a bit.

Usually, the sea did that for him. He found a secluded spot at the west side of the castle and stripped down to nothing before wading into the cold water. Immediately, his body found a reprieve from the desire that was hammering him, but his mind did not quiet. He dove under the waves, hoping the cold would numb his thoughts, as well, but even in the complete silence found only beneath the water, his thoughts were still loud. And all of them were of Patience.

Sixteen

What in Heaven's name just happened?

She'd not meant to get angry, but he'd vexed her. Still seething, Patience stomped toward the kitchens, aware of William striding silently behind her. But even if she were not so angry, she did not know what to say to the man. He was Brodee's friend. She inhaled slowly, trying to calm her roiling thoughts and order them. Once her heart quit racing, she tried to analyze the morning from when she'd awoken in bed alone.

She'd roused herself and dressed quickly with the intent of finding Brodee and spending time with him. She could not imagine after what they'd shared in his bedchamber that the man would not want to attempt to open up to her as she wished to open up to him. To really get to know him and learn of his life before he'd met her. His hopes. His fears. To snatch up the shiny future that dangled in her sight.

How could she have been so wrong? And how the devil was he so stubborn? Maybe there would be no reaching him. Maybe all she would ever be to him was a duty he had to fulfill. An enjoyable one, at least at night. The man could not deny that. He'd groaned just as loudly as she had last night, but now that she'd tasted passion, tasted what could be, and seen the tenderness in him that lurked under the armor he wore, she wanted more. She wanted what she'd never believed possible. She wanted to love her husband and be loved in return.

Tears filled her eyes, and she quickly blinked them away and swiped the evidence off her cheeks. *A duty.* He'd called her a duty. And worse than that was his demeanor this morning. He'd been cold, withdrawn. Absent were the gentle touches of last night, and even the tender looks he'd given her during the day before. It was as if what they had shared scared him, and he'd closed off some part of him. And she had no notion how to get back to the place they'd just found.

Blast, this tasting of what could be was worse than never having known it. As they neared the kitchens, she wanted to scream her frustration. Instead, she balled her hands into fists and forced a smile to her lips. "Thank ye," she said, turning to William.

"I'd have thought ye had more fight in ye than that, considering what ye have endured," William said, crossing his arms over his chest.

"I beg yer pardon?"

"He's waging a war," he said, staring at her with an expectant look.

"Who? Brodee?"

The expectant look turned to one of exasperation. "Who else?"

"Indeed," she said, a trifle irritated herself now. She was not a seer, after all. He acted as if she could read his thoughts! "And with whom is he waging this war?"

"I kinnae say. That would be a breach of trust, and I owe the man my life. I would nae ever breach his trust."

"Certainly nae," she quickly replied, hope infusing her. "I suppose the war must be with himself," she guessed, given what Brodee had admitted to her. She held her breath, waiting for William to confirm it.

"I kinnae say," he repeated with a shrug. "But he did say ye are an intelligent lass, and I'd have to agree from what I've seen. When I am trying to seize a castle, do ye ken what I do?"

"Attack?"

"Aye. I attack the castle—and the men who are waging war against me. They put up the barriers, and I tear them down with persistence and determination. I use my best weapons, too—my mind and my sword. What do ye suppose is yer best weapon? I mean, if ye were ever to need to wage a war."

She thought about that and where William was clearly trying to lead her without saying things outright. "My mind?"

He nodded. "'Tis a good start. Men are simple creatures, lass." He paused. "Of course, *I'm* nae."

She laughed. "Nay, of course nae."

"But," he continued, rubbing at the stubble on his chin and looking contemplative, "I have seen great lairds defeated by their desire for a woman. Have ye ever seen such a thing?"

"Nay," she whispered, but she grinned. "Are ye telling me to wage war on Brodee with my…womanly charms?"

He shook his head and threw up his hands. "I did nae say that." Then he gave her a long, pointed look. "Ye did."

"He is different this morning, though," she said. "Withdrawn. Cold. As if he put up a wall."

"'Tis natural. I would think ye breached his defenses last night…"

"How do ye—"

"My bedchamber is two doors down," he said, matter-of-fact, his mouth twisting into a knowing smile.

Her cheeks burned with the knowledge that he'd heard them.

"When Brodee and I have attacked castles, and it seems we may nae win, he always retreats briefly, analyzes the situation, and regroups with a new strategy."

"I affected him last night!" she gasped. "I breached his defenses, and him leaving the bedchamber this morning was his retreat. And then he regrouped! And his new strategy must be to keep distance between us, to think of me only as an obligation he must satisfy."

And only at night.

"I dunnae have any notion of what ye speak," William said, turning his face away but not before she saw his grin. "I best be moving along now to go find Fergus. I imagine it will take me awhile, and I ken Brodee will be waiting for me on the west side of the castle. He'll nae swim for that long before he's irritated."

"Thank ye, William!" she said and impulsively kissed him on the cheek, before she whirled away from the kitchens and ran toward the seagate stairs.

In her haste to get to Brodee, Patience didn't even notice Kinsey until she was practically on top of the woman. Kinsey, it seemed, didn't notice her, either. She was standing at the turn in the seagate stairs, looking down toward the shore. Patience followed Kinsey's gaze, and in the distance, Patience thought she saw Brodee standing, looking out at the sea.

"What are ye doing?" she asked from the steps above Kinsey, curious as to why she appeared to be staring at Brodee.

Kinsey glanced up at her, a startled expression on her face. "Patience! I did nae even hear ye. I was lost in thought about ye."

Patience frowned. "Me?"

"Aye. I was just wondering how things were going with Blackswell. I did nae want to ask since, well, I was so foolish before, but I do want ye to be happy."

Patience tried to stop the smile from coming to her face, but at the pull of her cheeks and lips, she knew she was unsuccessful. "The marriage kinnae be dissolved anymore."

Kinsey smiled, though it did seem a bit forced, but Patience appreciated Kinsey's effort. "Are ye going to find yer husband now?"

Patience nodded, to which Kinsey motioned her along. "Off with ye, then."

Patience wasn't sure what to say to make it better for Kinsey, because she could tell by her tight face that she was still hurting, and she feared anything she might say at this point would only make things worse. So she nodded and brushed past Kinsey. One step beyond her, though, and she felt a hard shove against her back, which propelled her toward the ledge of the stairs.

"My lady!" she heard someone gasp, and then a hand curled around her arm.

Her heart pounded painfully in her chest as she stared down at the rocks below. She'd almost fallen. She felt ill. She turned seeing Kinsey's hand on her arm and Jane, looking horrified, above them both at the top of the stairs.

"I'm so sorry, Patience," Kinsey said, her voice shaking. "I slipped and fell into ye. Thank God, I caught ye!"

"Aye," Patience said, her stomach still roiling.

Jane came racing toward them, her face white with shock. "Are ye all right?" she asked Patience.

She nodded. "I had quite a scare, but luckily Kinsey is strong and pulled me back."

"Aye," Jane agreed, her gaze darting to Kinsey. "Lady Kinsey, I was just coming to find ye to tell ye I have drawn yer bath as ye requested."

For a breath, Patience could have sworn Kinsey looked like she wanted to throttle Jane, but then she smiled sweetly. "Thank ye, Jane." With a squeeze to Patience's arm, Kinsey said, "Careful on the stairs. They are quite slippery from the morning rain." With that, she released Patience and ascended the steps toward the castle.

Patience and Jane were left standing alone. "My lady," Jane began, "I wanted to thank ye properly for saving me." Jane held out what appeared to be a tiny figure to Patience.

"Ye've thanked me multiple times, Jane. 'Tis nae necessary to give me a gift."

"Beg pardon, my lady, but it is necessary for me. I would nae wish anyone dead normally, but I must confess I did wish Loskie would die. I did nae want to wed him, because I had a bad feeling about him, but my family needed the money he offered."

Patience was well acquainted with being used. She reached out and took the gift, and when she did, she squeezed Jane's hand. "You will wed again, and he will treat you with kindness."

"I hope so," Jane replied.

Patience turned the figure over in her hand. The carving was remarkable. "Did ye do this?"

Jane shook her head. "Nay. I've no skill with carving, but Cul does, and I asked him to do it. 'Tis Soteria, the Greek goddess of safety and preservation from harm." Jane fidgeted for a moment. "I thought, well, since ye have endured so much, it would nae hurt to have a goddess watching over ye."

"I love it, Jane, thank ye. Do ye mind placing it in my

room by my bed?"

"Nae at all, my lady." She took the figure from Patience, the women gave each other a quick hug, and then Jane set off back toward the castle and Patience descended the remainder of the stairs. Once she was on the shore, it didn't take long to make her way to the west side of the castle where she knew Brodee was. She picked her way across the rocky shore, and then she stilled, a delicious heat sweeping her body. Her husband stood near the water, and in one fluid motion, he relieved himself of the braies he wore, then stalked toward the sea, looking very much like a man with an enemy stalking him. She suspected Brodee's enemy was his memory of the woman he'd lost.

Jealously gripped her. How could it not?

His hair shone under the bright rays of the sun, and even from the distance at which she stood, she could see his body glistening with sweat. Muscles rippled as he walked into the blue-green waters, and once he'd waded to his waist, he disappeared under the water. She rushed toward the water, fearing that if he saw her, he'd stop her. She hurriedly kicked off her gown and slippers, leaving nothing on but her léine. He broke the surface once more, but his back was now to the shore. Still, her heartbeat raced as she ran into the water and dove under the cold surface.

As she kicked her feet and glided her hands through the water, she felt almost as if she were a different person. Never would she had been brave enough to do what she was doing now. She just prayed that it worked.

She was smiling as she broke the surface but let out a yelp to find herself face-to-face with Brodee. And he did not look pleased to see her. At all.

"What the devil are ye doing here?" he growled, his tone unfriendly but his eyes devouring her.

A shiver of wanting ran through her at his look. It was a new experience for her to feel desirable, and God help her, it made her feel powerful, as well. Now, if she could wield some of that power to break through her husband's shields, so they could have a chance at something wonderful…

His hair was slicked back from his forehead, accentuating his strong jaw, and the sun glinted off his broad shoulders. The drops of water beaded there enticed her to do something more daring, and a feeling of recklessness filled her. She swam toward him, slid her arms around his waist, and trailed her tongue along the top of one of his powerful shoulders. She could feel him instantly harden. Triumph filled her, but then he pushed her gently away, and an acute sense of loss took the place of her momentary triumph.

"Why are ye here?" he repeated, his voice thick. Thick with the desire for her he was fighting, the stubborn man.

"Dunnae it seem obvious?" she asked, heating with embarrassment at the boldness of her words and actions, yet she refused to retreat.

"Lass," he said, swimming backward to put space between them.

She could hardly believe a man known as the Savage Slayer was retreating from *her*. She almost said so, too. Almost. But she did not think it would help.

"I already told ye that in the daytime, my duty is to the clan."

If she'd had a pot from the kitchens she would have knocked her husband's thick skull with it. Maybe then he would have been sensible and realized what she had: what they had before them was a gift. One she'd never dared to hope for. "I am a member of yer clan," she said, swimming toward him, and almost giggling when he swam backward once more. She smirked at him. "At this pace, we will be at land soon."

He scowled at her. "I kinnae afford to be distracted by ye. I've duties."

"Is swimming one of yer duties?" She did not care that she sounded flippant.

"Lass." The single word held warning.

They could go on like this all day. She needed a different tactic. Either he was too stubborn to succumb to the charms she was offering, or now that he'd joined with her once, he was not nearly as interested in doing so again. She gritted her teeth, determined not to allow doubt.

"Are ye afraid of me? Of what I made ye feel?" She prayed that questioning him, his bravery, which she knew well he prided himself on, would prompt him to take what she wanted to offer, and then that would hopefully lead to him simply relenting to what was brewing between them.

"Afraid of ye?" He stilled in his backward motion, as if he'd just realized how he was making himself look. "Of course I'm nae afraid of ye." He swished his hands through the water, the cords of the muscles in his shoulders moving in sync with each stroke.

"Prove it." She hardly believed the words she'd said.

"Prove it?"

"Aye." She swam toward him until she was so close that she could see the droplets of seawater clinging to his eyelashes. "Kiss me."

He looked as if he would deny her. Frustration radiated from the thin line of his lips to his dipped brows. She was certain he'd simply swim away from her. Instead, his hand snaked around her neck so fast and she was tugged to him with such force that she only just registered her little victory when his mouth covered hers as she exhaled. He tasted of salt and bridled desire. She'd never tasted anything so sinful in her life. Her toes curled, her belly tightened, her heart fluttered.

His kiss was ravishing, possessive, intense. He claimed her mouth with hard pulls, nips, a swirl of his tongue. The kiss held an urgency that left her mouth burning with fire. Then his hand slid to her breast. He circled her nipple, which strained against the wet material of her léine. Her breast grew immediately heavy, and despite the cool seawater, her skin burned and ached. God, the ache. Only he could assuage it. He trailed his fingers lower, skimming down her belly and between her legs. He touched the place he'd brought to life the night before, and she dug her nails into his shoulders, unsure how much longer she could keep herself afloat.

"Brodee," she moaned.

He responded with a growl, and then he was swimming toward the shore, tugging her along with him. It seemed they reached shallow water much faster than it had taken her to swim out to him earlier, and as she stood, he swept her up into his arms. Water splashed around them as he carried her to an area of the shore that was smoother than the rest. He laid her down gently, then came over her, his powerful thighs caging her in at her hips, his hands splayed against the sand beside her shoulders.

Water dripped from his hair onto her chest as he leaned nearer. He brushed his lips over hers, one of his legs coming between her thighs. His fingers trailed over her breasts once more, before he sat up and stared down at her. "I'm nae scairt of ye," he said. "I believe I've proven it."

With that, he scrambled off her, gained his feet, and stalked toward her gown in the distance. Disappointment filled her as he picked up her gown and brought it back to her to thrust it at her. "Get dressed, Wife. I've training to see to today. Tonight," he said, his hand cupping her neck, "I'll see to yer needs." He claimed her mouth in a final kiss that left her breathless and more determined than ever to break down his defenses.

She refused to see this encounter as a total failure. She'd gotten him to kiss her. Clearly, the man needed a greater push. She didn't know what that might be yet, but maybe some of the women in the kitchens who had husbands could give her some advice.

Seventeen

"Ye must tempt him so greatly that he kinnae deny ye," Mari said late that afternoon, yanking on the gown she'd just helped Patience don. It was one that Ivan had given her after he'd ripped another gown from her body. He had thought to make up for his cruelty with the gift from his trip to Paris, but his sort of cruelty could not be forgotten with a gift, however lavish. Patience had never even truly looked at it. She'd only remembered it when Jane had said something about it earlier, after Patience had told the women in the kitchens of her futile efforts to soften Brodee. Jane had seen the gown in Patience's wardrobe and suggested she wear it.

Mari, Jane, and Ada smiled at each other as they looked at Patience and nodded. "This gown will surely do the trick," Jane said. "It shows my lady's assets quite boldly."

"Aye, she must be bold," Ada said. "She's doing battle with the laird. He dunnae wish to succumb to soft emotions, but of course, he must."

"Men rarely wish to succumb to soft emotions at first," Mari said with a cluck of her tongue. "They must be shown why it's necessary."

This was all very fascinating to Patience. She'd never experienced being part of a group of women's frank talk, and she was glad she now had them as friends.

"Dunnae forget," Ada added, "pay special attention to what other men say tonight."

"Aye," Mari agreed. "In fact, ignore the laird a bit. It will vex him, but it will also make him want ye more."

She didn't like the idea of playing games with Brodee, and she didn't think she would, but she didn't want to hurt the women's feelings by telling them that she would not heed all of their advice. It was one thing to try to catch his eyes by looking her best; it was quite another to court the attention of another man.

"Ye're stunning," Mari said with a grin and handed Patience a looking glass. Patience held it up to her, and then slanted it downward and her mouth dropped open. Immediately, she shifted the looking glass to one hand and tugged on the gown, which displayed entirely too much of her chest.

"I kinnae wear this gown like this," she said, her face heating. It was just like Ivan to have brought her such an improper thing.

Mari pushed Patience's hand away and tugged her gown down once more. "Ye most certainly can," she said.

"'Tis indecent!" Patience protested.

The three women surrounding her snorted. "Aye, 'tis, but our own queen was seen wearing a similar gown sent to her from Paris, so if the queen can wear it, ye can, too," Mari argued.

Just then, a knock came at her bedchamber door.

"Who is it?" she asked, as the three women with her giggled.

"If it's the laird," Jane whispered, "he'll likely wish us to leave yer bedchamber immediately."

A chorus of laughter broke out, and Patience waved the women to hush as she went to the door. She could not hear

the reply because of the women. She cracked the door open
to find Kinsey standing there holding a mead bucket.

"Come in," Patience offered, taking the bucket with a
frown. "I looked for ye to see if ye wanted to come in here
with us."

Kinsey nodded. "Eleanor told me when I went to the
kitchens just now. I was serving some of the men who have
been training all day. I thought some of ye might want
some mead?"

Everyone shook their head and Kinsey set the bucket
down then turned back to Patience, her eyes widening.
"What are ye wearing?"

"I—Well, Jane, Ada, and Mari thought this gown might
help me keep my husband's attention."

"Are ye already having trouble keeping his eye firmly
on ye?" Kinsey teased.

Patience quickly told her about how Brodee never
wanted to feel the way he once had ever again.

Kinsey looked thoughtful. "I would nae ever have suspected that a man such as he could have been so devoted to
a woman. 'Tis romantic that he loved her so much that he
dunnae believe he can repeat it. She must have been verra
beautiful. I did hear the men say she was. Fair haired and
blue eyed, I think they said, with skin like freshly fallen
snow."

It was everything Patience was not, and her gut
clenched. She had scars, inside and out. Perhaps she was a
fool to think she could capture Brodee's heart. Mayhap she
should just be satisfied with the kindness, tenderness, and
protectiveness he showed her. She tugged the gown off her
shoulders. "This was a foolish idea." Even as the other three
women other than Kinsey protested, Patience yanked the
ruby gown off her body and picked up her discarded pale-

green gown.

"Ye're nae going to wear it?" Mari asked.

"Nay. I'm nae so much in the mood anymore to try to compete with a ghost."

"I, for one, think that's wise," Kinsey said. "Do ye mind if I wear the gown?"

Patience frowned. It wasn't that she minded, she didn't, but... "Why do ye wish to wear it?"

"Well," Kinsey said, her mouth tugging into a secretive smile, "I'm trying to gain the attention of one of the men in the guard."

"Oh," was all Patience could manage through her surprise. Since coming to the castle, she never noticed Kinsey giving particular attention to any man.

"Who?" Jane asked, looking and sounding as stunned as Patience.

Kinsey bit her lip. "I'd rather nae say unless I manage to succeed. I'm too embarrassed."

"Here." Patience held the gown out to her friend. "I hope all yer wishes come true tonight."

"Ye're nae giving up on the laird, are ye?" Jane asked.

Patience shook her head. She wasn't going to give in that easy, but she didn't particularly want to set herself up for another disappointment today. Her emotions felt raw, her heart tender, and her confidence lacking since hearing how beautiful the woman he'd loved had been.

Kinsey patted her on the arm. "The simple gown ye have on suits ye," she said sweetly as she tugged off her own gown while the supper bell rang. She turned her back to Patience and the other women, and held up her hair. "Will one of ye lace me?"

Patience stepped forward and quickly laced the gown. "Finished," she said.

Kinsey turned and linked her arm with Patience's, surprising her. "Come," Kinsey said brightly, "let's go to supper together, but first we must take the mead bucket back to the kitchens. We will make quite the entrance!"

Patience wanted to decline, but Kinsey gave her such a hopeful look that Patience agreed and all the women made their way out of her bedchamber and the main keep and to the kitchens. Once Kinsey deposited the mead bucket, and they helped get the food on the serving platters, Mari waved them both away.

"Ye two scurry and make a grand entrance. We'll bring the food."

Patience nodded.

"After ye," Kinsey said and waved Patience in front of her.

They made their way from the kitchens to the courtyard, which was deserted because everyone had already gone to the great hall. In the distance, Patience could hear the laughter of men in the gardens, likely the archers still practicing. They always were last to supper. Kinsey was rambling about the gown, the weather, and the upcoming tournament.

"Oh!" Kinsey suddenly exclaimed and bent down. "I've a rock lodged in my slipper." Patience started toward her, but Kinsey waved her on. "I'll catch up. Ye dunnae wish to make yer husband vexed by being late for supper yet again."

Shamefully glad not to have to listen to any more chatter, so she could think in peace on Brodee, Patience said, "All right. I'll see ye in there." She got halfway across the courtyard when Fergus called out, "My lady!"

With a glance around, she located him coming from a path just behind her and to the left.

"My lady," he said, huffing with his effort to reach her,

"I was sent—" Suddenly his eyes went wide as something hissed by her head.

"Holy God," Fergus bellowed, pointing in the direction of the gardens which were behind her.

She turned toward the gardens where the men were still busily training. "What was it?"

"An arrow," he croaked. "An arrow nearly hit ye in the head. Someone must have misfired."

"Those damnable fools!" Kinsey said, pointing toward the gardens. "I saw the arrow coming from the garden, but I was frozen with fear! Good thing whoever shot dunnae have true aim."

"Aye," he said, wiping his brow. "The laird sent me to find ye, my lady. He's vexed with me for letting ye out of my sight."

"Oh, Fergus, I'm sorry," Patience said, reaching out a trembling hand to pat the man's arm.

"The laird will likely kill someone for this," Fergus said.

Patience gasped. "What?"

He laughed. "'Tis an expression, my lady. Everyone will keep their lives, I vow it. But it will nae help his mood which is sour."

Mayhap his bad temperament had something to do with his trying to resist her. The thought gave her hope. "Let's nae mention it," she blurted, not wanting him to become grumpier and not wanting anyone to get into trouble on account of the incident.

"But—"

She gave Fergus a stern look. "Nay. 'Twas an accident."

"Aye," Kinsey agreed when Patience gave her a pleading look for aid in convincing Fergus.

He scowled. "But they need to be more careful."

"Then ye can mention to them to take greater care, but

please dunnae tell the laird," Patience implored.

Fergus rubbed at his neck, then sighed. "I suppose there is nae any harm in that."

"Nae any," Patience assured him. "Right, Kinsey?"

"Nae any," Kinsey agreed.

Patience linked arms with Kinsey and fairly dragged the woman toward the great hall, calling behind them for Fergus to follow.

From the moment Patience appeared in the doorway of the great hall, it was as if everyone else disappeared. The din of the noise around Brodee died, and his vision tunneled to her. She was a vision in her pale-green gown. Even with all her skin covered, she the most tempting creature he'd ever seen. Despite her dark hair, dark eyes, and olive skin, she exuded a light and warmth to rival the sun. He wanted to go to her, to bury his face in her neck, smell her lavender-scented hair, run his fingers across her silken skin, and hear her husky laughter.

Instead, he gulped down a glass of wine, and then as William, who was sitting immediately to the laird's right, raised his wine goblet to drink it, Brodee relieved his friend of it and drank those contents, too.

"What the devil?" William growled. "Ye dunnae even normally drink wine. What's vexing ye?" He leaned closer to Brodee and arched his eyebrows in expectation.

"Put yer eyebrows down, Will," Brodee managed in a tone that sounded calm, though he felt anything but. Patience did that to him. Her mere presence set the world that he'd worked so hard to make orderly into disarray. As she walked slowly toward the dais with Kinsey by her side, one thought came to mind—he wished supper was over. He wanted to shove his trencher aside, grab Patience, and carry her upstairs to their bedchamber so he could repeat what they'd done last night. Multiple times. It was, in fact, the only thing he'd thought of all day.

He was so filled with yearning that he half-feared he would be too passionate, too wild, too uninhibited when next they joined, and he'd scare her with the feelings he was trying to keep inside. He had to maintain control not just now but later tonight, as well. Yes, she'd matched his passion last night, but he had still restrained himself a bit so as not to scare her. It was as if she had caused a violent storm inside him, and if he released it and let it consume him, it might just frighten her away.

When Patience reached the dais and curtsied to him, his eyes went, of their own volition, to her body. He grew instantly hard, his blood heating, and desire pounding painfully within him. Incensed that he could not control his reaction to her, he jerked his gaze away from her and to Kinsey, who stood awkwardly by Patience. Brodee frowned, realizing the woman thought to sit at the dais with them. It was on the tip of his tongue to tell her to take a seat with rest of the clan, but Father Murdock offered his chair, and then somehow, Kinsey ended up in William's seat and William took Father Murdock's, who had given an excuse that he was ready to retire.

Brodee could not even say how the seat switching came to be. It took all his concentration not to stare at Patience. Instead, he looked straight down at his trencher of food, as if it was the most interesting bit of meat and bread he'd ever eaten. As conversation started to flow around him, Patience talking to William, Fergus, and Cul, who was finally well enough to join them, Brodee motioned to the kitchen lass

Ada to refill his wine goblet. Once she did, he reached for it, unable to help himself from stealing a sidelong glance at Patience when she burst into laughter at something William had said. Their heads were close together, and jealousy ripped through Brodee. His attention was quickly diverted, however, when his hand touched another's on his wine goblet. He looked to the goblet to find Kinsey's hand upon it. She blinked, appearing surprised as well. "I'm sorry, Laird. I thought that was my goblet."

She lifted it toward him, even as she grabbed the one to her right. "Here ye go. Ye seem as if ye need this. Ye looked vexed."

"Thank ye," he said. He was being a damnable fool to be jealous of his wife and his closest friend, yet he *was* jealous. God's teeth, he needed something else to think about, anything besides the growing irritation at how interesting his wife seemed to find William.

"If ye would indulge me, Laird," Kinsey said, leaning toward him, "I have some suggestions for the tournament that I think would help unite our clans."

"Speak freely," he said, only too glad to have the distraction. As Kinsey told him of her ideas, he realized she actually had some good ones. Maybe he truly had judged her too quickly and harshly. His gut felt nothing odd in regard to her at this moment.

"I could help Patience use my ideas for the tournament," Kinsey offered, her voice low. She darted a look at Patience, who was still talking to William, much to Brodee's annoyance. Or at least he thought Kinsey had looked to Patience. Maybe she'd looked to William?

His brow furrowed. His thoughts felt muddled. It had to be the wine. He didn't normally drink wine, only mead. He'd not really considered that the informal tournament might need any planning, but apparently the women had.

"I think it will overwhelm her," Kinsey said, touching her hand to his forearm. He frowned at the contact, but when he went to brush her fingers away, his movements were sluggish. Devil take it, he should not have drunk three glasses of wine. Still, he was surprised how much it was affecting him and how quickly. He was a big man, and even though he normally drank mead, he had consumed wine before and had never been so affected.

"Brodee?"

He looked to Kinsey, who he saw two of. "Aye, ye can help her," he said, wincing because his words sounded slurred. He shoved away from the table. He needed a cold swim. He didn't want the clanspeople or Patience to see him like this.

Patience watched in frustration as Brodee left the dais without a word to anyone. He stalked to the door of the great hall and took his leave. Then Kinsey quickly excused herself, claiming a sudden headache. Patience wanted to leave, too. She wanted to go to her bedchamber and bury herself under the covers and not come out. Hurt and anger pulsed through her as her husband had only looked at and spoken to Kinsey during the entire meal.

"Patience," William said beside her. His tone of sympathy was plain.

Blast, if he'd noticed Brodee's attention to Kinsey, as well, Patience was not simply being jealous. William must have been attempting to divert her attention at supper so she would not notice what Brodee was doing. Her gut clenched. Or worse, William had seen what was occurring and diverted her out of pity.

"I dunnae want ye to feel sorry for me," she said in a low voice. Her cheeks burned with her shame. She suddenly felt just as she had whenever Silas or Ivan had humiliated her. "I'm tired," she said, trying to rise, but William grabbed her wrist.

"'Tis nae what ye are thinking," he said, keeping his voice low. "Brodee would nae ever betray ye."

She would not have thought it last night. Or the day before. Or even this morning. Why, though? She did not truly know him, and that was still the problem. She'd given him her trust because he'd given her kindness and passion and a few hints into his past. Was she a fool?

"Ye are nae a fool," William said, as if he knew her thoughts. "Sit with me for a moment, and then I vow I'll walk ye to yer bedchamber myself."

"I dunnae want to sit here," she replied, feeling as if the room was suddenly too small.

"Then walk with me," he suggested. "We can stroll the ramparts."

She nodded and followed William out of the great hall and toward the stairs to the ramparts. "Ye are right to trust him," he said.

"Am I?" she asked, trailing behind William.

He stopped on a step and turned to look down at her. "Aye, ye are. Did I tell ye the story of how Brodee and I came to ken each other?"

"Nae in much detail," she admitted.

William tugged a hand through his hair, then motioned for her to join him on the step he was on. She did, and together, they started to climb the long, spiral staircase for the ramparts. "I had gone off like a fool to be trained by the Dark Riders."

She gasped. "The Dark Riders? But I thought men who sought to train with them rarely came out of the forest alive."

"That's true. Most dunnae. But Brodee's brother, Broch, did, and I wanted to also. I have… Well, I have some things in my past that haunt me. We shall leave it at that."

She nodded and let him go on as he wished.

"Suffice to say, I found the Dark Riders, and they did train me—and well. But one kinnae leave their company without a price, one that they name. And the price for me to leave was five missions for which they had need of me. I kinnae tell ye what they were, but the first one nearly killed me. That is when Brodee found me. He did nae even really ken me, but he offered his services for the other four missions if they would let me leave. I was verra sick by then and needed a healer. They agreed, Brodee took me out of the forest and to a healer, and he completed the missions in my name. Dangerous missions that could have verra well taken his life. I was nearly a stranger, but he did it because he'd made a vow to the king to find me and bring me home." William pushed the door to the ramparts open, and cool air washed over Patience. She stepped outside into the dark night that twinkled with stars. "He made ye a vow, as well, my lady, and he'd nae ever break it."

She nodded, feeling somewhat foolish for being so jealous. Turning toward the courtyard, she looked down, and suddenly she couldn't breathe. Below stood her husband, face-to-face with Kinsey, each of them holding on to the other. Patience could not move. She wanted to turn away, but shock and betrayal had rendered her immobile.

When Brodee heard his name being called, he whipped around so quickly that the courtyard momentarily tilted and specks of bright light danced in his vision. He blinked, seeing Kinsey come into focus, and as she reached for him, he grasped her to steady himself.

"I think I may be ill," he mumbled, but the world seemed to right itself long enough for him to feel the wash of disappointment that Kinsey was before him and not Patience.

"Shall we sit?" Kinsey asked him.

He shook his head. "I need to go for a swim. To cool off and clear my mind."

"Ye dunnae look well, Laird. Let me aid ye—"

"Nay, I'm fine," he said, releasing his grip on her. The truth was, he felt far from it. He was sweating as if he'd just finished a fierce battle, and his head felt filled with mud. His thoughts were sluggish, and his movements even slower than they'd been in the great hall. He was definitely ill.

"I'll just walk beside ye, then," Kinsey said, sounding as if she were standing at the end of a long tunnel, though he saw and felt her beside him. "I wanted to talk to ye about something, but I dunnae ken how to tell ye what I saw."

It took until they reached the seagate stairs for him to process her words and say, "Simply tell me."

"Do ye trust William MacLean?" Kinsey asked as he descended the stairs to the sea.

Brodee paused, swaying slightly halfway down. He glanced at Kinsey, who was one step behind him. "Aye. With my life," he said, trying and failing to identify what he was detecting in her tone. God's teeth, he was a fool for drinking so much wine.

"I see," she hedged and brushed past him. "I, well, never mind, then."

He caught up with her on the bottom step as she reached the rocky shore. "Kinsey," he said, his voice sounding far away to his own ears. "Why did ye ask me such a thing?"

She turned toward him and cocked her head, staring at him. What was that look? Triumph? No. That made no sense. He desperately needed to clear his head in the cold water. Pinching the bridge of his nose, he inhaled a long breath and tried once more to focus on Kinsey. "Why did ye ask me that?" he repeated.

"Well…" She shifted from foot to foot, and a look that *did* register—uneasiness—settled on her face. "'Tis just that I saw Patience kiss him," she said, her voice full of apology.

He trusted William. He did. But the rage that swept through him made him shake. He curled his hands into fists as an image of Patience kissing William taunted him. He had the immediate desire to find William and beat the man, his friend, to near death.

No, that was not right. His head began to pound as he tried to temper his reaction. William would not betray him. Would Patience? His gut told him no, and he always went with his gut. Still, he would hear the facts, and if need be, he would question William and then Patience. "When did ye see this?"

"Today," Kinsey said. "I'm so sorry, Brodee." She squeezed his hand.

His own current situation hit him. To anyone who saw them, it could appear something was occurring between *them*, and perhaps that's exactly what had happened with Patience and William. Brodee pulled his hand out of Kinsey's grasp and took a step back from her. "I'm certain what ye saw was an innocent thank ye or some such thing."

"Brodee, I dunnae think—"

"Laird," he corrected her, his words coming out sharp.

She had opened her mouth to say something else, he was certain, though he was having a great deal of trouble concentrating on her, but at his curt tone, she snapped her jaw shut. A long silence stretched, and then she finally said, "Aye, I'm certain ye are correct."

He got the distinct impression she was only saying what he wished to hear, but given he did not want to extend their standing here alone talking, he did not make mention of it. "Do ye need me to walk ye back to the castle?" he asked politely, hoping she would decline. He no longer wished to swim because, frankly, he felt too unsteady on his feet, so he was heading back to the castle anyway. Though if she declined his offer, he would let her go first. He'd rather they not enter the courtyard together.

But at her nod, he clenched his teeth on his frustration and focused all his effort on simply getting one foot in front of the other. By the time they reached the courtyard, he could feel himself swaying, and he was so distracted by how odd he felt that he did not realize Kinsey was reaching for his hand until she had it in hers, their fingers tangled together. In that moment, all he could think upon was the pleasure of the simple, intimate gesture of hand-holding that Patience had returned to him. It was a gift. She was a gift. Wasn't she?

His muddled thoughts irked him. Everything about this night irritated him.

He tugged his hand from Kinsey's hold, and she frowned at him. "I only meant to tell ye if ye need someone to talk to—"

"I'll talk with my wife," he assured her, though as he said the words, he felt a small bit of doubt regarding Patience. Damn Kinsey and her claim.

Her lips pressed together, but then she offered him a smile. "Of course. I bid ye good night, Laird."

He inclined his head in answer and waited until she was in the castle and would have had time to make her way to her room before he entered and headed up the stairs toward his bedchamber. But when he neared the top of the stairs and heard his wife's and William's voices, Brodee stilled, listening.

"Vow to me ye will nae say a thing," Patience said. The desperation in her voice filled Brodee with sudden doubt that maybe he really did not know her. Or William.

Sweat trickled down his back, and his vision blurred. He pressed a hand against the wall as William responded. "I'll nae, but—"

"I dunnae wish to hear anything else," she interrupted, her voice trembling. Was it because she'd betrayed him with William? He gave his head a little shake to rid himself of his unfounded jealousy, but a flash of wild anger ripped through him. "I hate him," Patience said.

"Laird!" Fergus's voice at Brodee's back caused him to flinch. Brodee didn't even turn to acknowledge Fergus. He took the last step between him and the landing where his wife and William stood, and they both looked toward him as one.

All the color drained from Patience's face, and William's eyes narrowed upon Brodee. He curled his hand around the hilt of his sword, even as he reached for the wall to steady himself. "Ye're such a good friend, William," Brodee said, hearing his own slurred words. "Thank ye for seeing *my* wife to *my* bedchamber. Ye're dismissed."

When William glanced at Patience and she shook her head at him, Brodee felt black rage sweep through him. Something was most certainly occurring between the two

of them. Brodee stepped toward Patience, thinking to slide
his hand around her waist, but William moved in front of
him. "I believe yer wife is tired, and ye are actually standing
in front of *her* bedchamber."

It took all Brodee's strength not to hit William in the
face, and if he'd not been seeing double of the man, he may
have done it. He moved to step around William, who was
blocking his view of Patience, but William started to move,
as well. "I'd nae do that if I were ye," Brodee said, hearing
the lethalness in his tone. A look of shocking indecision
settled on William's face, one that made him seem guilty to
Brodee. But he'd learned long ago not to rush headlong into
decisions, so he'd decide what to do about William in the
morning.

Patience suddenly stepped out from behind William.
Her spine was straight, and her chin lifted. Christ, he felt the
need to step toward her, gather her in his arms, even now.
"I wish to sleep in my bedchamber," she said, her voice
clear and strong. "Alone."

He didn't want to be without her. The realization hit
him hard. He started to reach for her, and she flinched
away. "Will ye force me to yer chambers?" she demanded.

"Is there another ye prefer in there?" he growled, swiv-
eling his gaze to William.

He heard Patience's gasp of outrage. Her door opened
and slammed, but he refused to look away from William.
He was looking for a sign of guilt, betrayal, deceit.

William scowled at Brodee. "What the devil is wrong
with ye?"

Brodee opened his mouth to answer, but the floor tilted
under him and everything went black.

Sunlight streamed into his room, waking him. The first thing he realized was he was desperately thirsty, his head pounded, and his mouth felt as if someone had filled it with sand. He'd seen men drink too much wine, heard them complain of the effects, and he was disgusted with himself for having apparently done such a thing. Though, as he lay there and recounted the night, three goblets of wine should not have done such things to him. But it had.

He sat up, grasping his head at a wave of pain in his skull. His brain felt five times too large for his head. It seemed it was trying to push its way out of his skull.

Squeezing his head and his eyes, he stumbled to his washbasin, rinsed his hands and face, drank a cup of mead, and then returned to the edge of his bed. He looked beside him, wondering for a brief moment why Patience was not there, and then the events of the night came back to him in painful, nauseating flashes.

I saw Patience kiss William. Kinsey's words rang in Brodee's head. He felt the same disbelief and rage he'd experienced last night, except now he was better able to keep his temper. Was what he saw as it seemed? He couldn't honestly say. What he did know for certain was that Patience had not wanted to sleep in his bedchamber with him, and William, a man he thought he could trust above anyone, had acted as if he would try to stop Brodee if he thought to make Patience go to his bedchamber.

Brodee wouldn't do that. Of course he would not, but that was not the point. The point was that William had been acting as if Patience needed protection from Brodee. He could not think of a reason William would do that, unless the man thought that Brodee had discovered there was something occurring between William and Patience.

Christ. The pounding in his skull was relentless. There

had to be another reason. Another explanation. But he could not come up with one, and all he could see in his head was his wife and his friend locked in passion. He could demand the truth, but he held little hope he'd get it.

One thing he'd learned in his life was that guilt affected everyone. A guilty person would reveal their duplicity in little ways they did not even recognize. Brodee would wait and watch. He would keep his distance from them both. If nothing had occurred between Patience and William, Patience would surely want him back in her bed to reclaim the passion they'd shared two nights earlier. Mayhap she'd merely been tired last night. Hell, mayhap she'd been fearful because he'd imbibed in too much wine. Perhaps one of her late husbands had done such a thing. He had the sudden urge to go to her and ask, but pride kept him from doing so. She needed to come to him, and if she didn't, if neither she nor William approached him... He didn't want to dwell on what that meant. Nor did he want to linger on the acute hollowness in his gut at the thought that Patience could have been unfaithful. He was not meant to care so much about her that it made his chest ache so painfully.

Eighteen

The day of the tournament, just as the sun rose in the sky, Patience watched from the ramparts as Brodee rode across the bridge to partake in a quick hunt before the planned afternoon tournament. A contingent of men—that did not include William—rode behind her husband. She could see William at the other side of the ramparts talking to one of the guards. He had not been in her sights for four days now; it was more like he kept her in his sights. He was her new guard now, apparently assigned by Brodee without Brodee even telling William himself. Her husband had passed his order on to William through Fergus, who could not say or would not say why either of them had been reassigned, just that they had.

She suspected greatly it was because she had asked William to keep the secret that she had seen Brodee and Kinsey standing so intimately in the courtyard, that she'd stared in horrible disbelief as they had gone down the seagate stairs to the dark, rocky shores below. That she'd waited—with a twisting gut and cheeks burning with shame—for them to return, praying it would be quickly. Praying that Brodee would mention something to her, offer explanation and tenderness. But that had not happened in all the days since then.

Hurt roiled inside of her. Not only had he ignored her

that night in the great hall when she had entered with Kinsey, who had been wearing that red gown, but he'd held hands with Kinsey, left the castle with Kinsey, and when he had returned, his words had been slurred and his demeanor off. He seemed to have drunk too much wine, which shocked her. For a man who prided himself on control, there had been quite a lack of it. Still, she knew he'd had a long day of training hard. That was forgivable. Or it would have been if not for the rest. And to add insult to injury, he'd apparently that night given Kinsey leave to organize the tournament festivities.

As the lady of the castle, that duty should be Patience's. She would not have minded sharing it, had he asked her, but he'd not asked. Nor had he even told her that he'd given the responsibility to Kinsey. Jane had been the one to tell her when Kinsey had announced it to all the women she'd gathered the morning after that fateful supper in the great hall. Kinsey had not even told Patience, and when she'd asked her about it, Kinsey had apologized profusely and confessed that Brodee had asked her to walk with him after supper the night Patience had seen them in the courtyard. Brodee had apparently told Kinsey that he wanted her to oversee things because he had been worried Patience could not handle it, given she had no experience as the lady of the castle.

Patience pressed her fingertips to her aching forehead. She was so confused. Had he been trying to help her, or had he decided he no longer had use for her? Or was all this an effort to keep distance between them? Had his attentions turned to Kinsey? From the way Kinsey acted so uncomfortable and embarrassed, she did not seem to want them, yet she had once again taken on the duties of lady of the castle with gusto. Patience felt like an outsider, just as she always had before, as if she did not belong. Except it was worse this time because she had *wanted* to belong. Brodee had breached her defenses and had gained her trust, along with a bit of her heart, and now she felt like a fool.

Since that night, he'd not said more than a few polite words of greeting when she had seen him, which had not been much. Between training with the men and hunting to stock the kitchens with meat for the winter, he'd been busy day and night. He had not been in the great hall for supper, nor had he come to her bedchamber to share another night of passion. She now doubted her decision to turn him away the night she'd seen him with Kinsey, but she'd been hurt and angry and she had not wanted him in her bed if he had been with Kinsey.

If what Kinsey had told Patience was to be believed, she and Brodee had simply talked, but it was what Kinsey had been clearly trying not to say that Patience had to pry out of her. She'd finally admitted in tears that it seemed to Kinsey as if Brodee had wanted something from her that night, something of a passionate nature, and that confession had stopped Patience from going to him. No matter how many times Patience went through possible reasons why Brodee had acted as he had, none of the outcomes were good. He wanted Kinsey. He wanted distance from Patience. He held no stock in being faithful. Bad. Terrible. Horrid. Sickening. That's what all the answers to her confusion seemed to be.

She'd thought she could not feel worse than when Ivan had beaten her, and then she had learned at Silas's hands that emotional punishment could be more scarring than physical punishment. After that, she'd believed she could never feel anything worse than that, but what she felt now was an utter loss of the joy she had experienced in Brodee's arms. Had it even been real? She clenched her teeth at her cowardice. She was afraid of the answer, and that was truly why she'd not approached him yet.

She saw William turn her way and stride toward her, so she forced a smile to her face, but the look of pity he gave her let her know he saw through her mask. "Let me tell him what we saw," William said, repeating the same request he'd put to her for days. "There is surely an explanation, and I dunnae like keeping things from him and avoiding him. I'm certain he kens I am doing so, and frankly, I'm shocked he's nae come to me and demanded to ken why."

"Mayhap he has nae done so because he is guilty. Mayhap he's avoiding ye," she said, her voice trembling, "because he kens ye would nae approve." She swallowed past the sudden tightness of her throat. She had not told William the entirety of what she'd learned about Brodee, but the need to do so now, to have someone to talk to, to analyze it all, spilled out in a rush of words with the hope that William would tell her she was being foolish. That Brodee's closest friend would reassure her once more that Brodee would never betray her, shame her, make her feel worthless.

Instead, William stared at her openmouthed for a long silent moment, and then he surprised her by stepping toward her and giving her a brotherly hug. "I'm certain it will all sort out," he said in a tight voice. Yet he didn't *sound* certain. He sounded angry, as if he believed Brodee had betrayed Patience—or wanted to—and the look of pity he gave her sealed it. She mumbled an excuse about needing to get to the kitchens to help prepare the tournament meals, and then she pulled away from him, quickly leaving before the tears started to fall.

As she made her way down the stairs and out of the castle to go to the kitchens, where she really did need to be helping, she nearly ran straight into Kinsey, who was coming from the woods carrying a basket. They both yelped, and Kinsey dropped the basket, then fell to her knees to gather the herbs that had tumbled out. Patience kneeled down to help. She wanted to hate the woman, but it was not Kinsey's fault if Brodee was attracted to her.

"I'm sorry," Patience said. "I did nae see ye."

Kinsey stilled in gathering the herbs, and her gaze came to Patience. "I'm sorry, too," she said. The three words sounded heavy with cumbersome regret, as if the two of them nearly running into each other weighed on Kinsey. It was odd.

They both stood. "I was just coming to find ye," Kinsey said.

Patience frowned. "From the woods?"

Kinsey laughed at that. "Nay. Well, aye. I was planning to come find ye after I gathered the herbs in the woods for Mari." She set a hand on Patience's arm. "Brodee came to speak with me before he went hunting with the men."

Brodee. When had Kinsey started calling Brodee by his given name and not using his title of laird? Her heart squeezed in anguish at the implication.

"Did he?" she managed to say, her voice sounding normal, though pain was flowing through her.

"Aye. I... Well, he thinks it best if I'm the one to sit at his side at the start of the games today."

"I see," Patience said, her chest aching.

"'Tis simply because I represent the Kincaide clan and he represents the Blackswell clan, and the tournament represents bringing the two clans together. 'Tis nae anything to be fashed about."

"Of course nae," she lied. "If ye'll excuse me, since I'll nae be needed at the start of the tournament, I dunnae think

I'll go to the ceremony. I'm awfully tired." And shamed. And hurt. And something else that was brewing. Something making her hot and shaky.

Kinsey gave her an understanding smile. "Of course, I understand. Go have a rest. The castle will be nice and quiet since we will all be at the tourney, and ye can have a nice long nap."

Patience nodded and quickly made her way to her bed-chamber. She flung open the door and strode in, but then stopped cold. Her bedcovers were rumpled, though she'd left them perfectly made. She was certain of it. It looked as if someone had sat or had lain on her bed. The hairs on the back of her neck stood suddenly on end. Behind her, the door swished shut, and fright swept through her. She reached for the dagger sheathed at her hip, her fingers touching the cold steel, but before she could properly grasp it, pain burst in her head as she was hit from behind with something hard. Bright-white light exploded before her eyes, and then everything went black.

⚜

Brodee could not recall a time he'd been so distracted. Every moment awake was filled with thoughts of Patience. He longed to talk to her, to make her laugh, to bring her pleasure. Yet he could do none of that, not without knowing if she and William had betrayed him. Each day that went by with both of them avoiding him made him more certain that they were guilty.

The purpose of the hunt had really been to distract him, but with every animal he killed, he saw William's face. Brodee knew he would snap if he did not confront William.

As for Patience, he would confront her after he spoke to

William. No more waiting. She was his wife, betrayer or not, but he could not imagine keeping her near if she had betrayed him. The thought twisted his gut into a jumble of knots. He refused to analyze why her possible betrayal hurt so much. Instead, he settled on his pride.

As he rode in from the hunt, one of his men, Carrick, was waiting for him in the courtyard. Brodee had appointed Carrick to follow William and report back on his comings and goings. He knew William and Patience had been together. In fact, he purposely made it so to give them an opportunity to show him what they would do, and so far, they'd done nothing more than talk.

"Laird," Carrick said, giving him a look that conveyed he had information to share.

Brodee dismounted and motioned his men to ride on. The tournament was set to start at noon, and they needed to prepare. "I'll make my way there shortly," he assured Cul and Fergus, who lingered behind as the other men continued toward the stables. Both men nodded and followed the others.

"Speak," Brodee said.

"Nae long ago, yer wife and William stood on the ramparts and she was in his arms."

"In his arms?" Brodee repeated, his blood beginning to boil.

Carrick nodded. "Aye, Laird. They were talking, and then William pulled her into his arms, and they stood that way for a few minutes, and—"

"Brodee!" William's voice cut across the silence of the courtyard, tipping Brodee's anger to an uncontainable point.

Brodee's hand went to his sword, and as he pulled it out, he handed it to Carrick. "Take this for me, and it dunnae matter what I say, dunnae give it back to me until ye see I have cooled."

"Aye, Laird," the man said. He quickly took the sword and scrambled back.

Brodee whipped around toward the sound of William's heavy footfalls. The man, his supposed friend, was scowling at him. Brodee began to tremble with the need to launch his attack, but he first said, "Disarm."

William stopped, a confused look coming to his face. "What?"

"Disarm now, or I will call my men to disarm ye."

"Ye'll what?" William still looked confused.

Blood rushed in Brodee's ears, and the fury coursing through him made him break out in a sweat. He curled his hands into fists and took a step toward William. "I will fight ye man to man, nae with weapons. For if I have my weapon, I will kill ye."

"Ye'll kill me?" William repeated, still seeming confused. *The swine.*

"Aye. Disarm."

William unsheathed his sword and tossed it to the side, his narrowed gaze steady on Brodee. "Just what is it ye wish to fight me about? I'm here to speak to ye!"

"I imagine ye are. It took ye long enough, ye cuckolding coward." With that, he closed the distance between them, and in a flash, he smashed his fist into William's nose.

With a grunt, William's head jerked back, and he came forward once more, his fist connecting with Brodee's lip. "Ye think I'm bedding yer wife?" William roared, shooting out a fist, which Brodee dodged.

Brodee landed a jab to William's jaw, but the man surprised him with a hard hit to his ribs. Pain danced up Brodee's left side. With a sharp inhale, he snarled, "Aye. I ken ye are! She kissed ye!" He kicked out and caught William at the knee.

The man's legs buckled, but William was a fighter. He grabbed Brodee as he went down, and the two of them fell together, fists flying. For one breath, they rolled, then William came up on top of Brodee. He punched him in the nose, and Brodee tasted blood immediately.

William glared down at him. "Yer wife kissed me on the cheek out of gratitude for advice I gave her regarding ye!" he spat.

Brodee froze, his fist stopping mid-punch, as he'd been about to deliver another blow to William. "What?"

"Ye heard me," William said, then rolled off Brodee and gained his feet.

Brodee quickly followed. "What advice?"

"The ill-served advice that she should nae relinquish hope in ye. The encouraging words that led her to go find ye the day ye were swimming in the loch."

Instantly, Brodee recalled the day. He swiped at the blood dripping from his nose, as William did much the same. Brodee opened his mouth to question William further, but William cut him off. "I sent her to ye because I thought ye honorable. Ye dunnae deserve her!"

"And ye do?" Brodee growled, his heart beating so hard it thumped in his head.

"I dunnae want yer wife, ye clot-heid."

"Ye had her in yer arms today on the ramparts," Brodee said, hearing the rancor in his tone.

William's lips parted in shock, and then his face hardened. "Are ye having one of the men watch me?"

"Aye," Brodee admitted unapologetically. "Do ye deny ye had my wife in yer arms today? Are ye calling Carrick a liar?" Brodee asked, motioning toward Carrick, who stood to their left still holding Brodee's sword.

William turned to glare at Carrick. "I'll deal with ye later," he said, his tone threatening, and then he focused on Brodee once more. "I gave yer wife a brotherly hug because she was near tears from all ye have done to her!"

"What I have done to her?" Brodee said, his breath coming ragged with his anger.

"Ye ken." The words were punctuated with a righteous indignation that gave Brodee pause and set off warnings in his head.

"What do ye think I've done to Patience?" he asked.

"We saw ye in the courtyard holding hands with Kinsey after the night she wore that revealing gown. Do. Ye. Deny. It?" William asked, throwing Brodee's words back at him.

Brodee flinched as a flash of memory from that night came back to him. "We were nae holding hands," he said, his neck suddenly hot. "Kinsey followed me, and she grabbed my hand. I was slow to react because I'd drunk three goblets of wine at dinner, and they had an unusual effect on me."

"Ye expect me to believe three goblets of wine made ye act that way?"

It sounded ridiculous, but—"It's true," Brodee clipped. "I'd nae lie. And I'd nae be untrue to Patience."

William arched his eyebrows. "I suppose ye'd nae ignore her at supper either and instead talk to Kinsey the entire time? And gape at all the charms she showed in that red gown?" The fiery look William gave Brodee made his uneasiness grow tenfold.

"I dunnae recall any gown that showed any charms of Kinsey's because I dunnae see her that way." He only had eyes for his wife, but he refused to admit it aloud. Instead, he scrubbed a hand over his face. "I did ignore Patience that night, but it did nae have anything to do with Kinsey. I drew a line, and I have to stick to it."

"What line?" William asked, crossing his arms over his chest and scowling. "The one that sent ye down to the shore with Kinsey in the dark on the same night ye ogled her and held her hand?"

"Ye have it all wrong," Brodee said, suddenly suspicious that he did, too.

"Do I?" William sounded disbelieving. "I suppose I also have it wrong that ye were the one to ask Kinsey to walk to the shore with ye, that ye made comments to her that ye wished to join with her, that ye gave her permission to be in charge of planning the festivities for the tournament?"

The inflamed, belligerent tone William directed at him left no doubt what William thought, and Patience must have too, that he was pursuing Kinsey. That he might have already bedded her. Had he asked Kinsey to the walk to the shore with him? He frowned, trying to recall the events of the night. "I felt unstable that night. She offered to walk with me."

William snorted. "I have nae ever seen ye unstable, even when ye have been stabbed, but ye are telling me wine made ye so?"

Brodee slid his teeth back and forth, thoughts tumbling quickly now. Something was not right. "I have nae ever hinted to Kinsey that I wanted to join with her. I have made clear I dunnae, if anything. And I did nae even consider anything needed to be planned for the tournament until Kinsey mentioned it, and said Patience would be over-whelmed. I did nae give her Patience's role." He curled his hands into fists, recalling his initial wariness of Kinsey. "I think a talk with Kinsey is in order—one for which Patience is present."

"Likely a good notion if ye wish yer wife to ever speak to ye again," William said, his tone not nearly as sharp as it had been.

Brodee looked at his friend's bloody nose and busted lip. *Christ.* How had he allowed himself to believe William capable of such things? He'd never been a jealous man, but... An image of Patience filled his mind. Her head was thrown back in passion, rosy lips parted, slender legs splayed wide, eyes filled with lust for him. Her husky laugh rang in his ears. The soft lilt in her voice as she had confided in him, then boldly told him she wanted to stay with him but not to sleep, whispered across his mind. He'd been so busy trying to control what he felt that he had not even realized the extent of it.

She had him completely, body and soul—likely since the first moment he saw her in the courtyard spinning in circles. He wanted to know her, to learn her hopes and dreams and make each come true. Fear gripped him, but he shoved it down. Fear of losing her had driven him to almost doing so. Maybe not physically, but emotionally.

"Will, I—" He didn't know the right words to apologize for thinking his friend would betray him. "I'm a clot-heid."

"I warned ye that women could make ye that way," William said with smirk.

Brodee laughed. "Aye, ye did. Come. I think we've one more false Kincaide to rid ourselves of."

Nineteen

"Brodee," William said, his tone lashing through the black fright that gripped Brodee.

He jerked his gaze from a sobbing Jane, who stood in the courtyard facing him, along with Fergus, Cul, Mari, and William. He turned his gaze to William and away from Jane, who he'd just yelled at. "What?" he demanded, the word more a growl than anything.

"The lass kinnae calm herself enough to talk with ye bellowing at her."

Brodee nodded. Logically, he knew William to be correct. Jane stood trembling and weeping before him. Her face was buried in her hands, her shoulders shaking. Physically, he was having a hard time controlling himself from yelling more as the terror clawed at him. He knew it. He knew it would cause him to make mistakes. And now Patience was gone.

She'd not been at the tournament and neither had Kinsey. They both had disappeared without a trace. He didn't have a care about Kinsey, except for the fact that he was certain she was somehow responsible.

Every time he took a breath, all he could think was what if Patience was somewhere hurt? What if he never saw her again? He needed answers, and so far, all he'd received since gathering those who should have known where

Patience was, was babbling and crying from Jane. Of course, they had only just gotten here and he had raged at the poor lass the moment she'd entered the courtyard. Everyone else was staring at him with a mixture of fear and trepidation, except William, who gave him a look of understanding.

"Try less yelling," William suggested.

Brodee yanked his hand through his hair. "When was the last time ye saw Patience, Jane?"

Jane slowly looked up, her lips quivering. "Nae since this morning. I took a goblet of wine to her room earlier, as I always do, but she was nae there."

Brodee frowned. "Does she drink wine in her room every day?" he asked, simply trying to get an accurate picture of her normal day.

Jane shook her head. "Nay. My lady has nae ever touched the wine I bring her."

"Then why the devil do ye bring it?" he roared, his control once again snapping. Jane immediately started to sob, and he had the desire to bellow his frustration again. Instead, he clenched his teeth, breathed deeply, and said, "I'm sorry, Jane. I'm verra fashed about Patience."

Jane sniffed, swiped at her eyes, and said, "I take the wine because Lady Kinsey ordered me to do so when she first appointed me as Lady Patience's lady's maid. She dunnae drink it, but Lady Kinsey instructed me to continue bringing it."

Brodee frowned. "Why would Kinsey have ye bring wine to Patience when she dunnae even drink it?" He was thinking aloud, not expecting an answer, so he was surprised when Jane did speak.

"I dunnae ken for certain, except Lady Kinsey did murmur that surely Patience would at least once drink the blasted wine. 'Twas her words," Jane rushed out.

Brodee nodded absently as he thought about the wine that had made him feel so unstable. "Mari"—he looked to the older lady—"would ye smell or taste an herb if it was put in the wine?"

Mari's eyes widened at the implication. "It depends on the herb," she said. "But perhaps."

"Jane," Brodee ordered, "go fetch the goblet ye took to Patience this morning."

"Aye, Laird, but surely ye dunnae think Lady Kinsey would be trying to harm Lady Patience?"

The memory of Kinsey's hand on his wine goblet that horrid night came to him. "I dunnae ken what to think. At this point, I dunnae dismiss anything."

Jane bit her lip, and remained before him.

"Do ye have something to say?" he asked, assuming she would speak in defense of Kinsey.

"Well, 'tis probably nae anything, but Lady Patience did almost plunge to her death off the seagate stairs a sennight ago. Lady Kinsey was standing above her on the stairs, and she said she slipped and fell into Lady Patience. I happened to be coming down the stairs and saw it, and I screamed out. Lady Kinsey then grabbed Lady Patience and pulled her to safety."

A cold, hard knot formed in his stomach.

Fergus cleared his throat. "My lady almost got shot by an arrow some days ago, as well."

"What?" He whipped toward Fergus. "Why are ye just telling me now?"

"I'm sorry, Laird. I was still trying to figure out what had happened, but I should have mentioned it immediately."

"What do ye ken?" Brodee demanded.

"Well, I was coming from a stone path that leads to the

courtyard and Lady Patience and Lady Kinsey were in the courtyard some distance apart from each other. I stopped Lady Patience to tell her I was sent to find her, but before I could get the words out, an arrow swished by Lady Patience's head, nearly hitting her. I saw it come from the direction of the gardens, and Lady Kinsey confirmed that's where she saw it come from as well.

"Nae any harm," Brodee said, disbelieving. Had he known these things, he would have guarded his wife himself. His throat constricted with the certain knowledge that Patience was in imminent danger, and likely from Kinsey, whom she trusted. Though, who else was helping her? Someone must have been. But who? And why?

Fergus shifted his weight, cleared his throat, and continued. "I was set to tell ye, but Lady Patience did nae want them to be punished if ye were too angered, and I told her I'd find the culprit and speak with them myself. I'm sorry, laird."

"'Tis just like my wife to think of another before herself," Brodee said, his chest aching with the knowledge of how kind she was.

"They all vowed that nae any of them shot a stray arrow into the courtyard that night. I started questioning each of them individually, but I've nae finished."

"Laird," Mari stammered, looking positively terrified.

His gut sank. "Aye?"

"I saw Ulric in the castle earlier today."

"Ulric," Brodee repeated. He'd not seen the man since the day Brodee had him escorted off the land.

Mari nodded. "He said he came back to challenge ye at the tournament today for the lairdship, so I did nae think anything amiss."

It could be that it wasn't. It could be that Ulric truly had returned to challenge him, as Brodee himself said someone could do. It could be that there was a reasonable explanation for where Kinsey and Patience were, but that would not justify Kinsey's manipulations. And they damn well were manipulations. She had been clever and careful, and he'd been so absorbed with trying to deny how Patience made him feel that he had not seen the trouble brewing right before his eyes.

He struggled to take a breath past his rage. "Call the Blackswell men to the courtyard. I fear Lady Kinsey is trying to kill Patience, and whether Ulric is involved or nae, I dunnae believe she's working alone. When they get here," Brodee said, focusing on Fergus, "send them in every direction out from the castle in search of Patience and tell them to be prepared to kill her captor."

Fergus nodded as Brodee turned toward the stables, his blood coursing through his veins and his heart racing. Behind him, heavy, quick footfalls fell, and then William and Cul were at his sides.

"We're coming with ye," William said.

Brodee nodded. He could not speak. His throat was so tight he could barely swallow. One thought kept going through his mind: he could not lose her. Despite not wanting to risk loving her, he'd fallen. He'd been successful at defending himself against countless ruthless enemies, but as he strode toward his horse, he realized he'd never had a hope of defending himself against Patience. He was not a praying man, not anymore—not since Arabel had been murdered. But Brodee found himself praying now for Patience's safety. He would give up his lands, the castle, even his life, to find her unharmed.

A screech ripped Patience from the blackness that had consumed her. She opened her eyes, and the sunlight nearly blinded her. Squinting with a pain that split her head, she blinked several times as another scream—this one almost animalistic—resounded around her. She knew that voice.

Kinsey.

Kinsey was in trouble!

Patience's eyes flew all the way open, and she pushed past a nauseating wave of dizziness in order to scramble to her feet. The forest around her tilted precariously, and bright dots peppered her vision.

"Damn ye, Kinsey!" came a man's enraged bellow. "I'll kill ye!"

Patience gave herself a little shake as she reached for the hilt of her dagger only to find it gone. Then she remembered her fingers upon the cold, hard steel before someone had hit her from behind.

She looked around frantically, unable to place exactly where she was. Deep in the woods, yes, but where? Wind whipped her hair in knots, making her think she was high in the mountains. She turned to get her bearings, and her foot slipped on the wet rock beneath her. She went down hard on one knee, cursing. Underneath her fingertips, she felt the slick, jumbled mass of rock. Was this basalt?

A memory niggled, and her breath caught. Silas had spoken of a rock ledge called the Old Man of Storr. He'd said it would be the perfect place to push her to oblivion if she ever angered him enough.

A chill swept through her as she struggled to her feet and turned to face the east. If she recalled correctly, the pinnacle of the rock was to the east. But it could not be that she was here. She started up the sharp incline of rock toward the direction of Kinsey's screams, shoving branches out of her way and grasping roots growing out of the ground. Grass covered some of the rock in a soft carpet, and her toes squished into the mud. She had no notion where her slippers had gone.

"Come for me, Ulric!" Kinsey shouted from somewhere above Patience.

Patience frowned as she climbed as fast as she could to get to her friend, banging her knees upon the rock when she slipped. She clenched her teeth against the branches that cut through her gown and sliced open her arms. Then she realized Kinsey had sounded taunting not fearful. But that did not make sense. None of this did.

The higher Patience climbed, the harder the wind became, and as she huffed in a breath, she smelled and tasted the sea. The trees grew thin, and sunlight hit her face once more. A blue sky appeared above her, and then another bellow from Ulric resounded in the silence.

"Ye betrayed me!"

The eerie laugh from Kinsey caused gooseflesh to cover Patience's arms. Finally, Patience reached a plateau, and in the distance, several rocks jutted to the Heavens above. Beyond them was a drop—to the sea, she was certain—and Kinsey and Ulric stood at the edge.

She opened her mouth to call for Kinsey when Ulric lunged at the woman. Patience screamed, racing forward and watching as Kinsey seemed to leap out of the way at the last moment, Ulric disappearing over the ledge. All the breath left Patience's lungs as she reached Kinsey, whose pale-blue gaze settled on her with an odd look.

"Kinsey!" Patience choked out. "He tried to kill ye." She moved toward the ledge beside Kinsey and bent down, grasping her dagger from where it gleamed on the ground. Ulric must have taken it and dropped it. Rocks dug into her knees as she kneeled and looked over at the steep drop. Far below them, Ulric lay in a twisted mass.

An uneasy feeling swept over Patience. Why was Kinsey here with Ulric? What had he meant when he'd said Kinsey had betrayed him?

Just as Patience curled her fingers around the dagger, Kinsey shoved her hard in the back. But the woman clearly had not seen that Patience had a knee upon the ground, and she did not fly forward, Patience understood with horror, as Kinsey had intended.

Patience shoved backward with all her strength, hearing a grunt and a thud. She twisted to the side, seeing Kinsey on her back, and as the woman struggled to get up, Patience scrambled around her, gained her feet, and started to run from the cliff. Five steps later, Kinsey barreled into her with a bellow, and they both went flying forward to the ground.

For a breath, Patience lay there stunned, but when Kinsey jumped up, grabbed Patience's ankle, and began to drag her, she shook off her surprise and swiped her dagger at Kinsey's hand. It sliced across her skin, cutting it wide. Blood began to flow, and Kinsey released her with a moan. "I wish ye would nae have done that," Kinsey muttered. "It will be hard to conceal from Brodee."

"Brodee?" Patience repeated, standing and pointing the dagger at Kinsey. Her mind fluttered wildly, her heart doing the same. "Why did ye bring me here?"

Kinsey eyed the dagger. "I did nae," she said, matter-of-fact. "Ulric did."

"Why did *Ulric* bring me here, then?" Patience tried again.

When Kinsey stepped back, Patience grabbed her by the arm and set the point of the dagger at the woman's stomach. "I'll stab ye if ye so much as move again," she said, her voice shaking.

Kinsey snorted. "Ye'll nae. Ye're too soft to do such a thing."

"I stabbed Loskie," Patience reminded the woman.

"True. That was quite surprising. Ye've always been so fearful, so I think it was simply a moment of being braw. If ye were truly braw, ye would nae have let my brother treat ye like a dog. I kinnae ken why he thought he loved ye." Kinsey bit hard on her lip, causing blood to appear.

"Loved me?" Patience repeated, stunned. "Silas did nae love me."

Eyes filled with hatred settled on her. "Aye. I said as much to him," Kinsey spat. "Told him he was obsessed, nae in love. *He was obsessed*. And 'twas yer father's fault, of course."

"My father?" Now Patience was more confused than ever.

"Aye. He turned down Silas's first offer of marriage to ye until Silas increased the amount of coin yer father would get. He made Silas feel he was nae good enough for ye, and that made Silas obsessed with winning ye. And he betrayed me to do it!" Kinsey screeched.

Patience shook her head. "I dunnae ken. How did he betray ye?"

"He was supposed to watch over me forever. Love only me, forever." A sick feeling rose from Patience's stomach all the way to her throat. Kinsey's eyes narrowed on her. "He vowed to me that I'd be the lady of the castle. Secretly, of course. We had to be secret. But I would be the true lady of the castle and his heart."

"Oh, Kinsey," Patience said, feeling the nausea rising.

"He loved *me*." Kinsey stared past Patience, as if seeing Silas. "He told me so when he touched me."

Patience had to swallow to keep from being sick. Silas had been twisted and evil as it was, but he'd used his sister and corrupted her mind? Patience felt a swell of pity, even as she felt such horror.

"He made me vow to keep our love secret once ye arrived." A cold expression settled on Kinsey's face. "I told him I'd only keep our secret if he did as I said when it came to ye. And he did." She smiled grimly. "Because he loved me."

Patience clenched her jaw. He'd enjoyed the horrid way he'd treated her, and she knew for certain it had nothing to do with love.

"I wanted him to kill ye." Kinsey glared at Patience. "But he wouldn't. He said ye were good in a way he'd nae ever kenned."

Patience held in her surprised gasp. Silas had said such a thing about her?

"Once he was gone, I was determined to kill ye. But it could nae look like I had. I was going to rule the castle for Lamond. He was always weak, and I kenned I could manage it. But then Blackswell arrived and announced that the king had given the lairdship, *my rightful lairdship*, to the Savage Slayer himself. I had to think." She tapped the side of her head. "What to do? How to survive? I was going to wed him. And then I discovered he was betrothed to ye!" Kinsey hissed. "Always ye! Ye are *always* in my way." She cocked her head and gave a faint laugh. "Ye are funny, ye ken."

"Am I?" Patience felt almost numb from all she'd heard.

"Aye. Ye and yer plan to drive Brodee away. So foolish but so perfect! If ye had only stuck to it or at least done me the favor of drinking the wine I sent to yer bedchamber."

"The wine?" Patience mumbled, then comprehension struck. "Ye poisoned the wine."

Kinsey slapped the side of her head so hard, the smack resounded in the air. "Of course I did! I could nae decide if I wanted to kill ye or nae after I got to ken ye a bit. Ye are nice. Too nice. Annoyingly so, really. But in the end, ye must die."

Patience tightened her grip on the dagger. Kinsey was behaving as if it were still a possibility. "I hold the dagger, Kinsey," she reminded the woman.

"Aye," Kinsey said. "Ye do."

Something in the way she said it, as if the weapon could not stop her, made her grip the hilt so tightly her fingertips pulsed. "Did ye send Ulric to take me and kill me because I would nae drink the wine?"

"Ye are so verra perceptive," Kinsey said. "Finally." She thumped at her head again. "If ye had only used yer brain a bit sooner and opened yer eyes, ye may nae have been here. Ye could have just driven Brodee to get yer marriage dissolved, and I would have let ye go and wed him myself. But the two of ye," she said, disgust clear in her tone, "had to bed each other. Ye—" her eyes were like two sharp knives pointed at Patience "—have caused me a great amount of trouble. Now I will have to convince him that Ulric killed ye for vengeance against him. I will have tried my best to save ye, of course."

Patience trembled. She did not want to stab Kinsey, but she was getting a feeling the woman may force her to action.

"I've set it up nicely, though," Kinsey continued, almost as if she were talking to herself. "He hates ye now. I'm certain he thinks ye joined with William. Just as ye thought he had with me. Both of ye are too easy. I expected more from the Savage Slayer."

Patience felt her lips part, and she sucked in a shocked

breath.

"But I suppose a man in love is a blind fool easily led by jealousy," she muttered.

A man in love? Patience's chest squeezed. Did Brodee love her? Had he thought her untrue, even as she had thought him untrue? Had Kinsey truly orchestrated it all?

"When I return to the castle, I'll lead him here, dunnae fash yerself. And then I'll be there to comfort him. Wed him. Rule with him." She flashed a wolfish grin. "I'm the perfect match for him. And ye, ye are in my way."

As Kinsey leaned toward Patience, the dagger pierced the woman's flesh, and Kinsey screamed. But before Patience could react at Kinsey purposely getting herself stabbed, Kinsey grabbed Patience's arms, and swung her around, shoving her backward toward the ledge. It was too close. Patience tried to dig in her heels, crying out as she slid backward across the grass and dirt toward her death. Her arms were locked in Kinsey's clutches, blood growing in a ruby circle at the woman's waist.

The ground gave way under Patience's feet. Her heart dropped. Fear twisted through her, and with a hard shove to her stomach, she tumbled backward, arms flailing, and watched Kinsey grin at her as she fell toward the rock below.

Twenty

"Nay!" Brodee bellowed, tugging his galloping horse to a halt as he watched, stunned, as Kinsey shoved Patience off the cliff. She fell, almost as if in slow motion, and his heart fell with her. Noise rushed at him, fear hammering in his ears. Then his raw cries drowned out the fear as the desire to close his eyes and not see her hit the ground to her death was so great that water seeped out of his eyes. She fell, and then just as suddenly, she stopped. Her body jerking and then hanging. Limp.

He didn't understand it. He couldn't process it. He blinked, and then—

"Christ!" He dug his heels into his horse's sides, spurring it into an all-out gallop, William and Cul matching pace behind him. The wind whistled by him as he raced toward the mountain he still had to scale. He tried to take in all the details of what he faced to get to her, to save her.

Was there enough time? How long would her skirts, which had caught on a series of branches, hold her? Was she conscious? Was—

Her scream tore through the space between them, the fear buffeting him. He watched, unable to turn away, unwilling to turn away, as her legs swung down, the material giving. He screamed his rage, and then his relief when she did not fall farther but hung from the branch by her hands now. Soft hands. Small hands. How long could she maintain her grip?

He reached the mountain and dismounted before the beast had even come to a full stop. He climbed like a man crazed. He *was* a man crazed. Fingers digging into dirt. Rocks tearing skin. Sweat dripping in his eyes. Up and up. The terror for her was making him dizzy. He loved her. He *loved* her, and he'd not even told her.

"Brodee!" Kinsey standing above him at the ledge did not even make him pause. She had a dagger in her hand, and blood smeared her gown. "She tried to kill me! I think she's truly mad!"

Brodee scrambled to the top, and with a single glance behind him, he merely said, "William."

"I've got her," William replied, understanding instinctively that Brodee wanted him to take care of subduing Kinsey.

Brodee did not slow. He ran toward the ledge toward his wife, his *life*. He dropped to his knees, scanned the rocks for a way down to her, and swung his legs over.

"Nay!" she screamed from below him. "Nay! Nay, ye will die."

He could not waste time or breath arguing. The rocks slanted downward in a sharp series of dips, as if they had been laid one upon the other. He'd climbed enough mountains to know instinctively how to scale it, where to grab hold and where to place his feet for purchase. The wind whipped at him as he descended. Rock sliced into his hands, and fear shredded his heart, but the closer he drew to her, the faster he went. His palms grew wet with his blood, and he had to pause to wipe one and then the other on his kilt before continuing the descent.

She screamed, and he looked to her. Her horror-filled

eyes locked with his. "I'm slipping!"

"Dunnae ye dare let go," he ordered her, glancing back once more. *Almost there.* "I love ye. I love ye, and I refuse to lose ye." Hand over hand, one ledge to the next, and then he was bending. He grasped the rock he was on and encircled her wrist in a death-defying grip.

"I love ye, too," she said, tears flowing down her dirt-smudged face. "I did nae let go," she whispered as he pulled her up toward him with a grunt.

Once he had her on the ledge with him, he wrapped her in his arms, bringing her into the protection of his embrace. His heart thudded as he pressed her body to his, and wave after wave of emotions rolled over him.

"Am I too late?" he asked, shaking as he pulled back to look at her face.

Her eyes met his. There was no confusion there—only clarity. Only love. He could see it. He welcomed it with everything he was and everything he no longer wanted to be.

"Nay," she said, pressing her lips to his. He cupped her face and kissed her as if his life depended on it. She broke the kiss and put her palms to his cheeks. "Ye are just on time for me."

◆◇◆◇◆

Later that night, after Cul had helped Brodee get Patience from the cliff's edge, Kinsey was sent with two of the Blackswell warriors to be taken across the sea to an island where she would dwell guarded for the remainder of her years with other twisted minds. Once Kinsey had departed, screaming her revenge, Mari tended to Patience's wounds and tried to tend to those of an uncooperative Brodee, but the only thing he'd let her do was wrap his palms. As she was tending to him, Mari told them about the drugging herb she'd found missing from her supplies. It did not come as a surprise now. They bid Mari goodnight, and made their way to Brodee's bedchamber.

She watched him as he closed the door behind them. He took her hand silently and led her to the bed, where he sat and pulled her into this lap. His gaze bore into hers, and she could see a glimmer of worry in the depths of his eyes. He reached up and tucked a loose strand of her hair behind her ear.

"I dunnae have an excuse for nae believing in ye," he said.

"Ye do." She brushed her fingers over the stubble on his jaw. "Ye do, and so do I. We need to develop trust, and that comes with time and really kenning each other." She bit her lip, almost afraid to say more. Yes, he'd told her that he loved her, but that had been when she'd been hanging by a branch for her life. It was one thing to tell her when he was unsure if she would live, but could he repeat the words now? Would he open his heart to her? To all the possibility she saw for them?

"I love ye, Patience," he said, his voice catching. "I'll nae lie and say I wanted to, because I did nae." She frowned at that, and he turned his head to her and kissed her. "Nae because ye are unlovable or unworthy."

She bit her lip again. Perhaps he knew her a little better than she realized.

"It was because I saw immediately how worthy of love ye are," he went on. "How special ye are. Even though I have loved and lost before, it was a young love, a love of infatuation and passion. My gut kenned from the moment ye revealed to me all ye had endured, that what I could find with ye was an even deeper love—of two souls coming together. That scairt me like nary a battle ever has."

She forced herself not to interrupt. For too long, she'd wanted to know him, wanted him to open up to her, so she could sit silent now.

"All I could think was that I should nae allow myself to love ye so I would nae ever feel pain if I lost ye. But that is nae a choice. I already loved ye. I could nae stop it. Despite all my skill, all my strength, ye defeated me, broke down my barriers without ever picking up a weapon."

She smiled then, and he slid his palm under her gown and over her bare skin, making her shiver. "Well," he said, his voice suddenly thick with desire, "I suppose ye did wield yer womanly weapons quite expertly."

She chuckled at that. "Only because ye gently showed me how."

"Would ye like me to show ye again?" he asked, his fingers trailing over the curve of her hips, up her stomach, and to her breasts, which ached for him when he ran his thumb over the bud.

"I would," she said, finding it hard to catch her breath, "but first, I would like to say something."

He stilled and nodded.

"I love ye, too. I think it blossomed the first moment ye protected me and showed me respect. Ye are savage to the world, aye, but to me, ye are passionate, and kind, and worthy." His eyes widened, and she rushed to continue. "Ye are nae second to me," she said, running her hand over the tattoo he'd been branded with. "Ye are first. The greatest man I have ever kenned. Ye make me feel things I did nae ken possible, and ye make me want things I did nae ever dream to hope for."

"God's teeth, Patience," he moaned and covered her

mouth in a hungry kiss. His tongue swirled around hers as his hands moved to the back of her neck and delved into her hair. "Ye have brought me to my knees." And then he released her, set her on the bed, and moved between her thighs, which he gently opened. "Let me worship ye."

A delicious warmth spread through her as passion rose like an uncontrollable fire. "I will, but let me worship ye first."

His eyebrows arched high. "Do ye ken how?"

"Nay," she said with a blush and a shake of her head. "But I trust ye, my Savage Slayer, to show me."

"Ah, Wife, this may be one time ye should nae trust me too much. I think I'll greedily take as long as ye are willing to give."

She chuckled, but her laughter died as he stood and stripped off his clothes. Moonlight glinted over his beautiful, strong body. "What do I do?" she asked.

He offered a distinctly wolfish smile before telling her in a velvet-edged voice how to take him in her hands and then her mouth. By the time he was done describing the details, her body was strumming with need for him, and she was squirming to do what he'd explained. She motioned for him to lie on the bed, and he did, bringing his arms up to lace his fingers behind his head.

She ran her hands down his corded abs, reveling in the way her touch could make her powerful warrior husband twitch with obvious need. *For her.* He made her feel protected, yet at the same time, he evoked a feeling of power within her. She brought her hands between his thighs, feeling the hardness, the slickness, the very essence of what made him a man. Her blood thickened within her as desire pooled in her belly, pulsed between her legs, and made her want to climb on top of him and demand he take her.

She took her time, learning him, watching his reactions as she stroked him with her hands, her craving growing as his obviously did. His muscle grew taut, his jaw tense, but his eyes stayed gentle and focused unflinchingly on her. She kneeled between his thighs, and his hands threaded into her hair as she bent toward him to take him in her mouth. Every groan that slipped from him, every jerk of his body, made her feel more in control, more bonded to him.

When his hands tugged gently on her hair, she released him from her careful torture to look at him. "I dunnae want to spill my seed in yer mouth," he said with frankness.

"Nay? Is that nae done?"

"Oh, it's done, to be certain," he replied, his voice ragged. "But I wish to be in ye. To hopefully give ye a bairn and start our family."

Happiness burst within her, and she started to climb off him. But he stilled her and then guided her on top of him. When she was settled, she looked at him, unsure. Her hands were splayed across his chest, and she straddled his thighs with her own. "What do I do?" she asked again.

He grinned, looking very much like a mischievous lad. "Whatever ye wish," he said, locking his hands behind his head once again. "Guide me into ye, and do with me what ye will. Ye are in control."

She felt her eyes go wide. "I am?"

"Aye, lass. Ye have taken my heart, now take my body."

A brief shiver rippled through her, and then she did exactly as he'd instructed. He slid into her, filling her, and then his hands came to her buttocks. Before long, they were moving together, two swirling storms that had clashed and become one. Searing need built in her until she yielded with a cry, releasing all her fear, all her feelings of unworthiness, and welcoming love, strength, and the beginning of a new life.

In the early-dawn light, she lay cradled in his arms, marveling at how they had made love until the sun rose once more. When he stretched as if to rise, she assumed he was going to go to the courtyard to train as he did every morning. "Can I come with ye?" she asked, loath to be parted from him.

He looked back at her as he donned his braies. "Nay, lass. I'll return momentarily."

"Oh? Ye're nae going to train?"

He winked. "Nae today. William can lead the men. Today is for ye. For us."

She nodded, excited and curious. He returned not long later, and after having her don her gown, he allowed two of his men in, who carried buckets of steaming water for the tub. She could not help the grin that his thoughtfulness brought to her face. Once the men left, Patience and Brodee settled in the tub, her leaning back against him and him soaping her with luxurious strokes. She told him of her father's coldness when she lived with him, his wedding a woman who did not care for her, and he told her of his childhood, his tense relationship with his father, and his leaving to become the king's right hand in hopes of acquiring his own land and home. He confessed it was that desire that had driven him to become such a ferocious warrior, to keep going to battle. The need to prove himself had been with him all his life.

He grew silent, and she turned toward him. He had a thoughtful look upon his face. "What is it?" she asked.

"I dunnae feel it anymore."

"What? The need to prove yerself?"

"Aye. 'Tis gone. I think..." He ran his soapy hand over

her breast. "I think ye have silenced my ghost and gentled the beast."

"Probably," she said with a definitive nod. "I'm rather powerful, ye ken."

"A worthy opponent," he agreed, capturing her mouth with his for a long, drugging kiss. "And the most valuable wife I could ever imagine."

Epilogue

*P*atience waited at the bridge to their home, one hand gripping the missive that said Brodee was returning to her this day from the siege of the Gordon clan's castle, Cawdridge Castle, and the other on the gentle swell of her belly. She smiled as snow began to fall. She could hardly wait to see him, to touch him and know he was safe. She yearned to feel his arms around her and gaze in his eyes when she told him of the child she carried.

"My lady," Cul said beside her. "The laird will be vexed with me when he sees ye standing in the snow in yer condition."

Fergus grunted his agreement from her other side, and Mari, who was far less subtle, said from behind her, "Ye should go in and sit. Ye work in this castle too much."

She grinned at Mari. She had never quit mothering Patience after the night Kinsey had pushed her from the cliffs. "I dunnae work any more than anyone else in the castle."

"But ye are the lady of the castle," Jane chided gently.

"Exactly," Patience replied to the lass, noticing her staring overly long at Cul and him returning the admiration. Patience smiled, hoping the two of them would come together. Then she spotted Brodee's horse, and at the same time, she felt a trembling under her feet from the hundreds of horses galloping toward them. "There they are!"

When the men gained the bridge, the vibrations became so strong they tickled the bottoms of Patience's feet. "Look at the sight of my husband returning," she whispered in awe. Mist had risen and swirled white in the air as Brodee's destrier led the pack. He'd told her the leader should always go first, taking the greatest risk as was his duty, and Brodee was the most honorable man she had ever known.

His black warhorse seemed to part the very mist as he rode toward her. Very close behind him was another rider she assumed to be William. Behind him was a sea of warriors, once Blackswells and Kincaides, but all the men now called themselves Blackswells. It had not taken long for the Kincaide men to see what she had recognized almost from the start: Brodee was an exceptional man. The sort of man that became a legend, which he already was. The sort of man others wanted to emulate, as William and Cul so clearly did. The sort of man they trusted implicitly, gave their loyalty to totally, and would die for. He would never be second in his home, and she would never be worthless.

She rolled up the missive and handed it to Mari, who held her hand out for it, now knowing her so well. Patience smoothed her gown, licked her lips, and barely resisted the urge to pinch her cheeks. "Do I look—"

"Aye," Mari said. "But lass, he sees yer beauty clear to the inside of ye."

Patience nodded, her eyes welling with unexpected tears of happiness, as they so often did these days.

Brodee brought his horse to a halt a few feet from them and dismounted in one fluid motion, closing the distance to her before she could even take a proper step. He scooped her into his arms, her feet leaving the ground, and swirled her around to which Jane and Mari both shouted, "Stop!"

Brodee immediately froze and looked to her. "What is it? Are ye ill?"

"Nay." She gave the others a warning look. They knew she wished to tell him in private, and they all remained silent.

"Thank God." Brodee's mouth claimed hers in a kiss that curled her toes while making her belly flutter and conveying just how very much he missed her. When he broke the kiss, he said, "I have thought of precious little but ye."

William was almost upon them now, and there was a man now riding beside him. The other rider had a hood pulled over his head so she could not make out his face. "How was the siege?" she asked. "I fashed day and night that my father would betray ye…"

"Oh, he did," Brodee said, setting her down and pulling her snugly to his side. She knew it was to offer comfort if she should need it.

She slid her arm around his waist with a sigh. "I wish I could say I was surprised. Is he—" She swallowed hard. "Is he dead?"

"Nay, lass," Brodee said gently as William, who waved his hand in greeting, and the man beside him halted their horses some feet away. "But he awaits trial for treason against the king, and he will likely be put to death."

Tears did spill down her cheeks then, which she brushed quickly away. "I dunnae ken why I'm crying," she whispered and turned her face into Brodee's chest.

His hand came to her hair, a gentle, gliding caress. The touch instantly soothed her. "Because ye have a good heart, and ye are filled with kindness."

She nodded, took a moment to compose herself, and then looked to Brodee. "What of his castle? And my brother? Dear God, dunnae tell me my brother aided him. Dunnae tell me my brother is dead."

Brodee suddenly looked to William and the man with him who had both dismounted. "Yer brother was the one who warned me of yer father's deceit. He rode to me in the night with men he'd gathered to come for ye. It seems he made a vow to ye that ye would nae ever have to wed again. At first he intended to kill me, to free ye from my murderous clutches...."

Patience gasped and glared at William when he chuckled. "I will write to him and reassure him I'm safe."

"I told him ye would." Brodee smiled. "After we had a sound fight, that is. Yer brother is an excellent fighter and a good man. But he insisted he had to see ye for himself, hear from yer own lips that ye are happy, healthy, and wish to be wed to the Savage Slayer."

The man with the hood cleared his throat.

"Duff!" she cried, racing to him and hugging him. He hugged her back.

He pushed back the hood, his dark hair blending with the night. "Hello, Patience."

"Why did ye remain silent?" she asked him, so grateful to see him. "Why did ye wait to make yer presence known?"

Duff looked to Brodee. "Yer husband takes yer safety verra seriously. He said he had to be certain I did nae mean harm to ye before he'd let me approach ye. Can ye forgive me for failing ye? For nae getting here in time to save ye from yet another unwanted husband?"

"Forgive ye?" Patience burst out laughing. "Oh, Duff! I should thank ye! Brodee is the best thing that has ever happened to me."

"God's teeth," Duff said as he squeezed her. "I'm glad to

hear it! Ye must be happy. Ye feel as if ye are finally nae just bone anymore," he teased as only a brother would.

She met Brodee's intense gaze, which she could feel upon her suddenly like a bright ray of sun.

"Patience?" he asked, his tone husky and hopeful.

She broke away from her brother then and went to Brodee, took his hands, and laid them on her stomach. "Aye, my love. We have a bairn coming."

He pulled her to him and pressed his lips to her ear. "Ye are the savage one," he whispered. "Ye have enslaved my heart."

"That," she said, kissing him, "was my secret plan all along."

If you loved my *HIGHLANDER VOWS: ENTANGLED HEARTS* series then I think you will love my new Historical Romance series, *RENEGADE SCOTS*! The first book in the series, *OUTLAW KING*, is now available. juliejohnstoneauthor.com/outlaw-king

She's the weapon intended to destroy him. He's the key to her freedom.

Dark days have come to Scotland, and fierce warrior Robert the Bruce would do anything to release his country from English rule—and not just because he's the rightful heir to the Scottish throne. As the bloody war rages on, enemies on both sides of the fight surround him, and Robert must dance a dangerous line between truth and deception. One misstep could topple his nation and cost him his life, yet one woman tempts him—and threatens his mission—as no other ever has.

Elizabeth de Burgh longs for freedom in a time when women have none. So when she finds herself ordered by her ruthless father and her godfather, the King of England, to seduce the leader of the Scottish rebellion and reveal his secrets, she yearns to fight back against their cruel plot. But they threaten to kill her beloved cousin, leaving her no choice but to comply. As she grows close to Robert and the mask that hides the man who would be king is peeled away, she cannot imagine aiding in the destruction of the noble Scot bent on liberating his people.

Bound by duty and honor but ensnared by passion, Robert and Elizabeth must determine if they are each other's biggest threat or greatest source of strength. And moreover, they must decide how much they are willing to risk for the one thing neither ever imagined they'd find with the other—extraordinary, boundless love.

Prologue

1296
Northern Scotland

*R*evolt had its own scent. It was one of burning wood and flesh, fetid wounds and rancid sweat, and it lay heavy in the air. Robert the Bruce, Earl of Carrick, smelled it with every breath he took.

"Rebellion surrounds us," Laird Niall Campbell said, pride ringing in his voice.

Bright-orange flames leaped into the sky from the destroyed guard towers that flanked the raised drawbridge to Andrew Moray's castle, which Robert had been commanded to invade. *Commanded.* The word reverberated in his head, making his temples throb. He glanced to his friend who sat mounted beside him. Perspiration trickled down Robert's back beneath his battle armor, and the moans of captured men reached his ears. Gut-hollowing guilt choked him. "We're on the wrong side of the fight," he said low, acknowledging out loud what they both knew.

Niall hitched a bushy red eyebrow as hope alighted in his eyes. "Dunnae tease me, Robbie," he whispered, ever careful, though they were far enough away from Richard Og de Burgh that the King of England's man would not be able to hear them. "Dunnae say such a thing unless ye are ready to disregard yer father's dictate."

"I'm ready," Robert replied, meaning it. The desire to follow his heart and defy his father, who demanded blind obedience to a plan that no longer had worth, had been building for months. Now, in this moment, it felt as if it would cleave him in two, it beat so strongly within him.

The time was not yet ripe to act, his father kept claiming. It was, and it had to be, now. Today. He could not take up arms against his own countrymen. He could no longer submit to his father's foolish order to remain aligned with King Edward in hope of gaining the Scottish throne, which had been stolen from their family by the usurper John Balliol.

"I'm a Scot, for Christ's sake," he muttered.

"Have nae I been reminding ye of that verra fact for nigh a year?" Niall's hand lay on the hilt of his sword revealing the danger of what they were about to do.

"Ye have, my friend, ye have," Robert said, his mind swiftly turning. His father should now rightfully be King of Scots, but instead Robert sat here ordered by the ever reaching King of England to destroy a stronghold in the land he loved, while his father seemed perfectly content to stay in England amid the comfort of the Bruces' plush English holdings rather than venture back to the wilds of Scotland to rise against King Edward and risk losing everything. Robert could no longer deny the truth—his father lacked the iron will to do what was right.

War meant blood, strife, and possibly death, but subjugation to an English king was a different sort of death, one of the spirit. He could not live that way. "We'll no longer be safe if we rise against Edward this day," he said, accepting it, but wanting to give Niall, who was married and had a daughter, one last chance to change his mind and keep his submission to Edward intact.

Niall snorted. "I thrive on danger."

God knew that was true enough. Niall had always been right there with Robert at the front of every battle, even on the day the Scot's daughter had been born. Still...

"We will be hunted," Robert added.

"Let them try to catch us," Niall said with a smirk. "The devil English king will nae stop until he sits on the throne of Scotland. He will kill all who continue to rebel, and that includes our people. I'd rather be hunted than aligned with King Edward."

"We will be outlaws, enemies of Edward."

"Shut up, Robbie," Niall growled using the nickname only those close to him dared use. "Quit trying to dissuade me. Ye need me."

"I do, but yer wife and yer daughter—"

"My wife will dance a jig when she hears we've taken up arms with our countrymen. Dunnae fash yerself. Tell me what ye want me to do."

Robert slid his teeth back and forth, contemplating that very question. He needed to be canny and proceed in the best way to protect his men. The wind blew from the west, sending billows of white smoke and heat toward them and de Burgh—the king's closest friend and advisor—who was mounted on his steed, some thirty paces ahead of them. De Burgh looked away, but Robert faced the wind. He, too, would suffer every hardship he demanded his men to endure, and most of the men who had ridden here on his command were in the path of the smoke. It burned his throat, nose, and eyes, making breathing nearly impossible.

Death by fire would be an awful way to die.

Robert swiped a gloved hand across his watering eyes and focused on the falconry building that stood vulnerable behind them. It was on the wrong side of the moat—the land unprotected by the drawbridge. Counting, his gaze moved over the captured Scots lined up in front of the outbuilding by de Burgh's men. Twenty of the Scot rebel Andrew Moray's men would die this day on de Burgh's command, unless the Moray warriors lowered their drawbridge and sent their lord, a leader of the Scottish uprising against Edward, out. Robert could not allow their deaths or Moray's.

"Andrew Moray!" De Burgh bellowed toward the castle, which was separated from them by the moat alone. The powerful Irish noble's accent sounded especially thick with anger. "Lower your drawbridge and surrender, or we'll burn your men alive."

Robert's hands tightened reflexively on his reins as the captured men moaned their protest, only to be silenced by the swords upon their chests, no doubt pricking flesh in warning. There was no more time to ponder. He had to act. These men would not lower the drawbridge.

De Burgh was a fool to think he could ride here from England and command these Scots. They hated Edward for his attempt to put himself on a throne he had no right to occupy. "Ride to the head of my men," he said to Niall, "and wait for my signal. If I can avoid bloodshed I will."

"Och," Niall said, "blood will be shed this day, but it will nae be Scot's blood."

"We can nae guarantee that, Niall," Robert replied.

Niall nodded. "I ken," he said, his shoulders sagging a bit. "Try to prevent a battle then," he relented, "but I feel in my bones it's imminent."

Robert felt it too, but he had a responsibility to do all he could to protect his vassals. "Go to the men," he urged.

With a nod, Niall turned his horse from Robert and headed down the hill toward Robert's vassals. Three hundred and fifty of his men who were loyal to him stood mixed with three hundred and fifty of the king's men. Robert clicked his heels against his steed's side and closed the distance between himself and de Burgh who flicked his gaze at Robert and then yelled toward the castle, "You do not have long to decide!"

"De Burgh," Robert growled, "ye can nae burn alive innocent men. They follow Moray's orders."

De Burgh jerked his head toward Robert. "Innocent?" he snarled. "These Scots rebel against Edward, their liege lord. They deserve their fate."

"Edward is nae their liege lord," Robert said through clenched teeth. "John Balliol was their king." The words sliding from his tongue were bitter but true.

"They should be glad to see such a weak king as Balliol driven from the throne," de Burgh retorted.

"Edward's plan all along, I'm certain," Robert snapped.

De Burgh flashed a smile. "Your people are the ones who appointed Edward to choose the next king of Scotland, all those years ago, if you recall. And he saw Balliol as the man with the best claim to the throne."

"He saw Balliol's weakness, and my grandfather's strength, and that's why Edward chose Balliol," Robert growled.

"You sound as if you wish to rebel," de Burgh said, smirking. "Where is your father, then?" De Burgh made a show of twisting around in his horse as if searching for Robert's father before facing Robert once more. His lip curled back in a taunting smile. "Ah yes, your father does not have the fortitude to rule Scotland. If he did, he would have risen in rebellion with the people who would fight against Edward in Balliol's name. Fall in line with me, Bruce," de Burgh threatened. "You have no other choice."

"There's always a choice," he spit out, finding the hilt of his sword and flicking his gaze toward Niall and Robert's vassals some one hundred yards behind them. Robert looked to de Burgh once more and motioned toward the captured men. "Release them."

"You insolent, foolish pup!" de Burgh growled, spittle flying from his mouth. "Stand down! Moray!" de Burgh roared. "I give you to the count of ten before I order my guards to fill the outbuilding with your men, and we can all watch them burn."

A window at the front of the castle banged open, and a woman—Lady Moray, Robert realized—appeared. "My husband is nae here, so we kinnae send him out."

De Burgh snorted. "She expects us to believe Moray did not come here to gather more men?"

"Perhaps he did nae," Robert said, seeing a chance to prevent bloodshed. "Moray rebels by the renegade William Wallace's side, and Wallace's men keep to the woods. Perhaps Moray went there first."

"I don't believe it," de Burgh snapped. To Lady Moray he shouted, "Lower your bridge. I will see for myself if you speak the truth."

"Nay, ye Irish scum! Ye simper and cater to the English king!" Lady Moray bellowed.

Robert's fingers curled tighter around the cool iron of his sword. There would be war today, after all. Lady Moray had just shot an arrow of barbed words at a man who wore his pride like a cloak.

De Burgh's face turned purple. "Burn them!" he cried, his voice trembling with rage. The two guards standing near the door rushed to open it, and as they did, de Burgh flicked his hand to a slight guard who held the torch. "Set the fire when the door is closed."

Shouts erupted from the captured warriors, and Robert's blood rushed through his veins and roared in his ears. His life was about to change forever. But his honor would remain intact. He would rise in rebellion, not for Balliol to be returned to the throne as king, but for the people of Scotland to keep their freedom. He could worry of nothing else now.

The terrified shouts of Moray's men as they were locked in the falconry pierced the roar of blood in his ears. "Tell yer men to halt," Robert yelled to de Burgh. "Do so now and take yer leave from Moray's land, or I'll kill ye." His heart beat like a drum.

De Burgh bared his teeth. "You have misplaced your loyalty, Bruce."

Robert flicked his gaze past de Burgh, over the rocky ground that separated the two of them from the warriors in the distance, to Niall at the front of Robert's vassals. He raised his right hand and swiveled it round, giving the signal to rebel.

Niall smiled, a flash of white against his sun-bronzed skin. He raised his own hand and returned the signal. They would live or die this day, but they would do it with honor.

Tension vibrated through every part of Robert's body as he yelled, "To arms for Scotland!"

All at once, the hissing, scraping, sliding, and singing of seven hundred blades filled the air, and the clashing of steel sounded in the distance. A woman's scream ripped through the noise, shocking Robert by how close it was. De Burgh swung his sword at Robert, but Robert parlayed the blow and unseated de Burgh with one move. With no time to waste, he turned his horse toward the outbuilding, and he gaped at the scene before him. The squire who held the torch was running from de Burgh's guards and toward

Robert. The young man suddenly swerved toward the moat and threw the torch toward it. The bright flame disappeared into the water, and Robert raced to save the man who would likely be killed for his actions.

Robert met the guards halfway to the squire, who was now running back toward him. He parried a blow from the left, then the right, and caught a glimpse of Niall riding fast toward him.

"Release the trapped men!" he yelled to the Campbell, but in a breath, de Burgh's warriors descended on his friend, now engaged in a battle for his life.

Behind Robert, the loud grating of the drawbridge being lowered stilled all motion for a moment. God's teeth! Surely, Lady Moray was not lowering it in surrender. Within a breath, the thundering of hundreds of horses' hooves against the wooden bridge set a buzz in the air that seemed to vibrate into Robert's very bones.

When he glanced around for the squire, he saw nothing but English knights heading toward him. He raised his sword in defense of an oncoming hit, knocked the blade out of the knight's hand, and nudged his mount out of the way of another Englishman. It had turned him directly toward the bridge where Lady Moray herself came riding out, her red hair billowing behind her as she led her husband's warriors in a charge. They appeared to number almost two hundred, not near enough that they could have withstood an attack from the combined forces of the Bruce men and the English garrison, but they had more than enough to overcome the English if the lady intended to join forces with Robert. But did she?

As she rode, she shouted, "Free our men. Free our men! Someone free our men!"

Robert swept his gaze back to the outbuilding, and the

breath was snatched from his chest. The young squire had somehow managed to get to the outbuilding. Niall was there, as well, along with six more of Robert's men. They held the English guards back, but one broke free and raised his sword to strike down the squire as he stepped toward the door and seemed to be opening it. Robert ripped his dagger from its sheath and flung it with all his might toward the knight. The dagger pierced the man's hand as he was bringing his sword down and he dropped his weapon. The squire, who'd turned toward his attacker, eyes wide with fear, twisted back around to the door and slung it open. Moray's men poured out, weaponless.

Robert unhooked his shield from his saddle, and then dismounted amid the chaos, his sword in one hand and his shield in the other. He raced toward the stumbling Moray men and the squire, parrying blows as he went. When he reached the boy, a call to fire at the lad and the Moray men went out from de Burgh. Cursing, Robert looked to his right to find that a line of knights had covered the distance from the scrimmage below to the castle, and they were lined up to shoot. Robert shoved the boy behind him, as a volley of arrows flew through the air. They clanked against his shield.

"Again!" de Burgh shouted, clearly not caring if he struck down his own men.

Robert moved to shield the boy once more, but the squire stepped out from behind Robert and ripped off his helmet. Long blond hair tumbled out over his—no, her—shoulders. Robert could do no more than stare in shock at de Burgh's daughter, Elizabeth de Burgh. Her clear blue gaze met his for a brief moment.

"Cease fire! Cease fire!" came de Burgh's frantic call.

The chit's eyes, bluer than any Robert had ever beheld,

widened with what appeared to be shock. Had she thought her father may not save her?

She turned to Robert. "Thank you for your aid, my lord." The words tumbled from her mouth in a rush, and then to Robert's surprise, she dashed, as graceful as a deer fleeing a predator, past him and toward her father.

Robert stood dumbfounded for a moment at the young chit he'd seen at court but had never met. One of his men lunged toward her, and Robert shouted, "Leave her!"

She raced through the melee, surprisingly agile and quick, and she managed to reach her father unscathed. At once, she was snatched up by the hand she stretched toward her father and slung on the back of the destrier he had mounted once again.

Lady Moray and her husband's warriors came into the fray of the battle that was now moving ever closer. English arrows flew toward them. She raised a hand as she raced forward, and Robert looked to the rampart of the castle, relieved to see four dozen or so bowmen. Within a breath, more arrows soared through the air, but this time toward the knights lined up to shoot at her. As she reached Robert, he said, "My lady, I would stand in defense of yer home if ye will allow me to."

She arched her eyebrows over glittering gray eyes. "It's about time a Bruce came to his senses," she said with a nod. "I'll fight alongside ye, for this day ye have saved many Moray lives."

Robert glanced around at the already fallen men from both sides and made a decision. "De Burgh!" he bellowed, before any more casualties came to pass. "The Moray men fight with me. Stand down and leave, or be prepared to die."

De Burgh twisted his mount toward Robert while calling an order to his men to hold, and Robert did the same to his and Lady Moray's men. De Burgh was an astute man. He had to see he was outnumbered and that the best option would be to flee as Robert had graciously offered to allow.

"I name you traitor, Bruce, and I'll inform King Edward of your treachery."

"I can nae be a traitor to a man I do nae call king!" Robert reminded de Burgh. A roar of approval arose from his men and the Moray men alike.

A command to his men to depart was the answer from de Burgh, and the English garrison quickly complied, taking their mounts and turning to ride out. As Robert watched them leave, Elizabeth de Burgh twisted in the saddle, her unwavering gaze meeting his.

Beside him, Lady Moray spoke. "That girl forever has my debt. I pray the punishment for her deeds this day are not too grave.

Robert nodded. Elizabeth de Burgh had mettle, that much was certain. It would remain to be seen if it was not beaten out of her after today.

"What will ye do now?" Lady Moray asked.

Robert thought briefly of his father ensconced in Durham at one of their English manors. He would need to send a messenger to give his father fair warning of what had occurred this day. What he did with that information was on his head.

"My lord?" Lady Moray said.

He caught the lady's inquisitive gaze. "I'll send word to my father of my actions—"

"*Honorable actions*," she said, reaching out and squeezing his forearm.

He inclined his head in gratitude, certain his father would not feel the same. Swallowing a sudden swell of emotion for the rift he had placed between himself and his father this day, he said, "then I'll ride to Hugh Eglinton's Castle. I've received word that the nobility leading the rebellion have been given safe haven there to meet and plan, and amongst the party is also William Wallace."

Lady Moray's eyebrows arched. She bit her lip for a moment then spoke. "Ye ken many of those men fight in the name of Balliol. They fight for his return to the throne."

"Aye," Robert replied. "But Balliol abdicated and I have heard that the Comyns—" saying the name of his family's bitter enemies who years before had put the force of their great power behind their cousin Balliol to have him named as the man with the best claim to the throne over Robert's grandfather, always made Robert's throat tighten. "—are imprisoned by Edward. I go to fight for Scotland, as I did this day."

She nodded. "I pray for ye that it will be enough to see ye well."

"I'll gladly take yer prayers, he replied, sensing deep within that he would need them.

"I'll send a messenger ahead of ye with word of yer deeds for me to my husband who is at Eglinton Castle," she revealed with a secretive smile. "That way, ye are more likely to keep yer head when ye approach the Scots. Many think ye a traitor."

"I know it well," Robert said, "but I will face it and prove them wrong. Do nae risk yer man."

"I owe ye," she whispered fiercely. "Ye saved my men. I will pay my debt by aiding ye in hopefully saving yer life when ye approach Eglinton. Grant!" Lady Moray bellowed and within a breath a young Scottish warrior appeared. Lady Moray smiled at the young man mounted beside her. "Grant rides like the wind. He should reach the castle before yer large gathering of vassals." Robert inclined his head at her words. To Grant, she said, "Ride to yer laird. Take word of Bruce's actions here today, and tell my husband, Bruce is our friend."

"I will, my lady," the warrior said, before turning his horse and galloping away. They watched him in silence for a moment before Lady Moray spoke again. "Dunnae tarry, Bruce. Scotland needs yer fighting strength. Ride hard."

"I vow it!" he swore, turned from Lady Moray, and gave the signal for his men to follow suit. Niall brought his horse beside Robert's and together they led the men away from Moray's castle. As they did, Robert felt Niall's steady gaze upon him. "What is it?" Robert finally asked.

"Please tell me this means we dunnae ever have to go back to the English court and pretend to admire the English king nor like English food."

Robert chuckled, some of the tension unknotting from his shoulders. "God willing. Niall, I will ride to Eglinton with my men to join the rebellion are ye certain ye wish to ride with me? What of yer clan, yer wife, yer daughter?"

"My clan is secure under my brother's care in my absence. As for my wife and daughter, it is thanks to ye that my daughter is alive. Dunnae think I've ever forgotten, nor has Calissa, how ye saved our Brianna when those English knights captured her. Brianna is safe at home with Calissa, and I will stay with ye and fight for our land and to free our people."

"If ye ride with me, ye may ride to yer death," Robert said, his tone grave.

"I've ridden next to ye since we were young and trained together at the Earl of Mar's castle, Robbie. If I'm to ride to my death, there is nae anyone I'd rather be beside, but I think we ride to freedom. Let us see it together, aye?"

"Aye," Robert agreed. There would be no changing Niall's mind, and Robert both appreciated his friend's loyalty and feared for him. But Niall's decision was set, and there were no arguments left to be made, so Robert urged his steed into a gallop to which his men matched the pace.

They rode relentlessly through the remains of the day, over hard terrain, under the baking sun, and into the early evening hours. When he finally spotted Eglinton Castle in the distance, he ordered the party to halt and turned to Niall. "I'll venture up alone," he announced, determined to protect Niall should the other Scottish nobility greet them with swords and wish to fight, despite Lady Moray's sending word. Many saw them as traitors, thanks to his father's orders to continue obeying Edward even when the Scottish nobility started to rebel against his rule, and Robert was not convinced Lady Moray's words would have much effect on those who distrusted him.

"The devil ye will," Niall replied, his tone hard. "I'm nae going to linger back here with the men and let ye get all the glory. I'll go with ye, thank ye. All those who dared to call us traitors will ken the part I played in striking against de Burgh and, therefore, the English king."

Robert opened his mouth to argue and then promptly shut it. It would do no good. "Ye're as stubborn as a goat," he grumbled instead. "And I do nae have time to mince words with ye. Come along."

Niall chuckled as they moved their horses down the path that wound up to the castle gates. As they rode, Niall said, "It's heartening to see that ye have finally learned I'm the stronger of the two of us."

"If ye think I'd ever believe that," Robert teased, "ye must have hit yer head."

"Name yerself," a guard bellowed, interrupting their

banter as they approached the gate.

"Robert the Bruce."

"Laird Niall Campbell," Niall added.

"The turncoat arrives," the guard hissed.

It was as Robert had expected. He whipped his sword up to the man's throat. "I'm nae a turncoat. My family did nae support Balliol, but that does nae mean I will nae fight for Scotland against Edward."

"Come along, then," the guard relented in a begrudging tone. "The others will decide if ye should keep yer head."

"Everyone always wants my head," Robert said light-heartedly, "yet it still sits upon my shoulders."

Niall chuckled, and the guard glared at the two of them. He guided them up the stone steps, past more guards, and into the torchlit castle. Silence blanketed much of the estate at such a late hour, but muffled voices drifted from down a dark corridor. A flicker of light flamed at the end. The guard stopped and motioned toward it. "The leaders of the rebellion are in the great hall discussing strategy."

Robert nodded, and he and Niall fell into step behind the guard once more. As they made their way down the corridor, the voices coming from the great hall grew louder and more distinct.

"I'm nae going to risk my life to put Bruce on the throne!" someone bellowed.

Robert flinched, knowing they were referring to his father.

The guard who was with them snickered, and Robert glared the man into silence.

"Bruce is the rightful claimant," came another voice.

"Bah! Bruce swore fealty to Edward as overlord of Scotland!"

"Ye ken he did that to avoid swearing allegiance to

Balliol!" someone else shouted.

"Where is he, then?" the other man thundered. "Balliol has abdicated, and Bruce, the elder, does nae return to Scotland to help us stop Edward. What does he do instead? He sits in his lavish English estate! He has no backbone to rebel! Let us look to John Comyn to lead us in Balliol's absence. He has managed to escape the imprisonment that befell many in his family."

Their words were like harsh blows to Robert's chest. John "the Red" Comyn came from one of the most powerful families in Scotland—Robert's being the other—and that was the heart of the conflict between his family and the Comyns. The Comyns wanted all the power, including the throne, but not for the good of Scotland—for greed. Comyn cared for the rebellion only insomuch as he wished to protect his vast estates and current power. He did not truly care for the people and their freedom.

Robert gritted his teeth. He would have to fight beside a man who wanted to destroy him in order to save the land he loved. He shoved the guard out of the way, but a hand came to his arm. He turned to find Niall staring at him. "I'll nae bend the knee to a Comyn," Niall said. "Ye ken as well as I do that they will do all they can to gain the throne if there is nae any hope to return Balliol to it."

Robert nodded. "We will fight for Scotland." He didn't say that he hoped his father would join them, though the hope lingered.

Suddenly, the door was flung open, and a giant of a man appeared at the threshold. He had to duck to exit the great hall. He strode toward Robert and Niall, his boots thudding against the floor. He stopped in front of them and smiled, a genuine expression that reached his clear blue eyes and made them crinkle at the edges. "I thought I heard a noise out here," he said in a deep, friendly voice.

"Ye heard us despite all the commotion within?" Robert asked, exchanging a quick glance with Niall.

"Aye." The Scot nodded as he scratched at his russet beard. "I've had to learn to listen carefully, especially when surrounded by chaos. 'Tis how I still survive though the English hunt me. I'm William Wallace of Elderslie."

"We've heard of ye," Niall replied. "I'm sorry to hear about yer wife."

Grief swept over Wallace's face for the space of a breath before murderous rage replaced it. "I thank ye. The English are suffering for the murder of my wife and will continue to do so. And ye are?" His curious gaze took in both Robert and Niall.

"Niall Campbell."

"Carrick," Robert said, giving only his title, as was customary.

"Ah, Bruce," Wallace said, ignoring the given title. "Word of yer deeds have been brought to us by a messenger from Lady Moray."

Robert nodded Wallace grinned. "Seems ye made a friend in the lady and she thought to save yer head should anyone want to take it off." He gazed intently at Robert. "Why have ye come here to us?"

"To help retain Scotland's freedom, just as ye, Wallace." Wallace looked unconvinced, so Robert added, "I've heard some things about ye as well."

"Aye? What do they say?" he asked, a twinkle in his eyes.

"That ye fight like a brute beast."

Wallace chuckled. "How would ye have me fight?"

"To win," Robert replied easily enough.

Wallace set a large hand on Robert's shoulder. "I do

believe ye are the first noble I've met that I have actually liked," Wallace said, winking at Robert. "Let us see if my opinion is enough to keep yer head on yer shoulders."

Robert nodded and fell into step with Niall by his side behind Wallace. Wallace entered the room of disagreeing Scottish nobles and rebels, and when Robert and Niall followed all arguing ceased, chairs scraped, and the singing of swords being unsheathed filled the air.

England

Elizabeth pressed her hands against the cold glass of her bedchamber window, which overlooked the beautiful gardens at the king's court. Her breath caught when her father and the king turned to look up at her as one. She scurried back from the window and bumped into the table behind her. The vase teetered, and she lunged for it, catching it before it hit the floor. But her foot slid out in front of her, and she went down with a hard *thud*, the breath whooshing out of her and the water in the vase spilling down the front of her gown.

She sat there with her bottom pulsing in pain, and her mind awhirl with horrid possibilities about what punishment the king was demanding her father dole out after what she'd done at the Moray's castle. Banishment from her parents, her brothers, and sisters to some remote place? A nunnery for life? She shuddered. She may only be twelve summers, as her mother and older sister always loved to remind her, but she did know some things, contrary to what they seemed to believe. She understood fully that she had far too much zest for life to spend hers in a nunnery or someday be a docile wife, for that matter. She inhaled a long breath and tried to slow her racing heart. Her father loved her. He would reason with the king. He would protect her.

Wouldn't he?

Worry niggled at her as she set down the vase beside her and drew her legs to her chest, shivering with a chill of which she could not seem to rid herself. The memory of her father giving the order to burn men alive filled her mind. There had to be some explanation. There simply had to be. Because if there was not, then her father was not the man she believed him to be. And if he was not good and honorable, then how could she trust he'd protect her?

Still quivering, she set her palms to the cold, wet floor and scooted over enough to see in the slash of sunlight coming through the window. She could recall her father's face just before he had locked her in this bedchamber, and the hairs on the back of her neck prickled. Never had she seen such rage from him. He'd been nearly purple and unable to speak, and it said a great deal that he had not come to see her even once in the past sennight, nor had he allowed her out of her bedchamber. She had thought he would have by now. In fact, she had been sure he would visit so he could tell her he was vexed, very vexed, but that he loved her and had been compelled somehow to give the horrific order to burn the men.

She twined her hair around her finger, her agitation increasing. She was not sure how much longer she could endure being locked in here alone. The only person she had seen since returning home was the chambermaid who brought Elizabeth a tray of food three times a day and emptied her pot. She let out a ragged sigh. Perhaps she should be grateful she was being fed. She began to rock back and forth, going through the events which had led her to disguise herself as a squire and ride out with her father, his men, and Lord Carrick, Robert the Bruce.

It had been two things truly. She'd been irritated that her father had dismissed her request to ride with him that day so completely, loudly, and publicly. She'd not known the "mission," but she had known she wanted to be part of it, and she could not see why she should not. Father had always allowed her to do things other girls did not. She rode as a man did, she spoke her mind, and she had even accompanied her father and his men on hunts.

The other compelling factor had been Lord Carrick himself. She had not met him, though the young man had been at court for some time. He was always surrounded by other lords and lavishly dressed women batting their eyelashes at him, but it was the way his dark gaze looked through the ladies and the simpering lords as if they were not there—or perhaps as if he wished to be anywhere but there himself—that intrigued her so. Once she had overheard her father tell the king that Bruce concerned him. He feared the young lord harbored secret compassion for the wretched Scots' cause. Those words had burrowed into her heart, for she secretly thought that it was wrong of her godfather to try to make himself king of a land to which he had not been born, to a people who did not want him as their king. She did not dare utter such a thing out loud, of course; even she knew it was foolish to *always* speak one's mind.

A soft tap came at the door followed by, "Elizabeth?" in a low, worried murmur.

Elizabeth jumped to her feet at her cousin's voice, nearly slipping in her haste. "Lillianna!" she cried out, pressing her palms to the thick, dark wood of the door. Never had she been so happy to hear her dearest friend's voice.

Lillianna was more of a sister to Elizabeth than her three true sisters were. Lillianna was the only female Elizabeth knew who shared her leanings toward things that were considered restricted to women—riding as a man, archery, swimming, and learning more than how to select food for supper and embroidery. Her cousin also was an excellent eavesdropper, a talent she'd taught Elizabeth when Lillianna had come to live with them two years ago after the death of her mother.

"I'm so glad to hear your voice!" Elizabeth said. "What news do you bring? Is it terrible? Am I to be banished? What did you learn?"

"Not very much, I'm afraid," Lillianna moaned. "Whatever has been decided about your fate has thus far been discussed behind doors too thick for eavesdropping. I'm not even supposed to be here. Your mother and father expressly forbade me from coming to see you, and Aveline has been trailing me, keeping watch."

Elizabeth rolled her eyes at her sister older Aveline being her usual perfectly awful self. "How did you manage to escape her?"

Lillianna snickered. "I told her Guy de Beauchamp wished to see her in the solar."

"Oh, Lillianna!" Elizabeth laughed, feeling so grateful for her cousin and only true friend. "Aveline will be livid when she learns you tricked her. She has a tendre for Lord de Beauchamp. Though I cannot see why. There is something about him that unsettles me."

"Perhaps it's the way he is always staring at you as if you are a great treasure he wishes to add to his collection when you become of age," Lillianna said sarcastically.

"I will never marry a man such as Guy de Beauchamp," Elizabeth vowed. "I don't care if he is one of the wealthiest lords in the land. Aveline can have him!"

"As if you will have a choice of who you marry." Sadness blanketed Lillianna's voice.

Elizabeth wished she could hug her cousin. Lillianna was likely thinking of her mother, who'd been forced to marry her father. Uncle Brice had beaten Lillianna's mother for being unfaithful, and she had died from the beating. But being a powerful lord, he had gone unpunished for the death of a simple Scottish lass.

Elizabeth inhaled deeply, refusing to worry about problems that were years off. "We shall both use our very clever minds to come up with a plot to marry men of our own choosing. We will aid each other!"

"You are so naive and hopeful, Elizabeth. 'Tis one of the reasons I adore you so. I cannot linger, though I wish I could. I came to warn you that your mother is coming to see you today."

Elizabeth tensed. Her mother never had a kind word for her, only criticism, and Elizabeth could only imagine what she would say about ignoring her father's orders. Likely, she was livid. Not out of care for Elizabeth, of course, but out of fury over being embarrassed at court by Elizabeth's actions. "You better depart, then. I'd not want Mother to take out her vexation with me on you." And her mother would; Lillianna knew this. Mother cared for Lillianna even less than she did Elizabeth, which was barely at all. Elizabeth felt sure her cousin had only been permitted to come live with them because it had made Mother look charitable and warm-hearted.

"I'll return tonight if I'm able," Lillianna said.

"Only if it's safe. I don't want you bringing trouble to yourself on my account."

"I'll be careful," Lillianna promised, then the tap of her

footsteps fell on the floor.

Elizabeth stood there listening until the sound of Lillianna's departure faded. Silence descended momentarily but was broken once more by the tap of shoes upon the floor. She sucked in a sharp breath, fearing it was her mother. She hoped Lillianna had not been seen.

A distinct jangling of keys and the clink of a lock made Elizabeth's heart race. The door opened, and her mother, looking perfectly coifed and richly garbed, stepped into the room. Blue eyes that she'd been told a thousand times were the same color as hers narrowed on Elizabeth. "You cannot depart this room looking like that."

Her mother's unfriendly tone made her clench her teeth, but the news that she was to depart hit her like a ray of hope. "I'm to be released? I'm forgiven?"

"Forgiven?" Sarcasm laced Mother's words. She stepped in front of Elizabeth, close enough that she got a full whiff of the pungent oil her mother liked to wear. "You are not forgiven. You are lucky to still have your head, you silly, willful girl!"

The slap came fast and hard, leaving a sting that brought tears to Elizabeth's eyes.

"Marietta!" Elizabeth's father boomed from the doorway. "Don't raise your hand to Elizabeth again!" Relief flowed through Elizabeth, but as her father settled his dark, unfriendly gaze on her, it vanished. "She has to be taken through the great hall to depart, and I'll not have anyone seeing her skin marred with red welts that will remind them of her deed."

"She is the talk of the court!" her mother wailed. "Let them see we punished her!"

Elizabeth's stomach knotted at her mother's words.

"Clearly, you have not been in the Great Hall this

morning," her father said to her mother. "Elizabeth's deed is no longer on everyone's lips. Bruce is the talk of the court now," her father said, his voice lethal. "It seems he left the rebel Moray's castle and rode from there to join the other Scottish lords and renegades to rise against Edward."

"Pity," her mother murmured. "I had a hope to marry Aveline to Bruce but that won't do now. He'll lose his estates for certain."

Her father frowned. "I have a marriage in mind for Aveline already, so don't vex yourself. Now, wait outside. I wish to speak with Elizabeth alone."

"Richard," her mother exclaimed, "you promised me I would have charge of her now!"

The news made Elizabeth cringe.

"Woman!" her father roared. "You will, but you will have it *after* I have spoken to her."

Her mother, eyes wide and no doubt sensing she had pushed Father as far as he would be pushed, backed out of the room, shutting the door as she left.

Elizabeth pressed her back against the wall, wishing she could disappear into it.

Her father's eyes seemed to harden as he looked at her. "You have made a fool of me."

Elizabeth clenched her hands. "Father, no. I—"

"Silence!" The word whipped across the space and hit her just as hard as her mother had.

She flinched away from him and fisted the slick material of her gown in her hands.

Her father's gaze raked over her. "I always had a particular tendre for you, so I allowed indulgencies I did not with your brothers and sisters, ones I should not have allowed."

Color rose in his cheeks as he spoke, and Elizabeth stared at the rosy bloom that spread down his neck. Father saying that he'd *had* a particular tendre for her echoed in her mind. Had she destroyed his love for her, then? Her belly felt suddenly hollow.

He swiped a hand across his red beard, tugging at the ends. "Your mother warned me that I was ruining you, making you into the opposite of what a lady should be— willful, too curious, wild—but I told her to mind her place." He shook his head. "I let you linger when I should have sent you away, and because of my weakness, you believe you can do as you please!" He banged a fist into his open palm. "You—" He pointed a finger at her. "You seem to think you have a place at the table of men!" His hand gripped her chin so swiftly she gasped. "I tell you now, you do not. You are a girl and will grow to be a lady, obedient and lovely, and you will learn that your purpose is to serve my house as I command for the furthering of the family. Do you under- stand me?"

She fought against the tremor in her body. She under- stood. Her importance to him lay only with what wealth or connections she could bring to the family one day, just as Aveline had always claimed. Elizabeth had not believed it until now. What a fool she'd been! She had no freedom, only the rights her father gave to her. Did he feel no true affection for her? Was there no explanation for the order he had given that day? Her mind spun, making her stomach roil.

Her father squeezed her chin. "Do. You. Understand?"

She stared at the pulsing vein near his right eye. She knew she ought to respond immediately, yet such worry coursed through her, she could not make herself speak, even knowing her silence would have grave repercussions.

"Elizabeth," he hissed, his color rising again. "Your head is currently on your shoulders because I convinced the king that you could be useful to him eventually. Should I tell him otherwise?"

The king? Her father had convinced Edward that she would be useful to him? But how? Gooseflesh swept down her arms as her father's fingers curled even deeper into her skin. "No," she managed to choke out.

"Good." He released her chin, and she rocked back from him, desperately wanting to rub her aching skin. Instead, she forced herself to fold her hands together and prayed she appeared calm.

Silence stretched between them, and he watched her steadily before he smiled. "You are stubborn and prideful, and you don't know your place. But you will learn it. By God you will." He grabbed her suddenly by the arm, half dragged her across the room, flung open the door, and shoved her toward her mother. "Take her home to Ireland, and make her into a lady who will benefit this family."

The anger and hurt deep inside Elizabeth burst within her and overcame her fear. "You would have burned men alive to keep the king's esteem," she accused with a desperate hope that he would deny it.

"Yes," he replied, his wintery voice and open acceptance of the awful truth making her feel as if her legs would buckle. She placed a steadying hand on the wall as the floor beneath her seemed to sway. "Do you think I became this rich and powerful without currying favors?" he demanded.

"Favors?" She heard herself gasp, yet her voice seemed very far away. Her ears rang horribly. "It is not simply a favor to burn men alive."

"I cannot allow anyone to defy me. *Ever.* That is how I stay powerful. You'd do well not to forget it, Daughter."

She would not forget. As much as it pained her, she would hold close the memory that her father had traded his honor for the king's continued support and the wealth it would bring. Never would she marry a man who would do such a thing.

You can order OUTLAW KING NOW!

Series by Julie Johnstone

Scottish Medieval Romance Books:

Highlander Vows: Entangled Hearts Series
When a Laird Loves a Lady, Book 1
Wicked Highland Wishes, Book 2
Christmas in the Scot's Arms, Book 3
When a Highlander Loses His Heart, Book 4
How a Scot Surrenders to a Lady, Book 5
When a Warrior Woos a Lass, Book 6
When a Scot Gives His Heart, Book 7
When a Highlander Weds a Hellion, Book 8
How to Heal a Highland Heart, Book 9
Highlander Vows: Entangled Hearts Boxset, Books 1-4

Renegade Scots Series
Outlaw King, Book 1
Highland Defender, Book 2
Highland Avenger, Book 3

Regency Romance Books:

A Whisper of Scandal Series
Bargaining with a Rake, Book 1
Conspiring with a Rogue, Book 2
Dancing with a Devil, Book 3
After Forever, Book 4
The Dangerous Duke of Dinnisfree, Book 5

A Once Upon A Rogue Series

My Fair Duchess, Book 1
My Seductive Innocent, Book 2
My Enchanting Hoyden, Book 3
My Daring Duchess, Book 4

Lords of Deception Series

What a Rogue Wants, Book 1

Danby Regency Christmas Novellas

The Redemption of a Dissolute Earl, Book 1
Season For Surrender, Book 2
It's in the Duke's Kiss, Book 3

Regency Anthologies

A Summons from the Duke of Danby (Regency Christmas Summons, Book 2)
Thwarting the Duke (When the Duke Comes to Town, Book 2)

Regency Romance Box Sets

A Whisper of Scandal Trilogy (Books 1-3)
Dukes, Duchesses & Dashing Noblemen (A Once Upon a Rogue Regency Novels, Books 1-3)

Paranormal Books:

The Siren Saga

Echoes in the Silence, Book 1

About the Author

As a little girl I loved to create fantasy worlds and then give all my friends roles to play. Of course, I was always the heroine! Books have always been an escape for me and brought me so much pleasure, but it didn't occur to me that I could possibly be a writer for a living until I was in a career that was not my passion. One day, I decided I wanted to craft stories like the ones I loved, and with a great leap of faith I quit my day job and decided to try to make my dream come true. I discovered my passion, and I have never looked back. I feel incredibly blessed and fortunate that I have been able to make a career out of sharing the stories that are in my head! I write Scottish Medieval Romance, Regency Romance, and I have even written a Paranormal Romance book. And because I have the best readers in the world, I have hit the USA Today bestseller list several times.

If you love me, I hope you do, you can follow me on Bookbub, and they will send you notices whenever I have a sale or a new release. You can follow me here: bookbub.com/authors/julie-johnstone

You can also join my newsletter to get great prizes and inside scoops!
Join here: https://goo.gl/qnkXFF

I really want to hear from you! It makes my day!
Email me here:
juliejohnstoneauthor@gmail.com

I'm on Facebook a great deal chatting about books and life.
If you want to follow me, you can do so here:
facebook.com/authorjuliejohnstone

Can't get enough of me? Well, good! Come see me here:
Twitter:
@juliejohnstone
Goodreads:
https://goo.gl/T57MTA

CPSIA information can be obtained
at www.ICGtesting.com
Printed in the USA
LVHW090539080120
642897LV00001B/22/P